Hide N' Seek

Eden Emory

Ashley Pines

HIDE N' SEEK

EDEN EMORY
& ASHLEY PINES

This is a work of fiction. Names, characters, places, and incidents either are the product of the author's imagination or are used fictitiously. Any resemblance to actual persons, living or dead, events, or locales is entirely coincidental.
Hide N' Seek
Copyright © 2023 by Eden Emory & Ashley Pines

All rights reserved. No part of this book may be reproduced or used in any manner without written permission of the copyright owner except for the use of quotations in a book review. For more information, address: contact@ellemaebooks.com

Cover design by Opulent Designs
Edits by My brothers Editor

www.ellemaebooks.com

NOTE

This is a work of fiction. Names, characters, business, events and
incidents are the products of the author's imagination. Any
resemblance to actual persons, living or dead, or actual events is
purely coincidental.
Before moving forward, please read the trigger warnings on the next
page.
If you need help, please reach out to the resources below.

National Suicide Prevention Lifeline
1-800-273-8255
https://suicidepreventionlifeline.org/

National Domestic Violence Hotline
1-800-799-7233
https://www.thehotline.org/

Trigger Warnings

depictions of torture, alcohol as a social lubricant, choking (nonsexual), choking (sexual), blood play, gore/violence, knife play, weapon of convenience, family violence, gun violence, gunplay, overstimulation, orgasm denial, voyeurism (forced and unforced), murder, stabbing, sexual violence, biting, physical altercations, depictions of corpses being treated poorly, toxic capitalism, getting caught in machinery, drowning, attempted murder, verbal, mental and physical abuse by a parent, crimes of passion, vehicular manslaughter, depictions of a car crash, medical debt, cancer (past mentions), parental death, extreme poverty, gaslighting, ableist language, mutilation, misgendering, homophobia, head injury, stalking, transphobia/transphobic language, flashbacks, bullying, sharing of non-consensual nude images.

Before You Continue

The story you are about to read features two individuals who are EXTREMELY toxic and quite frankly, not well. Please don't take any of the actions that they say or do and apply them to your real life. This is fiction and most of these acts should stay on paper, where they belong.

Additionally, this is not an accurate portrayal of the BDSM community, if you are curious and what to learn more please conduct your own research and do not rely on what you find in this book as accurate knowledge of the BDSM community, their etiquette, and their ways. Things in this book have been dramatized and are not an accurate reflection of reality or my personal thoughts and opinions on these matters.

Pronouns & Nicknames

Kohl:
> **Everyday**: They/Them
> **Family**: Brother/Son
> **Lover**: Good Boy/Pretty Boy/Slut/Whore/Kitten

Vic:
> **Everyday**: She/Her
> **Family**: Daughter
> **Lover**: She/Her/ Mistress/Goddess

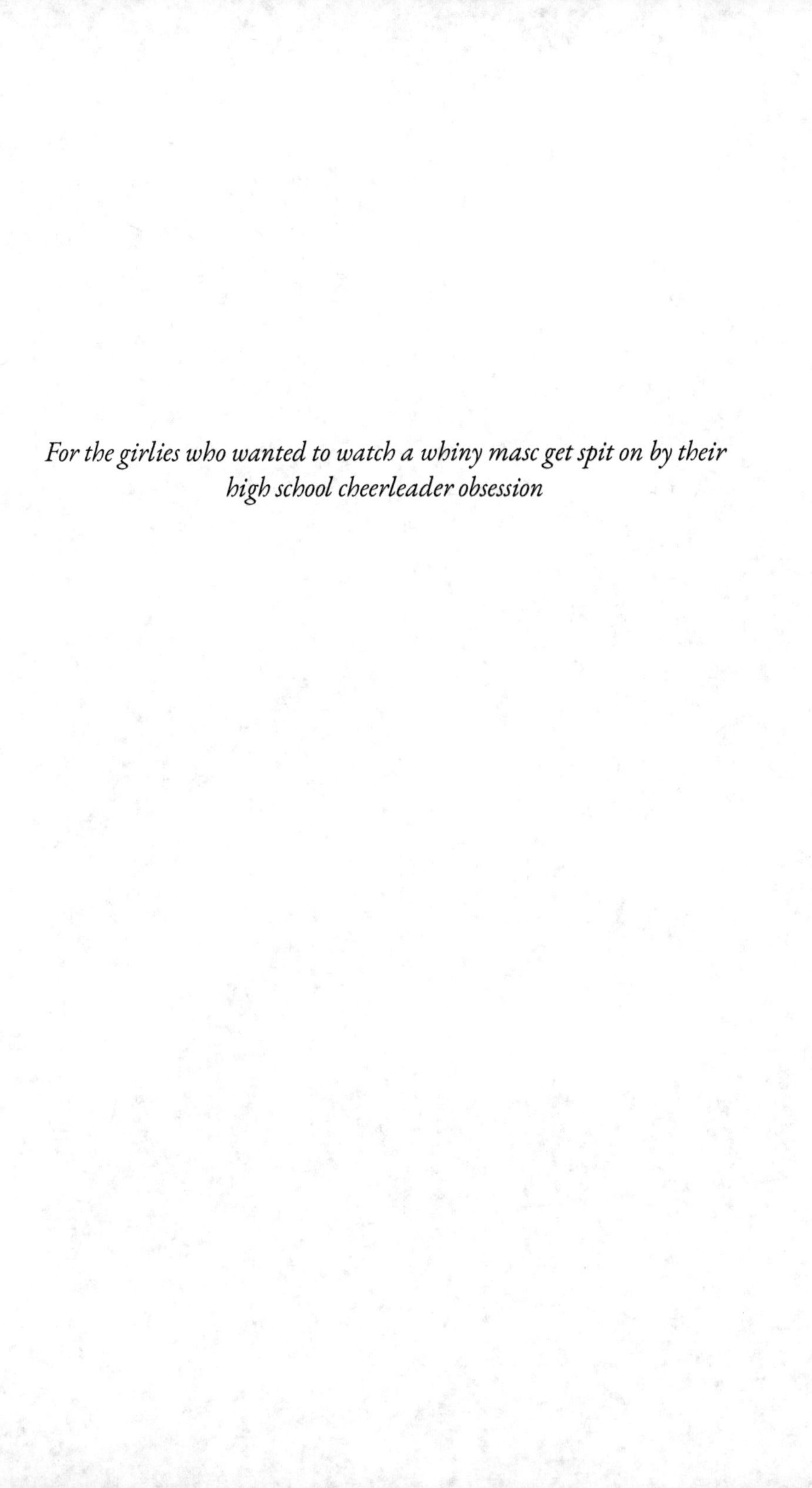

For the girlies who wanted to watch a whiny masc get spit on by their high school cheerleader obsession

KOHL

"What?" I snapped.

There are too many fucking people here.

The man in the wicket sneered, his crisp white uniform buttoned to the top of his throat, tucking away the ends of his quivering jowls.

It was like I'd insulted his dead mother or something.

The excited murmurs of the people in the line floated around me. The entire island was just vibrating with anticipation of what was to come as soon as the sun fell.

"Hiding or *seeking*?" he repeated, impatience threading his tone.

My eyes lingered on his gnarled hands where they clutched my plastic ID card.

I didn't have long to choose.

No big deal. It wasn't like this was life or death or anything.

Except that it *was*.

There were few moments in my life when it felt like I was speeding toward them, only for time to come to a screeching stop when they finally arrived.

The last big game of the football season.

Getting my license.

Graduation.

And now *this*.

Signing up to compete in the Devil's Playground.

The Games, to anyone with half a brain. That's all they really were anyway—games to entertain the filthy rich and to give the desperate *just* enough hope to keep going. Keep working. Keep *playing*.

Play hard. Die famous.

"There's a line, kid. You playing or not?"

I looked between the man and the black tent behind him, specifically angled to block contestants from seeing what awaited them in the arena. It was different every round. A new, fucked-up backdrop for stories of plucky underdogs and gruesome murders to keep viewers entertained.

I had gotten a glimpse of the looming island on the train ride over. A sort of fog-like cloud had covered it. As if the universe decided to join in the spectacle of it all.

The fog had slowly fallen to the ground, weaving between the players and chilling the air. It was the perfect setting for the disgusting crimes that would be committed inside the walls.

But what would *I* be? A coward or a monster?

Absentmindedly, I gripped the worn friendship bracelet around my wrist.

He snapped his fingers in front of my face, making me start. When my eyes flicked to him, he was already pulling his arm back through the slot. "Hiding or seeking?" Impatience licked through every syllable.

I couldn't blame him, not really. He had a ticking clock before the first event started and a long line of participants to get checked in.

I would've already registered if I'd decided to play before last week.

But I didn't, so here I was with the unwashed masses. Entering the games like a desperate loser.

Get your head in the fucking game, Kohl.

You were born for this.

"Seeking," I said, my hands fisting at my sides.

The man's eyes trailed over my ID, lingering on my name. A short, wheezy laugh escaped him as he set the rectangle of plastic on the wicket, his dirty fingernail pressing into my photo. "Can't believe it," he said with a smile that was anything but friendly. "Wolff, huh? You Hiram's boy? Dylan's brother?"

I tried not to flinch at my father's name.

Growing up, I'd promised myself that I'd be everything he wasn't. That I wouldn't let him turn me into a fucked-up mini-me of him like he'd done to Dylan.

I wanted to be *kind*.

I wanted to *love*.

And, most importantly, I wanted to be loved. To take care of the people who I cared about. To be their safety when things got hard.

That's how I ended up here in the first place. Fate either had a wicked sense of humor or a serious hard-on for reluctant murderers. Honestly, I didn't know which option was more depressing.

"Well, are you?" he asked, turning a thin magnetic keyboard toward me.

"Yes," I said, punching in my information while the attendant clicked through the screening questions.

If fate, the universe, or whatever fucked up god out there wanted me to be a monster, then I would become a creature like they'd never known. I'd rip my heart from between my ribs and leave my conscience bloody and bleeding in the street. A veritable river of carnage left in my wake, bodies stacked higher than Lady Liberty.

It didn't matter the cost. I'd do whatever it took to walk out of here alive with the prize money.

If love wasn't the answer, then violence was my only option.

I didn't care what it did to me on the inside, I could repent later. Tonight, I would feed the monster and then, once I'd made an offering to my goddess, all would be forgiven.

"Surprised to see you enter so late. Don't you Legacy types get the royal treatment?"

"Something like that," I conceded.

Do you really have to be so chatty?

I reached the last field on the form, username. The chattering behind me was getting louder.

My fingers moved before I could overthink it, typing in my usual moniker for PVP shooters.

KillerKohl.

"I remember your daddy's games, y'know. With genes like that, I bet you're a—"

I rolled my eyes and hit submit, a big red *ERROR: USER-NAME IN USE!* message flashing on the screen.

"Are you fucking kidding me?" I grumbled under my breath.

It's like my life was being run by two opposing forces.

One that desperately wanted me to jump into the arena and transform into the serial murderer of my birthright.

And the one that wanted me to run, as fast as I could, the other way.

But there was no running from fate.

I *needed* to do this.

Behind me, masculine laughter met my ears. I had seen them earlier. A couple guys signing up to be Seekers, if I had to guess by their stocky builds and deep widow peaks. Those dudebro small cock fuck-weasles always signed up for the opportunity to kill a couple civilians without going to jail.

Irritation skittered up my spine.

"Hurry it up," the attendant barked. "I don't have all night, even if you are a Legacy."

Cursing under my breath, I tried the next best thing.

Killer_Kohl.

To my relief, the tablet flashed green, *Welcome to Devil's Playground: Paradise Pier, Killer_Kohl!* sliding over the screen.

Ugly tossed my ID onto the small lip of the counter. I moved to pick it up and he grabbed my forearm, jerking me forward to fasten what looked like a smartwatch around my wrist.

As innocuous as it appeared, I knew that the watch would provide vital information to the Architects—*the sick fuckers who managed the games*—like my heart rate and where I was in the arena. It would also trigger cameras as I got close, letting the viewers stay up close and personal and providing me with a live feed of their comments and critical updates about the game itself.

"If you take that off, you're disqualified," the man grunted. "I'm not wasting my breath explaining the rules to a fucking Legacy, kid. Piss off and get into makeup. Hide and Seek starts in two hours."

A bundle of tarp-like material was pushed into my arms with a marker.

My nose wrinkled as I recognized what the lumpy object was.

"This is your body bag and a Sharpie. After this, you'll follow the walkway into the prep tent. Your stylist will be waiting for you there. Write your name, address, and the phone number of your next of kin on the paper tag in the front pocket. You'll then strip and place all personal items in the bag. Don't worry, *Killer_Kohl*, if you die, we'll ship your corpse back to your rich-ass daddy."

I stormed off toward the black tent just beyond the wickets, looking down at the mass of plastic with a scowl.

Like hell my father would be getting my body. They might as well ship me to a fucking Applebee's.

Printed signs led me down a canvas hallway that opened into a large circular area that reminded me a bit of my high school locker room—minus the lockers. Long metal benches sat in tidy rows filled with Seekers stripped down to their underwear, plastic body bags gripped in their hands as they waited for a stylist to collect them.

I tried to ignore the stares as I walked into the room. I had done it my whole life, but somehow their attention before the games was much harder to ignore. Because all of them had the same gleam in their eyes.

They were looking for an ally. One that could get them noticed. Too bad I wasn't one to play nice with others.

I found an empty patch of bench, trying to ignore the Minders dressed in all white stationed at either door with stunning batons strapped to their hips as I sat, pulling the paper card out of the clear front pouch of the bag. It wasn't unusual for a contestant to get this far and then try to pull out—unfortunately for them, once you'd signed the waiver and entered the playground, the only way out was to win.

The scent of permanent marker cut through the sterile, recycled air as I uncapped my pen, writing the name of the only person who'd given a fuck about me enough to care that I'd died—even if she'd probably drop my ass into a dumpster for lying to her and entering the games.

Kohl Wolff C/O Victoria Miller
    #7 Lanchester Avenue
    New Windemere, NY
    05467

When I was done, I stripped to my underwear, leaving my bracelet and the tracker in place.

If I was going to go through with this, I was going to need a reminder of *why*.

Her.

I caught a couple entrants eyeing my mastectomy scars. It should've made me nervous, but I didn't care. I was proud of the person I'd made myself into.

At least I was, before I ended up here. Before I signed up to be a fucking killer just like my father.

The games change people, Kohl. It's like... whoever comes out isn't who went in. I shook the memory from my mind, staring at the body bag in my hands while I waited to be called.

After a few of the longest minutes of my life, a woman with deep umber skin and long lilac knotless braids tapped my shoulder. "Kohl, right?"

"Unfortunately," I said, nodding tightly. My eyes flicked from her hand on my shoulder, taking in her closely trimmed nails to her eyes, ringed with elaborate golden liner.

"Come on, let's get you dressed. I'm afraid we are starting to run a little thin on time."

I stood and followed her through the curtain on the far side of the tent into a room full of stations with chairs. It reminded me a bit of a hair salon—if hair salons made a habit of keeping racks of clothes and cosmetics at arm's reach.

There were even a few weapons propped up in the back, ready for the contestants to pose with them and make sure their character was on point for the night's show.

Many of the Seekers were already sitting in their chairs, chatting happily with their stylists. My eyes lingered on a girl near the front as she gushed about her outfit.

"Isn't it just going to look beautiful with all the blood splattered on it?" she asked. "I know there are some fetish viewers out there that would pay big bucks to get a sneak peek under a bloodied skirt. What do you think? Is this too–"

"Oh, I just *knew* I had to grab you," the stylist whispered to me conspiratorially, flashing a wide smile as she pushed me into a chair. Her interruption was enough to pull me back to what was in front of me. "I was *so* disappointed when you weren't in the press junket. I'm Iris."

I smiled tightly, practicing acting like I was enjoying this. It was hard to ignore the buzzing in the room. Everyone sat happily in their chairs, picking out what would make them stand out the most, not even thinking twice about what was going to happen in the wall of the arena.

"Wasn't sure I was going to play," I said after a moment.

There were two main components to the games: gaining points and maintaining viewership. The more people watching you—*the better show you put on*—the easier the Architects made it for you. I needed this to be easy.

The stylist laughed like I'd told the funniest joke she'd ever heard. Maybe to her the idea that a Legacy wouldn't enter *was* funny. Or maybe I was more charming than I thought.

Something told me it was the former.

My information transferred to the mirror, the screen lighting digitally with a flood of data. My username, height, age, weight, hair texture, and skin undertone sailed by so quickly I hardly had time to read them.

Iris nodded thoughtfully, like she was considering the Mona Lisa instead of what was, effectively, my passport.

"God, I've wanted to get my hands on you for *years*," she said, moving forward to rummage through a case of cosmetics on the clear acrylic counter. "You have the best cheekbones."

"No makeup," I said quickly, feeling my skin heat with embarrassment, I added a hasty, "Please."

"Not like you need it anyway," she said, sending me another toothy smile that met her warm, dark eyes. "I'm more interested in what you'll be *wearing*."

She circled the chair so I could catch her face in the mirror as she studied my measurements on the screen. "Killers are so *boring* most of the time, you know. But this year they went with this edgy, cyber punk theme—you'll love it, it's very video game."

I doubted I'd love anything about this process but didn't bother to correct her.

"With a body like this, I'm sure we can put you in something that'll have you rolling in gifts. Viewers go crazy for a bit of skin, you know."

I let out a huff like I didn't give a fuck what the *viewers* thought, but in all honesty, getting their attention would only work in my favor. As much as I hated the attention of my lineage my entire life, it would come in handy during the games.

Especially if I could get a few gifts here and there.

And I *really* needed some help if I wanted any hope of winning.

I hadn't exactly made any friends to walk into the arena with, putting me at a disadvantage before we'd even begun.

Everyone knew the games didn't start when you entered the arena—it was when you registered. For someone like me with parents who'd won the games in a previous year, they started at birth.

That's why everyone knew my name. Why the kids I'd grown up with had their faces plastered everywhere for the last few weeks. In the early stages of the game, recognition was *everything*. The press junket just gave them a jumpstart on the competition, introducing them to the viewers before we even started.

My attention drifted as her mind spun. To the left of me was a particularly muscular man in nothing but a tight tank top and jeans. He held a large machete over his head, checking himself out in the mirror. His stylist leaned close to him, bright red paint on her hand, and pressed it flat just over his chest.

"Lift your tank top a bit, girls will go feral if they see a bit of blood when you raise your arms," she said to him.

"I think they'll notice the difference between fake and real blood," he said.

The stylist let out a laugh.

"Oh don't worry," she said, still giggling. "It's real."

Iris lurched forward and collected a tablet from a nearby rack, tapping it a few times before shoving it under my nose. "What about this?"

For fuck's sake.

My face had the audacity to heat at the image.

Usually, a pair of dark jeans and a hoodie was what I considered fashionable. This was... decidedly *not that*.

The avatar was wearing loose pants that cinched at the waist with pockets along the sides, paired with combat boots.

Those were safe, preferable even.

But the *shirt* was a strappy tank top that showed off the midriff with an even *shorter* hoodie on top of it.

It was the sort of thing that would draw eyes to me.

Paired with a mask, it'd be *perfect*.

She might be a little overeager for my taste, but I'd really lucked out with Iris.

"It's excellent," I praised, catching her eye. "But don't touch my hair."

She let out a surprised laugh, slapping her hand against my shoulder. "You got it! A green mask work for you?"

I wrinkled my nose.

She laughed. "Not green then, what would you prefer?"

A flicker of violet chiffon tugged at my memory, my mouth curving into a cocky grin as I looked into the mirror. "Purple."

The glowing mask felt heavy in my hands, the crossed-out eyes and stretched smiling mouth stared up at me cheerily in the dimly lit waiting area.

It was like it fucking knew what putting it on cost me.

Taunting me about what was going to happen behind those walls.

The second that mask covered my face, the games would start. Maybe not officially, but in my mind at least.

They had to.

I couldn't allow myself to stay the same Kohl who'd promised her I wouldn't enter. I'd have to be someone—*something* else entirely.

A killer.

Entering the arena as the Kohl pining after a girl who had *no* idea I was about to throw my life away for *her* was a death warrant. It wasn't just enough for me to play.

I needed to *win*.

To do that, I'd need to forget. My worries. My convictions. Who I wanted to be. All of it.

I'd need to become... *like him.*

No, I'd need to be worse. Second place wasn't enough for me.

"Whoa, are you Kohl?" a feminine voice behind me asked. "You're the second Wolff legacy, right? Fuck, I didn't think you were entering this ye—"

Damn it. I didn't get far before getting outed.

"And you are?" I asked without turning. Quickly, I fastened my mask on my face.

The last thing I fucking needed was a goddamn fan club. Viewer attention was good, but if I wanted to get the Ghosts, I would need to move quickly and without any baggage.

In the last couple years, I'd declined more press opportunities than I accepted, but I could never avoid the game-day coverage. The '*Where Are They Now*' segment was important for the image of the games, after all.

Hard to turn civilians into murderous psychos if you couldn't promise for them to be filthy rich, famous, and allegedly happy with a white picket fence and two point five kids.

I turned to see a pair of unmasked boys and a girl looking at me with mixed expressions of excitement, awe, and mistrust.

"I knew it," one of the boys said, nudging the guy next to him. "Their father is like *super* famous. It's practically a given that everyone after him will join. I mean, how could they not? Their dad is a Leg—"

The Devil's Playground theme song blasted through the speakers, abruptly cutting off the chatter.

Thank god. Ignore them and move on.

People swiveled their heads to try and catch sight of the noise, excitement crackling through the atmosphere like the beginning of an electric storm in the tense silence.

It's starting.

"Players! Please make your way to the starting area!" a cheery computer-generated voice called through the speakers.

I was the first to push through the crowd toward the back

entrance. The group that'd tried to talk to me followed close behind.

Fucking Perfect.

Just what I need, a bunch of no-name shadows.

Even if I hated coattail riders, I couldn't deny that I was in sore need of allies. If they were proficient in any aspect of the game... they could have value.

They continued to chatter behind me as if I wasn't even there. Going on and on about my father's accomplishments and nothing about the games that were about to start.

As I ignored them, they started to distance themselves. One guy lingered but shrunk away when I glared at him.

They wouldn't last. If money did things to people in the normal world, in there it was a thousandfold.

They'd turn on each other the second racking up points became more difficult.

Dozens of footsteps cut through the music along with excited murmurs, but all of that stopped when we reached the starting area.

It was a small half-circle paddock with a stage and screen set between two large steel doors. The telltale lights, sounds, and smells of an amusement park drifted toward us over the tall fences.

The sky was darkening and the fog that had fallen over the entire arena was clearing up just enough to make out the starry sky above. The area filled quickly, many rushing to take in the area up close for the first time.

Fucked up. But apt, I guess.

I could just make out a few of the taller rides, but besides that hint, inside was a mystery to be unearthed once I had no way back out. And beside the light music playing around us, there was an eerie absence of the normal joyous screams of an amusement park.

If I strained I could hear the creaking of the rides, the rush of wind, and a crackling, demented sounding carnival music.

It caused something heavy to sit in my chest.

Just beyond was a dead, soulless, amusement park that would

soon be crawling with Seekers readying their weapons and slitting the throats of helpless Ghosts.

In that moment, I stopped being a *Seeker*. As I looked around me, I saw the other players for what they were. *Killers and Ghosts.*

Property of the game.

Disposable.

Obstacles that stood between me and my offering.

I couldn't disappoint her, my goddess was waiting.

The late evening air should've cooled on my exposed torso, there was an eerie tension hovering over us that made my insides want to curl up and shrivel.

But there was something else.

A small but powerful electric wave of blood lust. It traveled the crowd, railing up the Killers and causing the offerings to curl in on themselves.

They were like lambs going to slaughter and all of us Killer were barely restrained wolves, gnashing our teeth at them.

And soon our leash would be cut.

A video played on the screen, lighting up the sky—the same footage we saw every year with highlights from the previous games —the only difference being the small sneak peeks of the area beyond. Less than a second each, it was crucial information about what lay behind that door.

The crowd was restless, whispers and fidgeting breaking out like a rash.

"Did you see—?"

"A Ferris wheel!"

"Oh my god, it's a theme park!"

The robotic voice came over the speakers again as a safety video began right after the first.

"Welcome to Devil's Playground: State Fair sponsored by *The Company*! Our first event of the evening, Hide and Seek, will begin in a few short moments. But first, The Company would like to remind you of a few key rules."

Images of carnival rides, games, concession stands, and a circus-like stage show slid by, all bright colors and flashing lights. All of them looked as run down as if this arena had been left abandoned for twenty years instead of just being created a few weeks ago.

I bounced from foot to foot and rolled my shoulder.

"There are a total of five hundred Hiders and five hundred Seekers. In a few minutes, Hiders will begin their seven minute head start while we assign them to their Seekers. Remember! For Hiders, you win the game if you make it until sunrise without being eliminated. For Seekers, you must accrue the most points."

I shifted uneasily, glancing at the tracker attached to my wrist. The screen was lit yellow, a tiny '*calibrating*' message along with a loading circle staring up at me.

"Your assigned Hider is worth the most points, but remember to be quick, as multiple people may be assigned your target if they find theirs first. As always, we encourage players to explore ways to earn extra points—voted by our spectators! If you have any questions, you may contact an Architect via your tracker's call function. Good luck, and remember—" the voice started, only to be drowned out by the crowd around me.

"Play hard! Win! Win!"

There was a shift as bodies moved to get closer to the doors.

In a few short minutes, the game would begin.

A flash of bright blue hair pulled my attention as it passed, disappearing toward the front where the rest of the Ghosts waited for their head start. Her fingers were laced into the hand of a player with a crop of short black hair, the pair of them in rabbit masks.

Blue and white.

Black on black.

Above the doors, the screen was pulsing with a red countdown starting at ten, warning the Ghosts it was almost time to enter the arena to find a hiding place.

I watched as the number crept closer and closer to zero.

It wouldn't do me any real good to watch where the crowd went, not until I could identify which Ghost was mine, but something was pulsing in my veins. The predator that I denied in my DNA stirred to life like a bear from hibernation.

Or like a demon crawling out of the pits of hell.

When the countdown hit zero, a siren blared to life along with flashing red lights as the door rose. The noise echoed through the small area and into the desolate park. It went on as they entered. Sounding more like an apocalyptic tornado warning, warning everyone in the area that danger was coming.

I had heard the siren time and time again, but it was nothing compared to hearing it in person and knowing that in a few more minutes one of those Ghosts would be dying at my hands.

Quick-footed Ghosts crawled on their bellies for a couple of precious seconds of extra time, others ducking under the door to get into the arena as quickly as possible. The sound of feet hitting the ground made my heart rate skyrocket, my instincts starting to kick in.

The blood rushed through my veins. The adrenaline pushing me to go after them.

My head was spinning by the time my tracker flashed, alerting me I'd been paired with a Ghost.

My eyes narrowed at the screen name.

bl@ck_r4bb1t.

It scraped uncomfortably at the back of my mind, not quite a memory as much as an impression. But where had I heard it before? I wasn't one to remember usernames, but something rang important about this one.

It didn't matter, copycat username or not, that bitch was as good as dead.

My eyes lingered on the tiny photo of her black mask. She'd been with the blue-haired girl.

Maybe if I got to her, I could go after the other one.

I shook myself, trying to push away the revulsion I felt at the thought.

So, this is what they meant. That once you entered the game, you became someone else.

I hadn't even picked up a weapon yet, and my mind was already trying to normalize this for me. I was already starting to *change*.

To lose myself.

But I didn't have time to worry about my humanity. The only thing that mattered from now until sunrise was how many points I could score.

It was time to get creative.

I'm coming for you, little rabbit.

VIC

I jumped the turnstile, sprinting to catch the train as the doors were closing.

Just my fucking luck that I'd miscounted my change. There wasn't even enough for me to make it to Paradise Pier—but I wasn't going to let something as trivial as *train fare* stop me. Not today.

This shit was do or die.

Emphasis on the die part.

The train was packed like sardines, bodies pressed together as we rumbled down the tracks. The smell of sweat hung in the air along with the stickiness forming on my skin at the heat. I was significantly shorter than most of the other passengers, making me an easy target for jostling as they swayed with every bump and turn. People talked loudly, their phones in hand as they watched the live entrant coverage on the high-definition screens.

I adjusted the bracelet on my wrist, trying and failing not to be upset that it'd turned from white to soft teal. My own damn fault for forgetting to take it off while I rinsed out my hair, but *still*.

It was my good luck charm.

And I *needed* a fucking good luck charm.

Above me, the usual advertisements for cosmetics, insurance, and antidepressants had been changed to fit a single theme, *The Games*. Faces of Legacies—players with a parent who'd won in a previous year—stared down at me with picture-perfect smiles and carefully coiffed hair.

Too perfect.

Especially since I knew most of them had coke addictions that would make Banff look like it was a tropical paradise.

Once upon a time, I could've called a lot of them my friends. I sure as fuck recognized enough of them from my classes and extracurricular programs. Got drunk at their parties. Hung out with them after school. Went to their families' long weekend barbecues.

But that's all they were now, *people I recognized.*

After they'd turned their backs on me, they might as well have been *nothing* for all I cared.

My eye caught on Jenna's photo, her dark hair carefully styled into waves that reminded me a bit of the flapper costume she'd worn last Halloween.

Surprise tickled my senses. *I hadn't realized she was playing.*

Okay, fine. There was one person in the arena that I could depend on. If I could find her. Of all of the useless pricks I'd called my friends before, she was the only one ever to check up on me.

She was kind, good in a way the others weren't.

Well, her and Kohl. I flinched away from that train of thought. I didn't have time to think about them now.

"Are you watching or playing?" a girl with a shaved head and a silver ring through her lip asked, her booted foot tapping impatiently against the sticky floor.

"How do you know I'm going to the playground?" I asked, narrowly resisting the urge to pull my hood up.

It wouldn't do me any good anyway. If I was sure of *anything*, it was that eventually, everyone would know *exactly* who I was.

Honestly, I was kind of counting on it. But it needed to be at the right moment.

She shrugged a bronze shoulder, blowing a bubble in her

violently purple, grape-scented gum that popped with a smack. "Look around you, sugar. Isn't that where we're all going?"

Fair enough.

I'd gone to a lot of trouble to be invisible tonight.

As a legacy, I should've been up there with the rest of them. But I'd registered late to avoid the press junket. In the arena, I'd have to rely on my mask to hide my identity. I just needed to avoid recognition from the other players until I got through the stylists. Then it would be fair game, the viewers were going to love a surprise *legacy* contestant.

It should've been easy, blending in with the crowd for a twenty-minute train ride. *Should've* being the operative word.

If I was normal like this girl—some no-name first-time entrant—maybe it would've been. But instead, I'd spent my entire life on a fucking pedestal, paraded around like an accessory to prove that the games *worked*. That you could rip yourself out of poverty for the tiny, insignificant price of your humanity.

It made me sick, to watch people praise my parents for the horrifying things they'd done in their games.

And yet here I was, offering up my soul just like them.

Not that I had much of a choice.

I needed that fucking money.

My face had been plastered on every magazine, gossip blog, and newspaper since before I could hold my own head up. That's what happened when *both* of your parents were Legacies.

I laughed lightly, my eyes flicking around the packed train car at the sea of black-clad young adults. Most of them were barely eighteen, like me, eligible for the very first time to play.

What did it say about this country that so few people could afford college that they were willing to kill for the opportunity to go? The chance was so slim of winning that you'd probably be better off trying for the lottery, but after the games took hold, more and more people started to bet on the outcomes of *that* than spend their precious few dollars on a lottery ticket.

"Well?" the girl asked, raising a split eyebrow. "Are you a viewer or a player?"

"Player," I said, my hand going to the bracelet on my wrist. "Hide and Seek. You?"

"Player," she echoed with a sarcastic peace sign. "Truth or Dare."

The games had three main events. All held on Paradise Pier, an island just off the coast that they refurbished every year into a new and exciting death trap. The first event, Hide and Seek, took place at sundown on kickoff day and ended when the first ray of sunlight hit the arena the next morning.

That was my event. The premise was easy enough, if you're hiding, stay hidden. If you're caught, you're *dead*.

Rat Race was next. Players needed to get from the start of a maze to the end without being killed by other contestants or any of the other dangers lurking around corners.

The last event, Truth or Dare, was a high-stakes game of impossible tasks and devastating secrets—and it was invite-only.

I'd gotten a red and black sealed envelope earlier that year that I promptly declined. I liked my secrets good and buried, thank you very much.

My eyes darted back up to Jenna's photo.

"Hot, right?" the girl remarked. "Pre-coverage says she'll be in your division."

"Yeah?" I said with a noncommittal laugh, my hand tightening on the overhead bar as the train bumped along the track to reach the bridge separating the island from the shore. From the pictures it looked to span miles from the underground tunnel to the island. An irrational fear of just one strong gust plummeting the entire thing into the ocean crossed my mind.

She grinned, showing a gap in her teeth. "Hiding or seeking?"

"I think you mean Killer or Ghost." I sighed. "Don't worry, it won't be you I'm haunting. I'm Vic."

That position was long filled by the dipshit that'd ruined my fucking life.

Hiram Wolff.

"A *vic* on both counts," she said, scrunching her nose. "I'm Della. Try not to die, okay?"

"Fuck, I can't wait to listen to them scream," a lanky, tattooed man said as he stretched his arms over his head. "Look at all the pretty prey—even the train is full of them."

His friend, just as tall and twice as wide, laughed unkindly. "Look at blue Barbie over there—I bet you she'll go for Truth or Dare. The slutty ones never want to get their hands dirty."

I straightened my back, looking out the window just as we emerged back overground and onto the bridge.

My breath caught in my chest.

Last year's Devil's Playground was Wild West themed—a fucking nightmare logistically, with way too much open space and not enough places to hide. I'd been hoping that this year would be a little bit more in my favor, but I'd *never* expected the flashing lights and bright colors of an amusement park.

It sort of reminded me of Disneyland.

A fog hung over the arena as the sky darkened. A large Ferris wheel turning slowly where it peeked over the high steel walls of the arena. Some taller rides, like the one that shot you up into space, and a two seater roller coaster were running, but even from this distance I could see there wasn't a soul on them.

The bright lights of the rides caused a halo-like effect over the island. Pitch black waves lapped at the cliffs of the island, clinging to the jagged rocks rising from the deep water.

It was eerie. Forbidding.

And we were heading straight toward it.

There wouldn't be a train back, not until the game was done. Once we arrived, we were stuck.

No way out.

Not like Disneyland *at all*.

"Oh, for fuck's sake," complained Della. "You think they'll dress the Killers like clowns? That shit creeps me out."

"I hope not," I muttered uncomfortably, my hand dipping into my pocket to pull out my nearly dead cell phone. Unconsciously, I pulled up the messaging app, clicking Kohl's contact.

KOHL

Sorry, gotta bail on our watch plans.

I'll make it up to you. Promise.

Don't do anything stupid.

My thumbs hovered over the keys. I hadn't replied, mostly because I didn't know what to say that wasn't, *It's cool, I wasn't going to show up anyway.*

My plan was to ditch Kohl in favor of catching the train. By the time they realized where I was, it would've been too late.

If they knew what was good for them, they were somewhere playing perfect little legacy with their father.

We'd promised each other that we wouldn't enter. It didn't matter what the expectations were. We were going to be the ones who stopped the cycle. Stop the games by refusing to participate.

That was before my life fell to pieces.

I couldn't afford to think like that anymore.

So, here I was, my affairs in order—at least as much as they could be for a nineteen-year-old with a dad in a coma and no other family except a fat, prissy cat.

The train slowed as it came into the station, finally lurching to a stop before the doors opened with a melodic chime. On the other side of the track, another train had just arrived, at least twelve full carriages dumping out onto the platform at the same time.

"Do you want to walk together?" Della asked, and I nodded gratefully.

Turns out that walking to your potential death was kind of scary as fuck, no matter how badly you needed the money.

It was nice to have some company.

She hooked her arm through mine, leading me out of the carriage and down the platform. I toddled along, looking around at the faces that I'd soon be fighting for survival. Either as fellow Ghosts, Killers I'd need to evade, or viewers I'd need to convince to keep me alive.

It was hard to breathe with so many people crowding together. Salty sea air from the ocean filled my nose, but it only made the air stickier, *thicker*. I tried to scan the crowd again, preparing myself for the Killers I'd have to run from.

Just ahead, a familiar stylized mullet came into view, blond hair partially obscured by a backward baseball cap. Even with the over-sized hoodie hugging their shoulders, it was unmistakable—Kohl was walking just ahead of me on the platform.

What. The. Fuck?!

My throat closed and I stopped walking. My hand snapped to the bracelet on my wrist—a bracelet that they had the partner of, given as a gift the last time we saw each other in person.

It was *stupid*. Obviously, a bit of string and magnetized metal didn't mean shit. Especially since I already knew I was lying when I gave it to them. But, still, I'd kind of hoped...

Kohl turned their head, and instead of their slightly rounded jaw and familiar smooth skin, I was met with another face—one that I knew all too well.

Dylan.

My ex-boyfriend and Kohl's older brother.

Shit.

"See someone you know?" a gruff voice asked me.

I whipped my head around, finding the tattooed guy from the train.

"N-no!" I stammered, grabbing Della's arm and pulling her down the platform and away from him as quickly as possible.

There were three kinds of people who entered the Devil's Playground:

1. The desperate, like me, who needed the money bad enough to risk being murdered for it.
2. The foolish, who hoped to obtain some kind of infamy by participating.
3. Sadists, people who wanted to hurt as many people as they could before the timer was up.

It was easy to tell what he was.

Option three, the same as Dylan.

My guts churned uncomfortably as I looked for him in the crowd but he was gone, swallowed up by the sea of unfamiliar faces.

Fuck.

He'd already played a couple years ago, so what the hell was he doing here?

Trying to fulfill his legacy by becoming the reigning kill score champion? In his first attempt, he'd missed the mark by only a couple hundred points.

That was the scary thing about Dylan. He was lethal, and he enjoyed knowing it.

At the end of the pier was a series of wickets, the words PLAYERS and VIEWERS lit above them in massive, red-painted letters framed by bare lightbulbs. It reminded me of ticket boxes at the fair—if the lines at the fair were fucked up queues to sign up for your inevitable gruesome murder, that was.

I cringed internally as Della and I stepped into the player line.

If I had to guess, my newfound friend was the second type of player. Looking to win big and make a name for herself. Truth or Dare had *some* risk, of course. But it was nothing in comparison to the bloodbaths during Hide and Seek and the maze.

I didn't bother to ask.

It wasn't smart to get attached. Not when we were both likely be dead by sunrise.

She shot me a thumbs up as she received her tracking bracelet— a sleek circular screen that looked like a smartwatch—and headed into tents beyond for hair and makeup.

"Identification?" a mustached man in a crisp white uniform asked, his belly protruding over the waistband of his slacks.

I reached into my pocket and pulled out my license, handing it to him.

"Event." It wasn't a question.

I cleared my throat, my palms slicking with sweat. "Hide and Seek."

"Hiding or seeking?"

"Hiding," I said, my hand wrapping around my wrist to touch my bracelet.

I'd been on the cheer squad and was counting on my flexibility to help me find a good place to wait this nightmare out until morning.

Or my agility if that plan went to shit.

More than knowing how to tumble, I also knew I could *hide*. I'd been doing it ever since the accident. Hiding from lawyers, the police, "friends" of Dad, you name it.

What was a couple more hours in the grand scheme of things?

At the very least, I could make it until morning.

I hoped.

He smiled nastily, his beady eyes widening as he pulled up my file and turned the keyboard toward me. "Oooh, always nice to see a little *Legacy*. What name will you be entering under?"

I typed the first thing that came to mind, the thing that no one who knew me would ever dream I'd use. The name my mom had used the year she won the games: *wh1t3_r4bb1t.*

Well, *almost* no one would expect it.

I knew that Hiram would see it on the roster and it'd make his miserable fucking blood boil.

Good.

"How nostalgic," the attendant praised, shoving a mass of plastic through the hole in the glass toward me. "Here is your body bag and a marker. In the next room, collect your uniform and put all personal items inside the bag. Write your name, address, and phone number on the bag. Or don't, if you don't care about your family getting whatever is left of you."

I nodded, feeling winded. The casual way this guy talked about my incredibly likely death was more than a little humbling.

He handed back my ID. "Wrist."

I sighed, offering him my right arm.

"This is your tracker. It'll let you know how long is left until sunrise, how many players are remaining, your assigned Seeker, and any other important information from the Architects. It also lets us know when to come collect your corpse. *Do not take it off.*"

"Got it," I said with an irritated edge to my voice. "Keep the jewelry on."

"Next!" he snarled, clearly not impressed by my cheek.

I breezed by, gripping the body bag and Sharpie as I stepped into the large tent beyond the wickets. I'd barely taken in the long metal benches when a stylist who introduced herself as Gwen tapped me to go into the room beyond to sit in her chair.

Around us, stylists ran between stations, pulling clothes from long racks and dusting glitter along cheekbones and on the tips of noses.

It was a little fucked up to me to apply highlighter that'd only be seen if you were dead, but hey, I was just a cog in The Corporation's twisted death game.

Looks like the Fixer tent—where the stylist's worked—was sponsored by Selena New York this year, with rows and rows of blushes, eyeshadows, lip colors, and whatever the fuck else lining workstations.

As much as I hated to admit it, a few years ago when LYX had sponsored, I *did* buy their setting spray after the games. If it could hold your smoky eye together while you were running for your fucking life, it could definitely handle cheer practice.

Given the event was being broadcasted on pay-per-view, it made a twisted sort of sense that The Company would do everything in their power to generate a profit off of it. That meant corporate sponsors. Ad revenue. Private investors.

Sick. Twisted. Evil motherfuckers who got satisfaction out of the suffering of the desperate so long meant a big fat check that paid for a third vacation home.

Fuck 'em.

As big of a part staying alive by your own merit was, you also needed to convince the viewers to help you—to follow your *storyline*. If you were *interesting*, or at the very least *desirable*, they might just choose to save your life.

Ugly people were worthless.

Uninteresting people were disposable.

That was the reality of the game I was playing.

I filled out the information on the body bag card and stripped to my underwear while Gwen picked out my clothes.

When she returned, all soft curves and bright pink hair, she was grinning. "Rabbit, right?"

I nodded tensely. "That's me."

"Great, get dressed. I love your hair. How do you feel about pigtails?"

I took the clothes from her, pulling on the black utility pants and matching sports bra before the cropped hoodie and zipper detailing crawled over my left shoulder, adding a bitch of an edge to the look. The pants were a little big, but they'd come with a belt that I tightened to the maximum.

Once I was seated in the makeup chair, I dumped my phone, wallet, and keys into the body bag and zipped it up.

Gwen applied moisturizer to my face before she started on my makeup. "Didn't a rabbit win one year?"

"Yeah," I said distractedly, regretting putting my phone in the bag already.

Not like it would do me any good to text Kohl *now*.

Once they realized what I'd done—that I'd lied to them and entered the games anyway—they were going to fucking lose it.

But I didn't have time to worry about that shit, I needed to get my head in the game.

That meant forgetting about them.

And all the shit I'd never say.

And the fact that the last thing they'd remember of me is that I'd used them.

Fuck.

I gripped the armrests of the chair, my fingernails leaving half moons in the soft leather.

No, I was going to survive this. And then I'd tell them everything.

Y'know, like that I'd been in love with them since the day we met. And that I didn't want them to be a casualty in my fucked-up disaster of a life.

Some of the other stylists were murmuring to their Ghosts as well and I heard an unmistakable sniffle through the noise. Drugs or crying, it didn't matter. It was time to get it the fuck together.

"Big fan?" the stylist asked, rushing through my contour and blusher.

"She was my mom."

The woman's lips formed a comical "o." "*Legacy* then. Did she enter as a Ghost too?"

I nodded, my lips twitching at the colloquial term. It was a nice way of talking about entrants to Hide and Seek who opted to hide. Either you were *dead* or *invisible*. Either way you'd be a *Ghost*.

"She must be proud," she said, applying a sharp coat of eyeliner to my closed eyelids. *She's dead,* I wanted to say, but I kept my mouth shut. "Honestly, I don't want to doll you up too much, you're so gorgeous as is. Besides, they won't see it under the mask anyway."

"Sure," I muttered, "Whatever you think is best."

Half an hour later I was done, my hair pulled into two long pigtails at the back of my head, a white rabbit mask clutched in my hands as I walked out of the tent.

The flash of a camera made me see stars, my bracelet humming to life.

Play hard, die famous, I thought bitterly.

As I made it to my gate, I scanned the crowd for familiar faces. I was just about to pull on my mask when a sharp bob of dark hair turned around, her eyes widening into saucers as she pushed toward me.

"Vic!"

"Jenna," I hissed, pulling my mask over my face. "It's white rabbit now."

"Right, sorry—I wasn't expecting to see you. God, I love your hair. You're going to clean up on gifts."

I adjusted the back of my white rabbit mask, making sure it was safely secured over my face.

"Right," I said slowly. "Are you ready?"

"Ready as I'll ever be," she said with a soft laugh. "I can't believe you're here. *Miss-I-Am-Never-Doing-That-Evil-Post-Capitalist-Bullshit* herself."

"Things change," I said tersely. "Is anyone else with you?"

She bobbed her head, pulling a black rabbit mask over her face. "Jack is here somewhere, and I'm pretty sure I saw Kohl too."

I scoffed. "Actually, I got a good look at him. It's Dylan."

"Fucked," Jenna muttered. "We should stick together for the first couple hours, then split up when the pack starts to thin."

Given I didn't have any other allies, I nodded in agreement.

I just hoped that we'd both find a way to survive this.

It'd be a bummer to watch the Custodians spray her brain matter off the concrete.

Kohl

Before the Games

I spat out the blood pooling in my mouth—right on the fucker's pristine leather shoes. Watching as it slid down to the gravel below.

Partly as a final way to defy him before they left me for dead.

Partly because I didn't want to look at my fucked up face in the shine.

My eye was swollen and purple, a deep cut in my eyebrow pouring blood down the side of my face. My teeth had shredded the side of my cheek after a couple blows to my jaw.

Lovely.

"What d'you say?" Murphy asked, his yellowed teeth bared in a shit-eating grin. His voice cutting through the silence of the dark alley way they had cornered me in.

"*Sorry,*" I forced through gritted teeth.

"Didn't quite hear that," he said, leaning closer to my spot on the ground. "Repeat it for me, sweetheart. One more time."

His associates—better referred to as *goons* given their paperboy caps and dirty jeans—laughed around him. It was easy to be brave when you had the upper hand.

Especially when the person you had the upper hand on was a scrawny high schooler. *Fuck*, I really needed to hit the gym.

The violent anger simmering beneath my skin came to a boil.

I hated him.

Hated him more than just about anyone in this world.

Adding insult to injury, Murphy wasn't even the one in charge. Not really.

He just couldn't pass up the opportunity to feel powerful for once in his pathetic life. To make a *Legacy* grovel at his feet.

As much as I was loath to admit it, I understood the urge.

Most of the Legacies out there were spoiled brats without a clue of what the real world was like. What lurked behind the cameras. Screaming fans and sponsorships.

Sickos who entered the games *for fun*, ignoring the very real possibility of their own deaths. Turns out it didn't matter how famous you or your parents were or how much money you had, a bullet to the brain would kill you just the same.

But I was nothing like *them*. Not like my father, who left whatever shreds of humanity he had in the first place in that arena. Not like my brother, who'd made a sport out of exploiting his title as a legacy for all it was worth. I hated everything that the games stood for. Hated how much they'd fucked up my life.

If not for them, I wouldn't be here, *embarrassing myself.*

If the games didn't exist, the man my father had become would be no more. Maybe he'd have been a normal parent fifty percent of the time. Show up to parent-teacher meetings. Drive me to football practice. Not spend all his time dreaming up ways to climb the ranks of the producers of a game that was a glorified for-profit prison where the only sentence was the death penalty.

And *Vic*—

"Cat got your tongue?" Murphy asked, pulling me back to the present.

It didn't matter what circumstances had led me here. At the end of the day, I still needed to get this shit over with. And quickly.

Another bout of laughter stoked the flames of my temper as I fought to rise to my feet. My ankle had to be busted, and if it wasn't my ankle, it was my knee. All I knew was that my legs and weight weren't mixing.

Where the fuck is Terrance?

The leader of this pitiful group of ragtag petty criminals had pushed me off to fucking *Murphy* as if I was some minor annoyance. Not someone he'd been doing business with for *years*.

It irritated me more than it hurt, but I couldn't write off just how easily he dumped me into this loser's lap.

Billy Murphy. Seasoned enough to know that no matter what my family name was, I wouldn't go running to Daddy. But stupid enough to think I'd take it lying down.

He was taking every advantage he could, failing to consider what would happen if I decided that *nothing* was worth—

Remember who you're doing this for.

But my problem wasn't remembering. There wasn't a second that went by that I didn't think about what happened to her. Where I wasn't trying to come up with a plan on how to help.

That's how I ended up here, as a fucking errand boy to the Jackals. They weren't even a high-level gang. It was fucking *pathetic*.

The problem was my own damned pride.

It was becoming more and *more* obvious that I needed to find money somewhere I wouldn't be getting my ass kicked on the regular.

I couldn't sit through beating after beating in some dirty back alley for some fucking pocket change. It was *insulting*. And not just because my allowance had been twice the pennies they offered me since I was *seven*. But because I deserved to be treated like a human, damn it. If I wanted to be treated like a show pony I would've just sold my soul and joined the games from the start.

The urge to stagger to my feet and slam my fist into Murphy's ugly, unshaved face was beginning to gnaw at the dwindling threads of my patience.

"I'm not going to fucking ask again, Kohl."

I gritted my teeth so hard my jaw ached, taking a deep breath through my nose. My raw fingertips dug into the gravel painfully as

I bowed my head, keeping my eyes locked on the slate pebbles beneath me.

My body shuddered with the force of my restraint—barely keeping myself curled in front of him, my bruised ribs searing with every breath of musty, garbage-filled air.

"I'm sorry, *sir*," I said, making sure my voice carried. The words sent a wave of nausea through me as they crossed my taste buds.

Fuck you, slime.

His gnarled hand ruffled the top of my bottle blonde hair—anything I could do to look less like my family. Pain flashed through my head as he dug his nails into my scalp.

It was the last straw.

His grubby, sweaty, *filthy* hands set off an explosion through me.

I jerked my head up, looking him square in the face. The crazed smile I'd been holding in spread across my face, stretching my cheeks until they ached. I let all the anger and frustration inside me bubble in my chest, making my body shake with anticipation and my fists clench.

"*Damn*," I said with a sigh that almost sounded remorseful. "I really wish I could've held out for just a bit longer."

Murphy's eyes widened, his lips parting as he realized I'd finally had enough. Before he could utter a single word, I sprung at him like a cobra, ignoring my aching body in favor of colliding with his round torso.

The world moved in slow motion around me, and his cronies left without so much as a second to react as I toppled their faux *leader*.

Murphy's steel-gray eyes widened comically as he tried to evade my raising fist. A futile move, but one I understood.

What I didn't understand was how they could really think I would just lie there and take their bullshit. They hadn't counted on just how *suicidal* I could be.

Sure, beating this fucking dipshit into a pulp would ruin my chance at securing this job, but I'd find another.

I'm sorry, my goddess. I'm so sorry. I promise I'll make it up to you in another way.

Hold on for me.

My fist slammed into the left side of Murphy's jaw, the same place mine was still aching. I couldn't help the laugh that slipped from my lips as his head snapped to the side.

Shouts echoed around us as people spurred into action, but I was able to ram my fist into the fuckers nose before multiple pairs of hands yanked me away.

"Come on, you little bitch! Can't you fight your own battles? Now that I'm not sitting pretty, you're *scared*, aren't you?"

Murphy cupped his bloodied nose, glaring daggers at me. But my view of him was short-lived as his men surrounded me.

Fuck me and my stupid fucking temper—

Fists rained down on me, pain shooting through the left side of my head. Then my lower back. Then my legs. There was no strategy to their attack, just to overwhelm.

And *goddamn*, did it work.

I was forced to my knees, unable to keep up with the assault on my already battered body. I tried to swing at the faceless men around me, tried aiming for their groins, even tried grabbing onto their arms to sink my teeth into... but there were just too many of them.

I didn't stand a chance.

Punch after punch was aimed at me. I got a few in myself, but then my arms were pulled back, stopping me from making contact and keeping me open to their assault. But I didn't let that stop me. I jerked my body and head back viciously, fighting even if it was futile.

That was the thing about Legacies—we never knew when to fucking quit.

Winning was in my fucking genes.

I will make it out of this.

"Hey!" a familiar voice shouted over the chaos. "If I see that fucking Wolff brat in the middle of this goddamn mess, there will be more than one body dropped at their father's feet tonight."

Just like that, their hands were off me. My muscles burned as I fought the urge to crumple to the ground. Each breath ached worse than the last, my vision blurred with blood and swelling.

Fuck, I probably had a concussion.

I rolled my shoulders and lifted my chin, putting on a brave face. That was the worst thing about shitbags like the Jackals, if they thought they'd broken you, things would only get so much *worse*.

Fuck, I *definitely* had a concussion.

Terrance pushed through the crowd. His dark eyes simmering with anger as he took in the mess they'd made of my face. He commanded the room without any words. As soon as his eyes drifted toward the men, they scurried away like the rats they were.

"Game pre-registration starts in two weeks. Which one of you idiots wants to tell Hiram that you busted up his kid's face before press photos?" Terrance asked, striding forward purposefully, his lacquered boots crunching the gravel beneath. He stopped in front of me, crouching to my eye level with a frown that caused something to shift inside me.

I'd never much cared for my father's disappointment, but his *hurt*. Terrance wasn't somebody I was forced into a relationship with because of my parentage. I'd chosen him.

And I'd let him down.

"I gave you this job because I like you, kid. Tell me why this is the *third* fight I've found you in?" His tone wasn't condescending, but that didn't stop it from feeling like the scolding that it was. Like a parent who'd found out that a child had gotten a C on their geometry test.

"I wouldn't *get* into fights if the worthless goons you hired didn't get a hard-on at the thought of a human punching bag," I spat, trying to ignore my bruised feelings.

Terrance frowned and looked back at Billy, his broad frame largely supported by his men.

A dark satisfaction curled in my stomach when I saw just how bloodied and wrecked his face was.

That's right, you fucked around and found out, asshole.

I wouldn't be delivering the final blow, I knew that. It was all Terrance. But at least my punches would make a painful memory for him. I wasn't the scrawny brat I was a few years ago, even if I had a long way to go.

I made a mental note to up my protein intake. I'd need it if everything else went to shit and I actually had to enter—

"They were short *two hundred!*" Murphy yelled, shakily pointing a finger at me. "I was teaching them a lesson."

"Come here and try again," I goaded, not caring anymore about fucking myself out of future jobs. Terrance was going to cut me—I already knew it from the look on his face when he arrived.

Might as well get a few final digs in before I disappeared.

"Wipe that fucking smirk off your face, Kohl," Terrance snapped.

I hadn't realized the smile had made its way back until he mentioned it. I carefully schooled my features into a look of mild apathy, steeling myself for what came next.

"You knew this was coming," Terrance said with a sigh as he stood, dusting his hands off on his tailored pants. "But I can't keep you around anymore. Not like this. You're too angry, kid. Too much of a loose cannon to be around the guys—"

"Then hire new people," I fought in a harsh whisper. "You know I need this job. Why else would I stay here just to get pummeled into the ground? You think I'm some kind of masochist?"

Okay, fine, I was. But I only cared to suffer at the hands of one person.

My *goddess.* I'd let her divine vengeance reign on me in any way she pleased.

For the first time, Terrance let pity show on his face.

"Your father—"

"Leave him out of this," I warned in a low growl.

Anything. I'd do just about anything so he wouldn't find out.

Anything except take those punches.

My former mentor—and as close to a real father figure as I had—gave me a sad smile.

"We both know I can't do that," Terrance said. "Your father was the reason I took you in. But the reason I'm letting you go is because I care about you, kid. Trust me when I say that you have better things out there waiting for you."

"Yeah, right," I muttered under my breath.

There was *nothing* waiting for me out there.

Not a job. Not a family. Not... *her.*

"I'm serious," Terrance said with a quirk of his lips, which was something like a fatherly smile. "Do something productive with your life. You're still young. Don't end up like these guys."

I sighed, looking down at the bloodied gravel.

"I don't want to end up like *him* either," I murmured.

Terrance squeezed my shoulder, the warmth of his hand sinking through my torn shirt and into my aching flesh.

"Then make your own path," he said, then added like it was a humorous afterthought. "If I ever see you on this side of town again, I'll bust your fucking kneecap. Then your balls."

I couldn't stop the bark of laughter that forced its way out of my throat. But I did manage not to correct him.

Whether or not I had balls to bust wasn't really the issue.

He helped me up, and then with a final squeeze of his hand, I was shuffling down the alley toward home.

How the fuck was I going to get that money now?

VIC

The lights above the doors flashed green, the doors sliding slowly upward. Jenna and I ducked below them, breaking into a run along with the rest of the crowd.

I grabbed hold of her wrist, worried we'd get separated in the jostling bodies as we sprinted.

We'd need to get as deep into the park as possible before the Seekers entered the arena after us, the countdown on my watch warning with every step that we were losing our head start.

For one wild moment, the arena reminded me of the last day of summer before senior year.

Kohl, Dylan, and I had gone to an amusement park to find some cotton candy and hit the rides. It was fun—as fun as spending time with Dylan ever was, at least.

But quickly the park turned into something sinister—*haunting.*

Rides towered above us, the metal beams used to support them creaking as we raced past. The salty ambrosia of buttered popcorn mixed with mold hung in a potent cloud. There was a film of dust and grime on everything. Overgrown vines running up the booths and cracked concrete underneath our feet.

Even the public bathrooms looked like they were barely

standing on their own. The wooden paneling splintered and cracked.

The shock of the environment made me want to stop. I'd expected the park to be frightening–but this looked like it had been here for years instead of just a couple months. Down to the rusted hardware and peeling paint.

The chill of the park seeped through my clothes, threatening to make me freeze.

But that was the *point*.

They wanted the Ghosts to pause as soon as they were in. To let the shock and fear fill them for even just a moment too long so they were easy to pick off.

As if I'd give them the satisfaction.

I pushed myself forward, ignoring the fear making my guts churn uncomfortably.

A quick glance as my watch warned that we'd already lost two and a half precious minutes.

We passed by a section of the park dedicated to fair games. Bright red flashing signs hung from the entrance, enticing a few Ghosts to try their luck in the measly amount of time we had left. Prizes hung from the stalls, but instead of colorful stuffed animals and inflatable hammers, it was full of guns, knives, spiked baseball bats, and explosives waiting like trophies. Some of them already had blood on them.

Even Jenna slowed like she wanted to try to make a grab for a weapon.

A stupid idea, as killing a Seeker always had consequences. The point was to hide from them, not to turn into a hunter yourself.

I shook her arm. "Didn't you watch last year? There is stuff hidden everywhere. We need to find a place to—"

That same, ear-piercing, shrieking alarm sounded warning us that danger was coming. The sound had been ingrained into my mind front the first game I'd ever watched. The same as the ones used for tornadoes and floods. Designed specifically to be unmissable—and to incite anxiety.

To make you want to *run*.

The Seekers are coming.

An electronically cheery, staticky announcement played over the speakers.

"Welcome to Hide and Seek! The game is *easy*. If you're hiding, stay hidden. If you're seeking, find and eliminate. Seekers have now entered the arena, prepare for combat."

Shit.

My memories blurred with the present. The smell of popcorn and burned sugar was bright in my nose, the sounds of whooshing rides coming to a halt, the pings of the carnival games around us. All of it so *similar* to the comforting thoughts I had of Kohl.

At least until the *screaming* started.

"We need to get out of the open," I said as we ran as far from the front door as our legs could take us.

This year, it didn't look like revolvers had been part of the uniform—thank fuck for that. But it didn't make the threat of stray bullets or *aimed* bullets any less serious.

"There!" Jenna shouted, pointing to a food truck up ahead. It was on wheels, but they had been rusted and bent, one of them almost falling off all together.

I didn't like it, but our head start was long over, and we'd need shelter to wait out the initial fray.

Like most Legacies, I'd watched every Games since I was a kid. It was just a part of my life. When I was little, it was like I didn't quite understand that they were real. It was too unrealistic to my pampered, childlike mind that people could really be desperate enough to sign up for their deaths. That they could possibly have something they needed so badly that dying was preferable to going without it.

What I wouldn't give to be that naive again.

How fucking humiliating to be here because I needed the money.

One of the benefits of being a Legacy was that it was supposed to afford you a comfortable life. Turned out that only worked out for *some* of us.

I wasn't supposed to have to enter the games out of desperation. It was supposed to be for family honor.

Duty. Obligation.

My birthright.

Fuck that.

At least my shitbag mom taught me one thing: *how to win.*

I repeated her strategy in my head as I kneeled to boost Jenna up into the truck.

Rule number one: Get out of the open.

She crawled over the counter, dropping down inside and offering me a hand to help me up. My boots slipped on the rusted metallic wall of the truck, but I managed to get in. The two of us sat with our backs against the cool cooking equipment as we listened to chaos unfold around us and our own panting breaths. Beneath us was that same splintered wood that seemed to cover the park. The discomfort of it was a welcome distraction—a good way to keep my head clear.

Rule number two: Don't hide somewhere a stray bullet could hit you.

The telltale sound of gunfire met my ears, making my stomach sour. There were so many Seekers infiltrating the park. I could hear their footsteps pounding against the concrete. Screams ringing out mere moments after the shots.

Fucking hell.

"I didn't expect them to get guns so fast," Jenna hissed as footfalls passed by.

"Of-fucking-course it had to be a goddamn carnival," I whispered harshly, fighting the urge to look out the windows to watch for Dylan.

He hadn't seen me, and I'd skipped the pre-season. There's no way he knew that I was here... *right?*

And why the fuck was he playing again?

He couldn't have known that I'd enter, so it had to be something else he was playing at.

I glanced at my watch, grinning as the white viewer count in the top right corner started climbing. I knew the hair would draw attention, but the outfit Gwen chose was positively *sinful*. Eye-catching.

Exactly what I needed.

Heavy footfalls approached around the side of the truck, warning me that other players were close by. Jenna put her hand over her mouth, trying to dull the sound of her panting breaths, and I followed her lead.

"Boost me up!" a feminine voice called. "I want to check if anyone is hiding inside."

Jenna and I shared a panicked glance.

Fuck.

Fuck. Fuck. Fuck.

No way was I going out like this, not in the very first fucking opportunity to prove myself.

I glanced around the truck, my eyes catching on a heavy metal frying pan hanging from a hook overhead. If I stood up, they'd see me, and if they had guns—I was fucked.

"What are you going to do, choke them to death? We should get weapons first..." another female said, her voice whinier than the first.

"I said, boost me!"

"Fine," the other girl snapped. "Your funeral."

Privately, I agreed.

Finally, rule number three: If all else fails, fight for your life.

These were odds I could tolerate. And information I was willing to gamble on.

As the Seeker's boots slid against the side of the truck just on the other side from where we were hidden, I lurched forward for the frying pan.

"Gotcha!" she shouted in triumph. "You're dead, blue."

I grabbed the handle, freeing it from the hanging rack, and turned, almost laughing aloud at the glow of the pink, heart-shaped marks around the Seeker's eyes.

"You think so?" I said, my lip curling as I pulled my arm back and struck her so hard in the face that her nose exploded on impact, the blood seeping from her mask. I grabbed her arm, pulling her into the truck with us—leaving her friend stranded outside.

Jenna jumped on her instantly, locking her arm around the girl's neck. "Pass out, pass out, pass out," she demanded in a panicked voice.

And for good reason, the clang of metal against her skull was already drawing attention, other Seekers approaching the truck.

I poked my head up, my skin going cold as my eyes locked onto the unmistakable form of my ex-boyfriend, glowing blue mask and all.

"We gotta dip!" I shouted, throwing the back door of the truck open and jumping down.

If Dylan got his hands on me—*if he realized who I was*—he wouldn't just kill me. He'd torture me first. Pay me back for the *'heartbreak'* I put him through.

Honestly, I'd rather take my chances with the hundreds of other Seekers waiting to murder me. At least for them it wasn't personal.

Game respects game.

Jenna dropped the girl, chasing after me as I rounded the truck, meeting me just as the first gunshot whizzed by.

"What do we do?" Jenna gasped, her voice high and panicked. "Vic, what do we do?!"

"Get a grip," I snarled, looking around for somewhere, anywhere, that we could hide.

The shooting range was like signing our death warrant.

The Gravitron was too spinny.

But then there was—yes! Just up ahead was a brightly painted info booth. The sides of it were just tall enough that if we crouched, we could hide out at least for another few precious minutes.

Beside me, Jenna was hyperventilating.

I don't know why I expected anything more from her, Legacy or not, she was always too soft for the realities of the games.

I dropped the pan, using my newly freed hand to slap her across the face. "Bitch, get your shit together. We aren't dead yet. But we're fucking going to be if you don't get your head in the game."

She gripped her cheek, tears streaming down her face under her black rabbit mask.

"Vic—"

"Run!" I shouted, hauling her behind me with my grip on her wrist as I sprinted. A bullet hit the ground too close to my foot for comfort and I pivoted abruptly, nearly colliding with a purple-masked asshole waiting beside the info booth that I hadn't even noticed until I was practically on top of him.

How could I be so fucking unlucky?

KOHL

THE GODS OF THE GAMES WERE ON MY SIDE.

I'd been criminally unlucky since I'd been born, forced into a family that only saw me as a way to continue their legacy instead of a person. But for once in my sorry life, that was all changing.

For the first time, something was going my way.

The white rabbit I'd spotted in the waiting area nearly collided with me as she ran by, with the black rabbit—*my target*—just behind her.

I'd been jogging in the other direction, hoping to cover as much ground as I could, when I came into view of the beat-up wooden stall that housed the info center.

When I turned, there they were coming right toward me, their attention fractured by whoever they'd been running from.

Greedy bastards.

With the size of the arena, I worried I'd never find my target, there's no way they'd already found theirs. That was the thing about Hide and Seek though: the more people you killed, the more points you'd earn—meaning you'd be more likely to *win*.

And I *had* to win.

It just proved to my twisted sense that joining the games was the right move. It was hardly an hour into the match, and here she was, my black rabbit.

My goddess had delivered her to me as surely as the sun would rise.

Or maybe my father's manic lectures about our superior genetics were actually true. Maybe there was *something* about how breeding Legacies would create children that were more suitable to hideous acts of violence.

That we were fitter. Stronger. The most likely to win.

That we'd do what we needed to do.

It was easier to get my head in the game this way. To turn myself into a creature that Freud himself would've flinched away from. Reigned entirely by my ego until I could quiet the feeble doubts that might've asked me to save her life.

I was born for this. Winning was in my *blood*.

And I couldn't wait to taste the failure in hers.

The white rabbit corrected course before I could grab hold of her, blue pigtails streaming by as she ran. It didn't matter. For the time being, she wasn't my target.

"Where are you going in such a hurry?" I asked the black rabbit, moving to get into her path.

She stumbled backward, her eyes widening behind the mask. "P-please! I'm—I'm a Legacy!"

I snorted a laugh as I approached her. "Like that means anything to me."

Adrenaline pumped through my veins, burning metal and salt flooding my nose with every inhale. The sound of the cheery music blaring through the crackling speakers—paired with distant screaming—only made my heart pound harder in my chest.

Begrudgingly, I had to admit that the Architects had outdone themselves. If I didn't know better, I'd have thought this was a real amusement park that'd been seeing families through its doors for years instead of a high-budget murder den. It could use some love, but the obvious ruin of the place made for a *much* better set for the show.

She moved to pivot, her dark hair swaying around her jaw as she rounded me to head for the information booth. I raced after her, putting as much power into my steps as possible. I was taller, my strides longer. It was only a matter of time before I caught her.

Like I said, *lucky.*

I thrust my hand out in front of me, grabbing the back of her long hoodie just as she made to jump over the counter. But she was already hauling herself over, and my grip slipped as she let out a scream of triumph.

"A bit early for that, isn't it?" I hissed.

I lunged forward, grabbing on to my victim's ankle and pulling her back over the decaying wood. The flimsy boards creaked as her nails gripped into them, trying desperately to hold on to her only chance of surviving this game.

*She won't live. It's destiny, just as **I** was destined to take her life so I could win... for her.*

All for you, my goddess.

"Not so fast," I sneered, catching the terror in her eyes behind her mask before I threw her to the dirtied ground. Black rabbit let out a moan of pain, the air pushing from her lungs.

She tried to gasp for another, but she was unsuccessful, the breath stopping just short. It almost made me feel bad, I could recognize the early stages of a panic attack a mile away.

Too bad it wouldn't do her any good.

"Please!" she huffed, hands clawing into the concrete as she tried to get back to her feet.

Not that there was anywhere to go. The Killers they'd been running from were coming into view, boxing her in on both sides.

Her desperation to get away from me made a smile pull at my mouth.

Little did she know there were *much* worse monsters than me. At least I'd make it quick.

And yet... there was something inside me. Something sick that loved the way she reacted with my every movement. I'd felt the same fear when I was weak and unable to defend myself from the bullies in my life.

My father.

My brother.

Murphy and the fucking losers he called employees.

But not anymore. Even the acknowledgment that I was no longer a weak, pathetic loser was enough to push me forward, eager to claim my power.

Not that I needed it with her on the ground.

Pitiful.

It was like watching a deer in headlights. They knew all too well the dangers that lay ahead, but they were unable to do anything but *stare.*

It was fucking intoxicating. Second only to the feel of *her* skin against mine.

The black rabbit's mask fell askew, only partially hiding her bruised cheek. She ripped it the rest of the way off, flinging it aside to gasp for air.

I froze.

Jenna.

My classmate's terror-filled face caused something to shift in my chest. Something that threatened to dismantle the high that was running through me.

A whisper, not quite a memory, forced itself to the front of my conscience.

It was an essay question, something that I'd seen a hundred times in my academic career. It wasn't like the systematic brain-washing of Legacies to turn us into murder machines stopped at home—it extended into our lives at school too. Especially since I went to specialized academy.

How would you win your games?

The question wasn't anything special, really. I'd had my answer down to a science.

They always try to knock you off your strategy by changing the arena, but really it was the same shit in a different font. Find your target and kill them before someone else does.

But it wasn't my answer that came to mind, it was hers.

I wouldn't.

I pushed it away, steeling myself. I didn't have time to feel. That was for after the games. Right now I needed to put this little *rabbit* out of her misery.

"Don't take this personally, yeah?" I asked and lurched forward as she tried to crawl away.

I put my weight on her, pinning her body to the ground.

I didn't like the way her body squirmed under me. Didn't like the way her voice was familiar as she pleaded for me to stop. But she would just be the first of many. I ordered the part of my brain that hesitated to harden.

If I didn't get used to it from the beginning, there would be no getting to the end.

I needed to forget what this felt like. Needed to forget what it felt like to be the one pushed into the dirt. What it felt like to *care*.

I cursed myself for not picking up a weapon before I found her. There was something... *personal* about using your bare hands to kill someone. Something I wasn't sure I'd be able to handle.

Maybe in a few more kills when the high was all I could think of... Maybe then I could get creative in the pursuit of extra points.

Remember why you are doing this. The Company gave you this opportunity for her.

"Please!" Jenna screamed. "Please let me go! I didn't have a choice. I—"

I searched the ground around us, looking for anything to use. When my hands grasped a cool, rusted piece of metal pulled off the information booth during our struggle, I raised it, ready to bring it down on the back of her head.

Before I could hit her, something hard hit the side of my face, sending pain exploding through my cheek. My body jerked to the side and my ears were ringing, the pain traveling through my body and dampening my high.

"*Fuck,*" I groaned and tilted my head back, hoping the starry night sky would do *something* to stop the pain enough for me to continue.

The distraction caused the victim below me to wiggle out of my grasp. I didn't have it in me to reach for her. I was barely sitting upright. I blinked a few times to clear my double vision.

"Go Jenna!" a familiar voice yelled. In the wake of what was likely a concussion, I almost thought it sounded like Vic.

I turned toward the voice to find the white rabbit had returned, her teeth gritting in fury. The shadows from the structure caused her body to be shrouded in darkness, but I could just make out her glare from behind the mask.

That little bitch.

Jenna was already running around the info booth, her breathing heavy and her mask in her shaking hands.

The little rabbits were terrified, but the *views...* I imagined them in the darkness, the screens lighting up their faces as they spent hours watching us wail on the victims. As they zoomed in on their phones to get a better look at their panic-filled faces.

They always loved when they fought back.

I wondered what I could do to keep their attention even more. What would make them click those little buttons that would guarantee me an advantage over the rest?

"Little rabbits, not so easy to kill, hm?" I asked, pushing myself off the ground with my metal weapon of opportunity gripped in my hands. "Let's get this over with. I have a game to win."

She stood there, her eyes narrowing behind the mask. Her friend was watching her, waiting for her signal, but the blue-haired rabbit was letting her eyes roam my body, sizing me up.

Fuck. She's strategizing, better nip that in the bud. Makes her more dangerous than the others.

"*Run,*" I said in an excited whisper.

She jerked back as if realizing what the situation was. No matter if they lived for a short while, they were in the presence of a Seeker who wouldn't stop until they were dead. She turned to run, grabbing her friend's hand as they booked it around the other end of the info booth and deeper into the park.

She wouldn't be as easy to catch as her friend... which made me wish she was my true target instead. I chased after them, rounding the booth and breaking into a sprint.

A ping cut through the air.

"Plus two for playing chase," a robotic voice said from my tracker. I couldn't hold in my laugh.

"Scared, rabbits?" I yelled at them. "A *Wolff* is chasing you."

Jenna looked back at me in fear, but the other rabbit didn't let my comment phase her.

She was small, but she sure as hell was fast. She zipped through the park with ease, her grip on her friend keeping them at the same pace. It was almost annoying how fast they were.

They wound between rides, snack booths and, souvenir stands while making their way down toward the games.

It was a smart move. The rides would be the perfect way to corner her, while the carnival stalls held something critical if they wanted to make it until morning—*weapons*. Ones that had the chance to turn the games around for a pair of desperate Ghosts.

A chance I wouldn't let blue get.

She has to be a Legacy.

Someone who had been around the games their entire lives. Had family dinners where all they did was talk strategy.

I knew because my father did the same, beating into us exactly what kind of bullshit Ghosts would pull to try and save their skins. His words were running through my mind. Reminding me how to corner them. How to act without hesitating so you didn't lose points.

It wasn't totally our fault, the games wouldn't exist if people didn't watch. The audience dictated how and when we earned points and privileges.

Really, it was *their* fault.

If they didn't watch, I wouldn't be here.

But since my view count was climbing by tens of thousands and they *liked it* the more bloodthirsty Seekers were... I didn't have much of a choice.

I was just following the rules.

Blood pumped through my body, my heart pounding in my ears. I was vaguely aware of screams around me, but I paid no mind. All they did was serve to push me forward, fueled by the idea that other Seekers had found their victims. If I didn't secure at least another point, I'd be left behind.

My goal was clear. My mind unburdened. And yet... for some reason I couldn't get the little blue-haired rabbit out of my mind. She excited me as much as she grated my patience.

A challenge, that's all it was. A reward for when I'd finished off Jenna.

I wondered which one of her useless, vapid friends she was.

In a move I didn't expect, the white rabbit took a sharp turn, pushing herself over the fence surrounding the carousel. Her friend followed clumsily.

Whoever she was, she was athletic at least.

There was nowhere to run back there, what's she thinking?

"You're wrong if you think that's going to save you!" I called as I jumped over the fence, attempting to grab the slower rabbit.

The white rabbit pulled her right out of my grip, the pair disappearing between the peeling pastel painted, rust stained horses as the machinery spun us. There was already a fair share of blood on almost every surface of the ride, thickening as it cooled.

"Not as fast as you think you are," the white rabbit called, disappearing around the bend of the ride. "What a *loser*."

I tried to follow, but when I arrived at the spot where they'd been, I found myself alone with only a discarded Ghosts body crumpled on the ground to keep me company.

The sound of my heavy breathing and the loud music from the ride were the only things I could hear. No footsteps, no breathing besides my own, nothing. It was deafening.

Panic inducing.

I saw a flash of blue right outside the ride. My head snapped toward it, just catching the end of her hair as she raced by. Grumbling under my breath, I followed.

Fucking. Legacies.

I paused when I came to a large tower of a ride. It was the sort of thing where you strapped people in, and it would climb higher and higher until dropping suddenly. It was rickety, like most of the rides I'd seen, making it all the more frightening.

The rabbits were nowhere to be seen, but I caught sight of something *worse*.

The group that'd been going after my rabbits was there, laughing as they held onto a struggling victim. The girl's cries echoed throughout the park as they tried to force her onto one of those rides that shot into the air and simulated falling, only this one had frayed ropes for harnesses.

I had a strong stomach and an even stronger need to win, but there were some things even I wouldn't do. Points were points, and I planned to *play* with my victims when the time came, but never *torture*.

"Please!" she screamed. "I'm not even worth that much to you, just let me go!"

The largest of them—who I dubbed as the leader of the group —threw his head back and let out a booming laugh. His golden-blonde hair stood out in contrast to the all-black outfit he was wearing, his blue mask glowing.

He waved her off and motioned for the other two to load her onto the ride.

"What do you mean?" he asked. "I already cashed out three points just by breaking your fingers. Can you imagine what they'd give me if we play a little target practice?"

My veins froze over as I heard his words. Not just because of how cruel they were... but because I *recognized that voice.*

The rabbits were forgotten in an instant, my mind whirling as I took a shaky step forward.

He can't be. Why the fuck is he—

Her guttural scream pulled me closer to them. They noticed

right away, pausing when I approached. At first, it looked like they were ready to fight, but once they caught sight of my mask, they calmed immediately.

"What the fuck are you doing here?" I growled and took a step closer to the leader, his happy blue mask and newly blonde hair mocking me.

The woman in his grip shook against him.

"Play nice, *Kohl*," he said, a teasing tone filling his words. "Gotta say, I'm surprised to see you."

I lunged forward, hooking my fingers behind his mask and tearing it away from his face.

A face similar to mine came into view, illuminated by the lights of the ride. The only difference was the slight stubble on his jaw, which was slightly more defined.

He even went so far as to dye his hair.

His presence here was like a punch to the gut. All the years of being beat into submission and being the joke of his friend group flashed across my mind in a haze of unwelcome trauma masquerading as memories.

I'd tried my hardest to forget about how he treated me. To forget the instinct to *fear* him.

But seeing him caught me so off guard that just a sliver of that fear forced its way to the front of my mind.

Dylan. My brother. Someone who'd already been through the games and shouldn't have been here in the first place.

I swallowed my feelings and grabbed on to the anger that swirled in my veins. I wanted to force my fist into his face. Wanted to lunge at him for everything he and Father caused.

It took more strength than I'd like to admit to keep my fists balled at my side.

I threw the mask to the ground.

The guys at his side shot looks to him. I couldn't make out the expressions behind their masks, but they seemed wary of my presence.

Good.

He pushed the girl into the arms of the pink mask. "Finish her."

"Wait, but I thought we were—"

"Do it," he growled back. There was a moment between them before he faced me again, a slow smirk spreading across his face.

How long had it been since I'd talked to him?

Long enough to forget how angry he made me, but not long enough that the instinct to murder him on the spot had been completely erased.

"Did you get yours yet?" he asked, motioning to the side of my face.

I lifted my gloved hands, wincing at the pain that shot through me when I touched the open wound, a fragment of my mask broken away. Biting my tongue, I glared at him.

I couldn't understand why he was here. Why he had chosen *this* game to get in on. If he'd just waited another year or two, he would never have had to enter again. Living a comfy life as a victor of his prior games.

"Your hair looks like shit," I spat.

He frowned at me, his hands coming up to pull at the fried edges. I wouldn't be surprised if he already had clumps of it falling out.

The girl's scream rang out. We ignored it.

"*Plus one point for the kill,*" the robotic voice said.

"*Plus one for mercy.*" This one came from my tracker.

Dylan's eyes roamed over me in the criticizing way he used to do when we were younger. He was deciding whether or not to instigate something. It reminded me so much of Father that it was unnerving, forcing me to pause.

"Huh," he said with a light tone. "I guess a point is a point, huh?"

"I won't ask again," I hissed, taking a step forward. My hand shot forward to tangle in his shirt. "What the *fuck* are you doing here?"

"*Someone* has to heal our family's broken image," Dylan said with a shit-eating grin. "How does it look for all of the Wolff bloodline to enter the games *except* you? We all knew you're a coward, but you don't have to show it to the entire fucking *world*."

I jerked him closer to me, getting up into his face.

"Is that what you're doing?" I asked. "Pretending to be me? Did that *bastard* put you up to this shit? I swear to fucking god—"

It was his turn to hook his hand behind my neck and jerk me forward to whisper in my ear.

"Stop it with this fucking tantrum," he hissed. "Don't you realize how bad this makes us look? They're watching. *Dad's watching.*"

I pushed him away with a glare. Unfazed, he smirked at me and picked up his discarded mask.

"They're joining us," Dylan announced to the group. Pink and Yellow turned to me, assessing.

And just like that, Dylan had me under his thumb again.

"No thanks." I turned to walk away, but Dylan was faster, his hand pulling me back.

"Imagine the views," he said. "Two brothers on the hunt for their victims? *Guaranteed interest.*"

This made me pause. As much as I hated it... he had a point.

Grumbling, I shrugged him off to face the others. They were looking at me with a mix of interest and hesitation.

"I guess," I said and leaned to the side, looking at the guy in the pink mask who held a knife, dripping with the blood of his victim. "Where'd you get that?"

He jumped, his gaze snapping toward mine. I didn't need to know. In fact, I had already guessed where he got it, but I wanted more than anything to end this conversation.

"Me?" he asked with a shaky voice.

"Who else, dimwit?" Dylan said with a cruel laugh. "Don't mind Shaw, he's a fucking idiot."

Familiarity nagged at my brain as I looked over Shaw.

Where was he...

Images of them gathered around the island in the kitchen passing Dylan's phone around filled my mind.

Renewed anger flashed through my mind.

Of course out of all the fuckers he had to bring... why him?

He slung an arm over my shoulders, pulling us forward. Because of the height difference, I was forced to bend down slightly so he wouldn't be hanging off my shoulders.

A smug fact I couldn't get over. For most of my life he towered over me, but now that I'd had a few years to grow into my body, I was *much* taller than he was.

"Let me show you where the weapons are. Maybe get you a gun," Dylan said. "In return, you just hang out with us for a bit. Sound like a deal?"

I hated him. Even more than father. I hated being stuck here with him... but maybe he had something going for him.

"You're just using me for views," I grumbled. "Don't try to make your motives seem altruistic."

"Can't an older brother help out their baby brother?" he asked with a laugh. "Hey, how many do you got by the way?"

I tapped on my tracker, making it light up. On the screen was my number of points, and in the right-hand corner was—

"Ninety thousand?! What the fuck? I barely have fifteen!"

"What are your comments saying?" Yellow asked, coming up to us.

"Comments?" I asked.

They all gave me bewildered looks.

"You've been in the game this long and didn't think to check your comments?" Pink asked. "You probably missed out on *so* many gifts."

Dylan grabbed my wrist, navigating the screen with ease, then a holographic-type screen popped up with comments going on at a hundred miles an hour.

B1GGYB0Y

They have more viewers because they're hotter

AUTHORBEXDEVEAU

No one wants to watch a sadistic fuck with little shrimp dick energy

ELLEMAEBOOKS

Kill him and I'll send you a semi-automatic

Clearing my throat, I closed out the window and put space between myself and Dylan's glare.

"So, about that gun?"

Vic

Before the Games

I was so sick of people telling me that they were sorry.

Sorry, the accident happened. *Sorry,* my dad was still in a coma. *Sorry* about all the moments we'd missed while he'd been like this.

Prom. Graduation. Getting accepted into Brown. Yale. Princeton. Having to choose where to go *alone,* knowing damn well I'd spent my college fund trying to stop us from losing the house and paying doctors when his insurance lapsed. Spending all my nights and evenings at the hospital in case he woke up. Realizing he probably never would.

Not gone, but not really here either.

It was exhausting.

Like *sorry* could actually do anything in this day and age. If anyone was truly sorry, they should've at least spared some cash. That was all that was important to me now.

The cellophane bag rustled as I tossed my dye-covered gloves inside, a little angrier than I meant.

Rinsing was going to be a bitch. We hadn't had hot water in three months, and I was getting fucking tired of shivering butt-naked in the stained tub while I tried to make myself presentable.

I looked myself over in the mirror, my hair slicked back as the vibrant teal did its best to hide my overgrown blonde balayage. Drugstore box dye was a far cry from the fancy downtown salon I was used to, but I'd scraped the bottom of my pathetically empty bank account for something—*anything*—that would help hide my identity.

How far the mighty had fallen. Kohl would love this.

They would tease me, tug at the ends of my hair, and make some off-handed comment about how I was going through some type of crisis.

Maybe I was.

I could *almost* hear their teasing laugh ringing in my mind. It still caused a warmth to spread through my body.

My fingers twitched toward my phone, a habit that I was trying to break. We weren't really friends anymore. Not really. Not after the accident. Not after I used them. Not after I lied about what I'd be doing tonight.

Not quite strangers, but not quite anything else either.

How could we come back from this?

The accident had done more than ruin my life, it'd shoved a wedge between me and one of the only people that seemed to actually *care* about me.

How fucked up was that?

I'd lived on this planet for nineteen years, and I could name on one hand how many people I had ever cared about—and one of them I couldn't even talk to anymore.

I sat on the edge of the tub, crossing one leg over the other.

Maybe if I'd been a nicer person, my life wouldn't have turned out like this. Maybe if I had actually tried to change for the better instead of letting the popular girl archetype strip my personality down, I would *actually* have some semblance of my life back.

Karma's a fucking bitch. Now all I'm known for is the short list of traits that I shared with Regina George and every other high school movie mean girl.

Even my parents' status did nothing for me after the accident.

Just like *he* wanted. We were pushed so far out of the spotlight that the world began to forget we ever existed.

But I would be changing that.

I would make sure to take back what I was owed, even if it meant risking my life in the process.

Beyond the door, my bedroom had a backpack and a mattress on the floor. It was all I had left to my name. I'd sold everything else to make one more mortgage payment. That was six months and four asset seizure notices ago.

I would do what I had to. Even if it meant throwing away everything and anyone that ever meant someone to me.

I tapped my phone screen, and it lit with the time, four o'clock. I'd have just enough time to get this rinsed before I needed to catch the train.

Sure, I submitted my documents online—copies of my ID, next of kin form, and a direct deposit for where they could send my winnings, if I had any. But I'd still need to go through hair and makeup before they'd let me set foot in the arena, which meant if I wanted to be ready for sundown, I'd need to hurry my ass up. I wasn't chancing being put in the fucking maze.

Bingsoo, my fat white Persian, jumped up onto the teal-streaked counter with a loud meow, and I sighed, picking him up and putting him under my arm.

"What are you going to do if I don't come home tomorrow to bring you breakfast?"

Bingsoo meowed again, his fluffy tail swishing.

"I guess Kohl would come get you, right? They'll have my face plastered all over if they manage to kill me."

It was the nature of the Game, you either won or you didn't come home.

They still cared about me enough not to let him starve, right?

The cat started to struggle, and I sat him down on the floor, groaning as he left little teal footprints. Not that it mattered. It would be a miracle if I came back and the bank hadn't already changed the locks. I wasn't ever going to have to try and scrub the dye out of the carpet.

Rinsing my hair was exactly as horrible as I thought it would be.

I used a T-shirt to try and get the bulk of the moisture out, grinning at my reflection.

A sort of manic excitement had started to eclipse my nerves, I was a Legacy after all. I was *born* for this.

And once I put on my mask, I'd be *invisible*.

Good—I'd have no lack of enemies in the arena. Players looking for fame and fortune as murderers or thieves. Being a Legacy had perks: a sign-on bonus, premium air time in the hopes that you'd be a content farm like your parent—or in my case, *parents*—were, and preferential registration. But all those perks came with one major downside: from the second you set foot in the arena, you were worth twice the points. It was better to be no one.

A Ghost.

I flicked the light switch out of habit more than anything else as I headed out of the bathroom and for the door. The power had gone off sometime over the summer. It was kind of like camping inside the house.

Bingsoo followed, toddling along on his short little legs. I scratched him behind his ears, offering him a cocky smirk I didn't feel. "I'll see you in the morning."

I swiped the change I'd left carefully counted on the kitchen counter into my hand, dropping it into the pocket of my jeans before I stepped out into the balmy evening air. There were only a few blocks and a subway ride between me and the games.

I just hoped I was ready to play.

KOHL

"Let me help you," Dylan said as he turned toward us, walking backward like he had the day he, Vic, and I had gone to the amusement park together. The sky was dark, the only thing lighting up the park were the dim lights splashed around the park. Every so often the bright blue lights of a screen would light up as we passed showing off our blood stained uniforms.

Careless idiot.

Though, I wouldn't be surprised if a fucking murder game was where my brother was most comfortable. He'd grown up with the Legacy title and all the douchebaggery that came with it.

His mask was back on, making it appear to the viewers that we were twins. We weren't that far apart in age, but being compared to him was one of my pet peeves.

It was fucking insulting. I was twice as smart as him, and I had it on *extremely* good authority that I was a better lay too.

As we walked, I just couldn't get over just how *stupid* he was. I'd never have guessed he cared enough about our *family's image* that he'd take it upon himself to enter the games a *second time*.

It just didn't make sense.

Even for Legacies, entering the games once was enough. Before the games, it was easy to buy into the fucked up fantasy that led us to believe that we could make it to the top without suffering from the crippling PTSD every player before us came out with. Only realize when we left that it was too late, we were going to be just as fucked up as our parents.

Stuck huddled in a bathtub, the screams of victims echoing on a loop like this fucking fair music, that's when we'd realize we'd made a mistake. Of course, that was if we made it out at all.

Most did, but not because of their skills.

Because of the millions of viewers that were watching them. Sending them gifts and supporting their stream. Those who had parents in the Inner Circle—the elite, even above the Architects— were even luckier. There was no way anyone in the Inner Circle would stand by as their Legacy died in front of the world.

It was a disgrace and would make their family a laughingstock for years to come.

Even *my* views were going up by the tens of thousands every few minutes, no doubt because everyone had clued into which family Dylan and I came from.

I really hated when he was right.

"I don't need your help," I said with a huff. The *'nice brother'* act he was trying to feed the cameras was even more irritating than if he'd just shown his true colors. I wished that switch of his would flip so everyone watching would see what a monster he truly was.

I should've known that I couldn't avoid my family for too long. They would find me, no matter what. Because to them, I was just another pawn in their game to use when they saw fit.

I could sense the disapproval radiating off him, even behind the mask.

I knew what he envisioned. He wanted the world to start tuning in. To look at the *two* Wolff children joining together to kill the less privileged and completely terrified Ghosts.

If we did well, it would be talked about for *years*. Our children's children would see our faces plastered in their textbooks and be forced to watch the highlights of this match as we killed for a chance at a big payout.

They would learn from Dylan. Take note of how he got my stream from ninety thousand to three hundred thousand in less than thirty minutes.

This was just how life worked. No use getting angry over something I couldn't control.

Or at least that's what I tried to force myself to think. In reality, I was hanging by a thread of patience worn thin like an over-stretched rubber band. A single crumb of pressure more, and I was fit to *snap*.

"Did you forget I've already done this once before?" he called, spreading his arms wide and turning around to look out at the park.

I followed his motion, catching a Hider and their Seeker weaving through the booths to the far right of us. The others didn't pay them any attention.

As much as I didn't want to turn into the murderer my father was, I needed to get away from them. Moving in a group as big as this would only slow me down.

I was here to win. Nothing else mattered.

Beyond the blaring music from the rides and screams of terror that filled the night every few minutes, I could hear the pounding of shoes hitting the pavement, scurrying to get away.

We were calling too much attention to ourselves.

My chances, *all of them*, running right past me while I yet again entertained my brother.

"Are you listening to me, you little shit?"

I jerked back, not realizing that I'd zoned out until Dylan's brightly lit mask filled my vision. His eyes were slitted behind the mask, glaring at me.

Ah, so now he comes out to play.

"Who needs to behave now?" I asked and quickly hooked my fingers under the chin of his mask, flipping it up hard enough to slam back against his face.

Before I could see his reaction, I made a hard right, leaving the group behind.

"You fucking—"

I knew he couldn't keep his temper in check any longer, nor would I be able to keep my lips sealed.

Unlike him, I didn't give two fucks about how this looked. If anything, I *wanted* the others to see. I wanted them to realize how fucked-up Legacy families were. That we were nothing special. That we were above nothing and no one.

This wasn't the genetic lottery—it was a fucking *curse*.

If people finally understood what it meant to be in here... maybe then the fantasy of winning the game would finally fall apart.

Blue flashed across my vision. It was so fast I almost missed it... but it was there. My gaze followed the hint of blue, lingering when I caught sight of her slower friend.

My little rabbit.

I didn't let Dylan's presence hinder me. *They could just fuck right off.* I took off running toward them, hope burning in my chest.

I could win this. I just need to get this one kill, and I'll have completed half the battle.

There was a shout behind me, followed by the rapid footsteps of Dylan and his friends. One of them let out an excited holler that caused my stomach to drop.

I won't let them take this from me.

The rabbits took off toward the haunted house, teal hair trailing behind them in the wind. The structure was tilted with a large sign hanging on by just its right corner. It looked just as menacing as the other rides, but was like a beacon, calling me to come take my prize.

"I knew you had it in you!" Dylan yelled from behind.

"Fuck off!" I shouted back.

The rabbits disappeared into the haunted house, I wasn't too far after them.

I pushed back the tattered cloth separating the fairgrounds from the haunted house, my heart pounding in my chest so fast the adrenaline was making my fingertips numb.

The fairground lights had been just bright enough that they forced me to a standstill as my eyes adjusted to the intensity of the darkness. I blinked a few times, willing the teasing shapes that hid in the darkness to disappear.

I walked further inside, following the single hallway leading through the ride—and hopefully straight to where the rabbits were.

The noise from the fairgrounds fell away with each creaking step.

After all the noise outside, the silence was almost deafening. The contrast so intense it made me uneasy, nearly looking over my shoulder.

Something jumped in front of me, causing my body to react without even registering what it was. I slammed the hunk of metal I had taken from the ground earlier right into it, only to come face to face with the most realistic skeletal-like animatronic I'd ever seen.

Half of its face still had skin on, the other half exposed bone. It jerked back and forth, and a crackling sound of maniacal laughter filled the air.

There was something about the way the exposed half shone in the darkness that made me pause long enough to realize that it *wasn't* just a normal animatronic. I cringed when a drop of *real* blood dribbled down its face.

The memory of the stylist speaking to the Seeker beside me as we got ready rang through my mind.

It was fucking real.

"What kind of sick bastards skin a person for a *game*?" I hissed under my breath. Bile rose in my throat, threatening that I'd be sick, but I pushed it down along with my feelings of disgust.

I forced my way around it, careful not to get any of the congealed blood on me, and headed deeper into the haunted house. Clashes of thunder filled the air. The same maniacal laughter seemed to follow me throughout the house as the hallway expanded into the first room.

I heard my brother crash through the front, one letting out a scream as the same animatronic jumped out at him. *Damn it.* Couldn't I just get five minutes alone to do what I needed to do?

Footsteps sounded from the room over, hurried but muffled, as if they were trying to sneak past.

A spike of excitement ran through me. I followed the sound, trying to keep my footsteps as quiet as possible.

The group was behind me, but they were too distracted by the jump scares their trackers triggered to come looking for me. *The game makers must be on my side.* Because my tracker only caused the single animatronic to jump out at me, but I heard multiple screams from the boys behind.

I ducked into the next room, my vision assaulted by strobing lights. It made my head swim, but just as I suspected, in the corner were two terrified rabbits.

They were talking to each other, the white rabbit's back toward me.

"We have to keep going, Jenna," the white rabbit said, her voice barely above a whisper. "You can't just tap out. They *will* kill you."

Her voice caused something to go off in my head, but I ignored it, my eyes narrowing on my kill. I'd get the white rabbit too, but for now my sole focus was the black one, hiding in the corner, shaking.

"I *can't*," she sobbed, louder than her friend. "You're cut out for this, but me? I won't make it out alive."

"Jenna, just listen to me. Get the fuck up, and I can help you–"

A crash in the next room sent the white rabbit whipping around to look at me, giving me the perfect opening. I lifted the weapon, aiming directly at my target.

"Move!" the white rabbit screamed and shoved her friend to the side.

But she was too slow. My weapon slammed against my target's shoulder, forcing a pained cry from her lips.

I shifted my body to stand over the rabbit. Her shaky hand was raised in an attempt to shield herself.

The strobe lighting made it difficult to follow her movements, but I wasn't going to let this chance slip by.

She attempted to turn over onto all fours to push herself up, but with one kick to her back, I sent her sprawling to the floor.

"Let her go!" the one behind me yelled.

Again, that same chest-tightening feeling hit me.

I wondered what I looked like to her, to the people watching.

A killer, ready to pounce on their helpless victim. Would they like the show I put on for them? Would it be enough to earn me extra points?

Kill her first, then go after the other. You need to win this for her.

Hold on, goddess. I'm coming.

"Don't be so impatient," I tsked. "I'll deal with you in a second."

But just like always, Dylan had found it in himself to insert himself into something he had no business being in.

He paused when his eyes fell to the woman on the floor. From his voice, I knew behind the mask he was smiling.

"Well, well, well. What delectable little treat do we have here?"

VIC

"If you don't hurry up, I can't help you," I threatened as we ducked and weaved between the rides.

The closer we got to the small booths filled with games whose prizes contained actual weapons we could use, the more densely populated the area got. I didn't have to stare at the screens around the park to know that at least a quarter of the Ghosts had already been killed.

The screams had become less frequent, which left the more experienced and more likely to win Ghosts to get smarter about their hiding spots—And would make the Killers more desperate, rushing to try and sniff out whoever was left.

We were running on borrowed time, and if Jenna didn't hurry the *fuck* up, all my chances at winning this thing would blow up in smoke.

At first, I thought it would be a comfort to have someone I knew here with me to navigate the games with, but Jenna was proving to be more of a liability than anything.

As much as I hated to admit it, I understood why Mom entered as a Ghost back in her day. It was exciting, every time we evaded that purple masked demon chasing us it was like a weight was being lifted off me. I was becoming smarter, faster with every showdown.

But Jenna? She was crumbling.

And my patience was wearing thin.

"I'm *trying*," Jenna whined as she tried to keep up with my breakneck pace.

She'd been lagging behind for far too long, and I had to quite literally *pull* her through the park to get from point A to point B.

Just get to the fucking weapons. If you get a gun, it doesn't matter how much she slows you down. Hard to chase you if you shoot out their knees.

But even as the thoughts ran through my head, I knew that was a fucking lie.

It was so early into the game, we had already had a close call. *Fuck*, she almost died right in front of me. If I hadn't hurled a rock at the purple-masked Killer, she would've.

I'd been more scared than I'd liked to admit. It just felt so... inevitable.

I knew coming in here would be difficult, but the fear that gripped my entire body when I saw how easily I'd been caught rattled my confidence more than I expected.

"Not hard enough," I huffed and then froze when I caught sight of the very same purple mask that haunted my worries.

Fuck me. They packed up.

Purple had three other people with them now, their masks glowing in the dark like a demented rainbow.

They looked like trouble. It was in the way they stood in the middle of the fucking arena like they were waiting for a smoothie at the mall. Too casual, *relaxed*. Like they had no sense of danger, because in their minds, they believed they owned the place.

Even I knew an apex predator when I saw it.

Just wait until the end when the Seekers kill each other off in hopes of getting the top prize, a dark voice in my mind whispered. *It would serve them right. Who in their right mind would willingly sign up to become a murderer?*

I shot a glance back to Jenna. Her eyes were filled with tears, silent sobs shaking her body.

I had to fight the urge to roll my eyes. It was hard to feel bad for her when we chose this.

Fuck, I'd be better off without her. At this rate, she was a liability I was quickly becoming unable to afford.

"You knew what you were getting into when you signed up," I reminded. "We're surrounded by it every single day, you can't feign ignorance now."

My eyes trailed back to the group, my body freezing when the yellow-masked man started to look around.

"I never wanted to—"

"Shh," I hissed and pulled her through the rides, my heart racing.

They didn't see. You're okay. Get to the weapons. You'll be safe—

Cheers from the group rang out. It was the only warning I had that they'd seen us. *Fuck.*

I picked up the pace, my grip on Jenna's wrist tightening. She could barely keep up. She was going to get us fucking killed.

If I was alone, I could have one shotted it to the games, but now that I had her to take care of, I had to think of a—*yes!*

The rickety haunted house came into view, and I couldn't help but send a quick thank you to the heavens for the perfect opportunity.

I wanted to stay out of attractions as much as possible so I wouldn't get trapped, but I had no choice, I had to find somewhere to hide.

What better than a darkened, haunted house? There had to be a nook that I could shove us into to wait out this shit show at least long enough for our pursuers to lose interest.

I pulled us toward it, the sound of the purple-masked Seeker following behind us.

I made sure to dodge all the animatronics as they jumped out at us. Jenna let out a few screams but stopped when we got deep enough that the noise from the outside fell away.

Though her sobs and sniffles weren't a much better alternative.

I pulled us as far into the house as I could manage before letting her collapse to the ground.

"We have to keep going, Jenna," I said, trying to whisper. The last thing I wanted was for that purple-masked maniac to find us. "You can't just tap out. They *will* kill you."

I looked off to the side and behind Jenna. The path continued making me believe that there was an exit out back. We needed to get out there fast before we were trapped—if it was me I'd have my pack coming from both sides.

"I *can't*," she sobbed, louder than I would have liked. "You're cut out for this, but me? I won't make it out alive."

"Jenna, just listen to me. Get the fuck up, and I can help you–"

A crash in the next room sent my head snapping around.

My heart stopped in my chest, my blood freezing as I caught sight of the damned Seeker that wouldn't leave us the fuck *alone*.

They'd been all but silent as they snuck up on us, nothing like their friends that I could hear bumbling through the ride beyond.

They lifted the weapon, aiming directly at Jenna.

"Move!" I screamed and shoved my friend to the side.

No. I hadn't reacted fast enough. The Seeker's weapon slammed into Jenna's shoulder causing a pained cry to come from her lips.

My body reacted on its own. My feet dragging me away from Jenna and the Seeker, I needed to get out of range. I could barely make out Jenna's raised hand in the strobing lights as she pleaded for her life.

Jenna tried to get on her hands and knees, but with one kick, the Seeker sent her sprawling across the floor.

"Let her go!" I yelled.

They turned to me, just enough of a distraction for Jenna to get onto her hands and knees.

"Don't be so impatient," they tsked. The sound of their voice so close caused the hair to rise on the back of my neck. "I'll deal with you in a second."

A blue-masked man came in, two more following him close behind.

Dylan.

He let his eyes fall to Jenna, and she pushed herself up.

"Well, well, well. What delectable little treat do we have here?" he asked, his voice sticking to my skin in the tight space.

Without hesitation, I reached forward and grabbed Jenna's hand again, attempting to pull us toward the exit, but that fucking Seeker was faster, and before I knew it, it became a sort of tug-of-war between the two of us.

"*Stop*! Please!" Jenna screamed.

Hands reached towards me from the other Seekers, blood and dirt caked under their fingernails. Panic clawed through me, if they got hold, I'd have no hope of getting free again. Not while they each had a good fifty pounds on me.

It was then that I realized how *fucked* I was.

My eyes shifted toward Jenna, and for the first time she looked at me with such hurt that it caused even my jaded heart to crack.

And then I... *let go.*

It was enough to send them all scrambling back, but the purple Seeker was fast. They twisted their body so Jenna was forced to the ground, raised their hand, and broug—

The sickening crack of their metal weapon hitting Jenna's skull was the thing to push me forward. They brought it down again and again and again, the noise ringing in my ears and I turned on my heel and sprinted down the hall.

Within a couple cobweb covered turns I found myself in a room positively crawling with rats, not that I had much time to be disgusted by them—not when my eyes landed on a glowing red emergency exit door just up ahead.

My lungs burned as I crossed the room, the animal skittering away from my feet as I pushed myself faster than I'd ever run in my life through the door and into the warm lights of the amusement park beyond.

She brought this on herself. I tried to tell myself. *If she was just the slightest bit faster—*

The yells from behind me forced all other thoughts from my mind. They reminded me why I was here. What I needed to do.

I *needed* to win this fucking thing, and if that meant having to sacrifice the life of a friend, goddamn I was willing to do it.

Kohl

Before the Games

I tried not to make a habit of stalking Victoria at school, but it became harder and harder to hold myself back after she started to spend more time at the house with my brother.

That useless scumbag didn't deserve to talk to someone like her, that he'd managed to convince her to date him was... *ineffable*. It didn't make any fucking sense.

Naturally, I started to wonder what her life was like outside of dating Dylan.

It was like an itch I couldn't scratch, all these questions about who she was that I didn't have answers to.

Who were her friends? What did she do in her free time? Was she good at school or kind of a slacker?

Today, we had free period at the same time. That's how I found myself lingering at the edge of the quad, watching as Victoria and a few of her friends from cheer gathered around one of the stone tables. Their laughter carried across the open space, making the back of my neck heat.

So this is what the little Legacy did with her downtime.

It was a bit disappointing. I don't know, maybe I expected something a little less... pedestrian.

I'd placed myself behind one of the large oaks that surrounded the perimeter of the quad, hiding in the shade while also being close enough to see them and hear what they were saying.

Vic and her friends often walked through the halls together, sometimes even wearing their matching cheer sets. It was criminal that I hadn't been able to get close to her before this.

The sunlight bounced off her golden hair as she talked, her hands moving to punctuate her excited voice. She looked at her friends with such a carefree, unburdened smile that it caused something in me to shift uncomfortably.

She never smiled like that with Dylan.

Victoria stood and motioned to her skirt. Her friends were sitting on either side of her, both of them leaning closer to her.

One of them reached out and tugged on her skirt, causing all the girls to grin.

What were they doing?

"See?" she said with a smirk. "This one is *much* heavier and hopefully won't blow up around my waist as much when I'm lifted."

One of the girls—Jenna, I think—laughed. I recognized her from my English class.

"I don't think it will stop the jocks from catcalling you or trying to peek up your skirt," she said.

"Even if you have the safety shorts on," the other girl commented with a small noise of disgust.

Vic opened her mouth to say something, but she was cut off by a boy in a football uniform sprinting across the quad and heading straight for their table.

"Vic, save me!" he cried, using the blonde as a shield.

Vic whipped her head around, trying to get a glance at the man but failing as he stayed planted behind her. His hands gripped her arms, locking her in place.

It wasn't long before another angry cheerleader came waving her fist at him, her normally all-white cheer uniform stained bright red. From this distance, I couldn't tell if it was blood or something else.

Vic gasped as she was jerked to the side by the footballer.

A burst of annoyance shot through me.

Why the fuck would she let him push her around like that?

She and her friends continued to joke around, but I couldn't stop looking at how he manhandled her. Even after the cheerleader was pacified, the boy kept his hand on her lower back without any hesitation.

Like it belonged there.

There was something else stirring in my stomach. Something bitter. A feeling that popped up way too many times when I saw her with Dylan.

My hands itched to touch her skin just like he had. To come up behind her, put my hand on her back, and whisper in her ear. For her to lean into me and laugh the way she did with the rest of the popular crowd.

Wait, am I—

I turned away from the group, embarrassment hitting me like a slap to the face.

What was I on? Getting jealous because of some stupid jock? Of my brother?

It was a fucking *joke.*

Before Dylan brought her home, I'd seen her plenty of times. Of course I had, we'd been in the same schools since pre-K. But never had I felt... *jealous* of the men around her.

Shame made my face hot as I headed back into the school, but I already knew I was fucked. Victoria had planted a seed in my mind, and it was growing, slowly causing all my thoughts to revolve around her.

My crush was quickly becoming an *obsession.*

And I wasn't interested in stopping it.

VIC

CAN'T I GET A BREAK FROM THIS PSYCHO?

A plan was a plan.

Jenna's... death—it wouldn't change that.

I knew what I needed to do.

Survive.

In the countless hours of game footage I'd reviewed leading up to stepping foot inside the arena, there was one clear advantage that every single winner, Seeker or not, had in common.

A weapon.

A lot of the players were bigger than me, stronger. So I'd need to make sure that I could level the playing field. I couldn't kill them without risking a penalty, but I could at least injure them enough to escape. That, or risk being a punching bag for a man who'd been waiting his entire life for a chance to legally kill a defenseless woman.

A man like *Dylan*, and he had no shortage of reasons to want me dead.

All the carnival games were fucked. Demented versions of themselves with rotating prize boxes that would open automatically if you won.

It was one of the craziest things about this setting—it was like the entire carnival was staffed from the shadows. The games, concessions, and even the rides all fully operational but not a soul walking around.

Turns out that Fixers didn't much care for being shot at—they stopped having civilians in the arena back in 1994 after one of the players detonated landmines and killed half a dozen. Hard to convince people to come work for you if they're worried an eighteen-year-old with a concussion is going to start setting up death traps at any time.

I kept low and moved fast, evading the dead bodies of ghosts who'd yet to be picked up. I expected any moment to be intercepted by Seekers looking for their next kill. The night was wearing on and they'd soon be getting desperate.

That's what didn't make any sense, the games area was like a ghost town—even with a fuckload of first aid supplies available at a few of the stations. I was the only person moving in and out of the shadows.

At least, the only person I could *see*.

The knowledge that someone may be out there, their form becoming one with the darkness as they watched over me, caused the hair to rise on the back of my neck.

Maybe it's just that the other Ghosts were looking to find prizes elsewhere?

I moved straight past all the lifesaving options, heading for the games with the guns.

It was a type of dart game where you'd throw a set amount of darts at the balloons, and depending on how many you got, the better the prize. Not particularly difficult, but damn, was it stressful to play a fucking fair game while keeping on the lookout for people who wanted to end my life.

I threw my first dart, a bright yellow balloon exploding with an audible pop. I looked over my shoulder, praying that no one heard. But still, the long walkway that led to the games was dark. No glowing masks to be seen.

The next dart hit blue, then green.

Victory.

The ding of the prize box unlocking was music to my ears as I hopped over the counter toward my brand-new handgun. My fingers brushed the acrylic container, excitement simmering in my veins.

Too easy. With this, I could—

Laughter, the kind that meant that multiple people were approaching, met my ears, and I ducked down, crawling to hide with my back against the counter.

Shit.

I was lucky to even get a prize unlocked, but I'd be risking my life if I crossed the space to grab it.

Wood dug into my shoulder blades as I pressed myself against the booth, using the shadows to hide me from view.

Get the gun. I could practically hear the viewers screaming at me.

I didn't dare check my watch.

Just wait. Wait while they walk right past you. Then get the gun.

I could hear a set of footsteps coming my way, the sound of boots crunching the gavel making my heart pound in my chest.

I prayed they couldn't hear it over the sadistic, high-pitched music that was blaring out of the booth's speakers.

But of course, just like the last few years of my life, the world just *had* to prove how unlucky I was.

Surprise rocketed through me as the purple-masked Seeker leaned over my hiding space, their fingers just barely grazing the butt of the gun.

Are you kidding me? Can't I get a break from this psycho?

Their mask was still stained with Jenna's blood.

I tried to stay quiet. Tried to mold myself against the wall in hopes they would just *pass me.*

But then their head turned to stare directly at me.

Fuck.

I acted without thinking, my fist connecting with the side of their head as I launched myself at them. Anger at their quickness to bludgeon Jenna to death combined with my fear mixed painfully, fueling the fight in me.

The Seeker made a move for the gun, but I was quicker, grabbing the weapon and aiming it directly at their chest. "Move, now."

"Hey—*hey*—just calm down. You don't have to—" They raised their hands, backing away from the booth slowly, and I put my foot on the counter, my eyes flicking down the aisles of games for their shitty, sadistic friends. They were close enough for me to see them but busy.

A gunshot would probably change that.

This was it. I could kill them. Get them off my fucking back, even just for the time being.

I wanted my motivation for killing them to be for Jenna. I knew there would be consequences, but I would hope that deep down, I'd be able to overcome my fear of them to shoot.

Tears stung my eyes and made my chest tight as my finger hovered over the trigger.

I'm so sorry, Jenna, I thought. It wasn't the fear of the consequences that stopped me, it was the need to *survive.* The need to win this thing and come out on top.

I cursed under my breath, throwing myself over the counter and making a break for it. My boots skidded in a pool of blood, nearly bringing me to the ground. I shoved the gun into the pocket of my hoodie.

"Should have killed me when you had the chance, rabbit!" the Seeker shouted, their footsteps mirroring mine.

My adrenaline-addled and panic-filled mind thought it sounded like Kohl.

But I knew Kohl. There's no way that they could've killed Jenna, not like that. They would be in here like me, a Ghost. Or watching.

If they were in here as a Seeker—I don't know what I'd do.

I'd made a point of hitting the gym pretty hard, the cardio machines especially leading up to the games. All that dedication served me well now as I whipped around the corner, speeding around a Tilt-A-Whirl and a rocking boat-like ride in my futile hope to find somewhere to hide.

Bodies littered the park, members of staff in their yellow bullet-proof vests helping to clean up. In a couple hours, when people really started to get desperate, this place would be deserted. Not even the Custodians would enter the arena the last couple of hours before sunrise.

My eyes caught on the sign for the building up ahead—the Mirror Maze.

The Seeker was still too close for me to be comfortable, and after I'd seen them take out Jenna without a second thought, I knew if they got their hands on me, I was a goner.

I couldn't exactly shoot them while I was running full tilt either, so basically, I was fucked.

I took the steps into the mirror maze two at a time, my pursuer coming at me just as quickly. I sprinted through the first stage of the maze, my masked face staring back at me as my hair whipped around corners. I looked every bit the anxious rabbit that my username promised.

Small. Panicked. Prey in the hands of a predator.

I gripped the side of the mirrored wall as I turned sharply around the corner, helping to propel me into the next hallway—and directly into a mirror. I hit it with so much force, it shattered on impact, tossing me to the floor.

The Seeker laughed, the sound bouncing off the glass. "That sounded like it hurt."

I rolled, pushing myself to my feet, but they grabbed the back of my shirt, yanking me backward before shoving me into another mirror.

"Come out, come out, wherever you are, little rabbit."

Glass littered the floor, cutting my hands and digging into my knees through my pants as I struggled to get back to my feet. I pulled the gun from my hoodie pocket, but in the adrenaline and nerve filled haze my hands shook so badly that I missed my shot despite the close proximity, a mirror exploding beside the Seeker's head.

They snarled, diving for me and knocking the gun out of my

hands so it spun away from us on the floor. The Seeker bared down on top of me, wrestling me onto my back. Their hands were in my hair, forcing my head back. I kicked and bucked like my life depended on it, grunting with the effort of trying to free myself.

I wouldn't scream. Wouldn't give this sick fuck the satisfaction of hearing how terrified I was.

You can't die like this! Fight!

I brought my knee up, nailing my attacker in the groin, and they hissed but didn't waiver.

"Fuck!" I shouted. It was just my luck that my attacker had the balls to murder me in cold blood, but no cock for my low-blow shot to make a difference.

Their hands wrapped around my throat, squeezing and cutting off my airflow.

Fuck, fuck, fuck, fuck!

I tried to pry their fingers away, but when their iron grip didn't budge, I picked a new target. Their eyes. I aimed a punch at the Seeker's head and then another until their mask loosened.

I'm so sorry, Kohl. Please look after Bingsoo for me.

My eyes were bulging, my ears roaring as my lungs begged for air.

I slipped my fingers into the band of the Seeker's mask and ripped it off, my entire world turning on its axis as the eerie purple glow illuminated a familiar face.

Kohl's lips were split into a smile I'd never seen before, the corner of their mouth hooked into a manic grin as they watched me struggle against them.

I wanted to scream, to tell them who I was, but I didn't have the air in my lungs to do it.

Tears slipped out of my eyes as the world shrank to their overblown pupils, the honey brown that I'd loved in their stare all but shrouded in a mass of black.

It was dark here, so dark that when their mask clattered to the ground in my limp arm, it illuminated them like a demon, casting great shadows under their features.

They lied to me.

They fucking lied.

And now they were going to kill me.

This is fucking bullshit.

With the last of my strength, I used my trembling fingers to pull my mask off.

Kohl froze, their fingers loosening immediately as shock and horror rocketed over their expression.

I took in a ragged gulp of air, sputtering and coughing. "You fucking—" I gasped, my voice raspy from being choked within an inch of my life, as I slapped them as hard as I could. "*Asshole!*"

Kohl

Should have killed me when you had the chance, rabbit!

The weight of the weapon in my hand doubled since attributing a kill to it. I gripped it tightly, afraid that the extra weight might cause it to slip from my fingers, leaving me defenseless.

I was at the top in this game. I had no reason to worry about losing a weapon. If I did, I'd just get another.

But every time Dylan got closer, every time one of his friends' voices got too loud... I found myself gripping it tighter.

Maybe that's why I hadn't objected when they pulled me along in their search for their own victims. Or why I just stood on the sidelines as they raced after a random ghost.

Yellow and Pink raced to the bottom of the Ferris wheel, ripping the victim away from the entrance to the ride that looked like a huge, haunted ship, swinging violently back and forth.

I had no idea what the ghost was thinking running there. Maybe they were hoping that they would be able to make it far enough and that the people chasing her were stupid enough to race right into the boat's path.

Something I would have much rather witnessed than what they were about to do.

Yellow tackled her to the ground while Pink readied the knife.

"We should find another of our own," Dylan said, the suddenness of his voice in my ear making my head to snap toward him in surprise.

Luckily, with the mask still fastened to my face, I didn't have to hide my disgust.

He was looking over the scene, his mask pulsing blue light in the darkness surrounding the park. Splatters of blood from when I'd struck Jenna decorated his face, causing gaps in the lights lining his mask like a paint splatter.

"There is no *we*," I hissed.

He turned to me just slightly. A move I knew all too well. One that was almost always accompanied with some type of annoying smirk.

"Then why are you still here?" he asked.

I held up my weapon to him.

"You said you'd show me," I growled. "I didn't think you'd lead me around the park with those idiots."

He turned in full, taking a menacing step forward.

"Those idiots are *Legacies*," he said, his voice lowering. "Legacies that are about to have more points than *you*. Watch your tone with them."

I turned to face him as well, standing straighter and looking down at him.

He paused, as if just noticing how much I had grown since we last stood face-to-face like this.

I wasn't a little kid he could push around anymore. Now, I was ready and willing to fight back—he'd already seen what I was capable of back in the haunted house.

If I was pushed, there was no doubt in my mind. I'd kill him. I owed him one for the bullshit he'd pulled last year anyway.

"So what?" I hedged. "What makes Legacies so special? Special enough that they can enter the games *twice* just for a little fun? Killing anyone they want? Don't think I haven't noticed your attitude. You don't care to win, so why else are you here, hm?"

He let out a laugh.

"I'm here to save our family's reputation. Save *you* from looking like a coward," he said. "Who knew your pathetic ass would show up at the last minute? Honestly, you should've just stayed home. You got a kill, sure, but you're embarrassing yourself."

My hands balled into fists at my side, itching to connect with his face. It would feel so fucking good to split his lip with my knuckles.

Finally, some blood to deliver to my goddess.

"You say that, but really, I think you're just trying to take advantage of the chaos. Maybe just like all the other winners, you got a taste of something you liked, and this has been your chance to let the world know what type of monster *really* hides behind that mask."

Dylan let out a scoff, his large hand squeezing my shoulder. He leaned in, lowering his voice. "Don't worry, Kohl, I won't tell your viewers how excited you were to catch your victim. Maybe then you can stay up on that high horse of yours. At least for another few hours."

His words shocked me. So much so, that when I opened my mouth to respond, but nothing came out.

Hypocrite. The word swirled around my head like a chant.

Of course I was excited. It was only natural that getting closer to winning felt good... But then there was something else.

A part of me hated it, this game that I was playing... but a bigger part enjoyed the act of chasing them down. Of ramming my metal weapon into them over and over again. Watching as the blood pooled in a sticky puddle at my feet. At the way that Jenna's stopped struggling as her eyes went glassy in death.

I even liked the attention from the viewers. The comments and praises rolling in for what I'd done, encouraging me to do more. Worse.

If I wasn't careful, I knew I'd totally lose the plot. I wasn't here to enjoy myself, this was a job. Like working for Terrance.

"Hurry it up," Dylan called, turning on his heel. "We gotta get this moron a weapon."

The other two gave their acknowledgments but stayed hunched

over the victim for a few more seconds. I should have pulled my eyes away, but I couldn't as her bloodied body came into view. Her skull smashed and leaking blood and brain matter onto the asphalt through tendrils of fiery red hair.

I was vaguely aware of the pings from the men's trackers and their hoots of excitement. It was the thing that tore me away from the girl's smashed skull and back to Dylan.

"Let's go, Kohl." he called, Pink and Yellow falling into step with him.

Just like that, my feet moved on their own, following him like I had been my entire life.

If I thought the area with the haunted house was creepy, the games were a downright horror movie.

The place looked decrepit. What looked to be once beautifully bricked roads with grass and weeds growing through the crumbling stones.

Games lined either side, stretching for blocks. There were two additional rows on either side of the main road, giving players a nearly endless amount of chances to get what they wanted.

Creepy music blared through speakers attached to the stalls, flashing lights and cheery paint doing nothing to stop from the whole place feeling weirdly haunted. There was just something about the lack of staff.

"The balloon one has a few good guns!" Dylan said loudly as he led passed the first group of stalls, largely full of medical supplies.

We walked around with ease, Pink and Yellow stopping to play some of the games that caught their eyes.

Many of the prizes were things that would help us gain points.

Knives, bear traps, and flamethrowers. Others had food, gauze, and medical equipment.

It was easy to see which games were meant for Killers and which were for Ghosts.

If I were more like my father, I would've set fire to the ones for vics. But that was a bit too evil for me… Barely. At least I thought I'd probably feel guilty about it.

"Over there." Dylan waved, pointing to a stall toward the end. "I'm going to try and get a stun gun I saw in another one."

I nodded and set off to my destination, happy to be rid of my brother, even if it was only for a little bit.

I frowned when I caught sight of the game. Most of the brightly colored balloons were destroyed, and the largest of the prizes gone. All that was left was some ammo and malicious accessories that would do me no good.

I was about to walk away when I caught sight of a glimmering piece of metal in the corner of the stall. Turning, I smiled as I caught sight of the gun.

"Architects sure love me today," I said with an excited smile.

With this, I will be able to make it through for you, goddess. Just wait for me.

Leaning over the counter, I reached for it. But it was just out of my reach.

"Are you fucking kidding me…?" My voice trailed off when I caught sight of a victim huddled in the corner.

But not just any victim.

My little blue-haired rabbit.

It was fate bringing us together again, it had to be.

She was just out of reach. With just one lunge, I could—

Her movements were quick, decisive. She lunged forward, grabbing the gun and aiming it right at my chest.

I held up my hands, shock running through me.

"Hey now—you don't have to do this—"

She used my pause to grab hold of the edge of the booth, hoisting herself over and out to break into a run.

I cursed. I should've known that she wasn't really going to kill me. That same rush of adrenaline flashed through me, and before I knew it, I'd pushed away from the booth and followed after her. She skidded in front of me, slipping on a bloodied patch of cement onto her ass. She looked back at me, slipping the gun into her hoodie before pushing herself off the wet ground.

She was *close*. So close that when I lunged forward, her long hair brushed the tips of my fingers.

"Should have killed me when you had the chance, *rabbit*!" I shouted, matching my footsteps with hers.

I didn't care that I was leaving Dylan and his stupid friends in the dust. If anything, I was glad to finally have the chance to get away from them.

Each moment that passed in the games was another moment I was stuck, losing possible points as Seekers sniffed out the remaining Ghosts.

I could hear it. Feel the weight of the impending sunrise like a ticking time bomb.

This was my *last* chance. Rabbit may very well be one of the last victims I came across.

Not only did I have to make sure to finish her off this tie, but I had to make it as memorable as possible. Get creative for maximum points accumulation.

"*Plus one point for playing chase,*" the robotic voice said once again from my tracker.

A positively feral smile spread under my mask.

Exactly what I needed.

She whipped around a corner, speeding around the Tilt-A-Whirl and a rocking boat-like ride, the same one I'd watched Victoria hurl into a trash cash after riding. Rabbit didn't pause as she dodged the corpses littering the ground, people in yellow bullet-proof vests zipping them into bags.

Briefly, I remembered that if I ended up like them there was a hastily filled out card with Victoria's address on it waiting for me.

It wasn't an uncommon sight at that time in the games. Bodies littered the park, and it only took a few minutes for the Vultures to come in and take away the eyesore—nothing fun and sexy about a minefield of the dead. Best for it to be tidied away so we could keep our minds on the freshest of the murders.

The closer sunrise got, the fewer people you'd find out in the open like this. In those last precious hours before the game ended—even the Seekers would begin to worry about staying hidden.

No one truly knew what was going on in a player's mind in those last few moments. It was essentially a free-for-all. Everyone vying for those critical last few points.

"You won't be able to run forever!" I yelled, and she turned toward the mirror maze.

Instead of my heart dropping, my excitement only heightened. It would be a challenge to get to her in there, but *damn*, would the viewers go crazy for it.

I couldn't have asked for a more cinematic backdrop.

She disappeared into the maze, moving quicker than I had expected her to. But I wasn't far behind, my lungs aching with the effort of keeping her pace even with my longer strides.

Like the haunted house the mirror maze provided a sort of buffer between us and the outside world. It was silent, save for our heavy breathing and the pounding of her footsteps, but even those quieted as she worked her way through the maze.

The glowing reflection of my mask shone back at me, redacted into multiples thanks to the floor to ceiling mirrors. I was unrecognizable, blood caked into my blond hair and splattered over my bare stomach and arms. My eyes wide and crazed beneath my broken mask, a thick chunk missing from when my prey had hit me.

I looked like a monster.

No, I looked *every* bit the killer I was.

I placed my palms against the cool mirrors, letting them be my guide through the path. As much as I wanted to race through the thing, the last thing I needed was to panic and make a fool of myself in front of the entire country.

As if I'd willed it into existence the sound of shattering glass and a gasp of pain met my ears, ringing against the mirrors and reverberating back to us through the space.

And this is why we go slow, I thought smugly.

I couldn't help but laugh. "That sounded like it hurt."

She was close, I could feel her even if I couldn't see her through the mirrors.

"Come out, come out, wherever you are, little rabbit," I sang, unable to keep the excitement from my voice.

The squeak of her boots against the floor was all I needed to figure out where she was.

Just around this corner.

What I hadn't expected when I turned the corner was a shot to ring out and embed itself right near my head, sending the shattered glass in a cascade onto the floor.

Not giving her time to correct her aim, I lunged for her, this time my hand finally closing around one of those damned blue pigtails to lurch her back.

I wrapped my arms around her as she struggled. One around her throat, the other around her waist to keep her still.

Her hands came to hold herself up before her strong legs found the mirror and pushed hard.

The move sent us flying backward, almost knocking the wind out of me.

Don't you fucking let this chance slip past you.

I kept a tight hold on her while flipping us around. She bucked against me, twisting in my arms until we were facing each other. She kneed me in the groin causing me to hiss but when it didn't have the desired effect she let out a snarled, "*Fuck!*"

She was going to die. I knew it. She knew it. It didn't matter how much more she struggled.

Her fingers slipped into my mask, tearing it off.

She paused when she caught sight of my face. It gave me the opening I needed to wrap my fingers around her throat.

Her eyes widened behind her mask as I choked the life from her. Her nails dug into my arms, shocked gurgles escaping her mouth.

My watch was going *crazy* with pings, the sound bouncing off the mirrors.

That's right. They wanted a fight, and I'm here to give it to them.

It was what the audience craved. They wanted to hope for the Ghost while cheering for the Seeker as they murdered them in high definition.

Sure there were few watching in horror, but the world we lived in had been *conditioned* for these games. They were celebrated. Revered for the money that they brought to the economy.

Once upon a time, companies wouldn't dare advertise on a death match, but now it was a *coveted* spot. Better than the Superbowl.

A spot that would earn me lots and *lots* of money.

Exactly what my goddess deserved.

It was enough to push away any lingering guilt for what I was doing.

Her hands loosened on my arms. She was giving up. Or at least I thought... until they fell to her face, where she used the last of her strength to tear off her mask.

Shock shot through my veins, burning where my skin touched hers.

I ripped my hands off her, unable to come to terms with what I was seeing.

The little white rabbit. The Ghost that I'd been chasing after this entire time... I knew her.

Not only did I know her... she'd single-handedly ruined any other woman for me.

Victoria.

Her brown eyes were wide as she gasped for air. Pink, full lips that I'd dreamed about kissing open as she tried desperately to right herself.

Fuck, fuck, fuck! What had I done?

No. I'd never meant to hurt her. This was all for *her.*

Her open palm connected with the side of my face hard enough that it made my ears ring.

I'd do *anything* for her. Kill anyone for her. But never had I thought that she would—

She pushed up to her knees, coughs racking her body.

"I can't believe you—" her wheezing voice was cut off by a particularly powerful cough. "I thought we promised—"

"You said you wouldn't do anything reckless!" I yelled, though it was more from panic than anger. "What are you *doing* here, Vic?"

"I could ask you the same!" she snapped, letting out another cough that caused my heart to twist in my chest.

I'd come seconds away from killing her. My hands were shaking under the weight of the realization.

"For you!" I plead. "I promised you I would find a way. What do you think I've been doing this whole time?"

She shook her head, loosing a derisive laugh.

"Living your comfy *Legacy* life?" she scoffed, shrugging. "I don't know. Whatever else it is you decided to do with all the money your father can give you."

"You thought I was just messing around?" I asked. "Like my promise meant nothing? Like what happened meant nothing to me?"

"How would I know?" she asked, seething with anger. "I was *struggling*, Kohl. I couldn't just dr—"

"And you changed your hair?" I asked accusatorily, reaching forward to grab onto it. The once-blonde locks now a mix of black and teal. "If I didn't know any better, I'd say you didn't want to be found. Is this your way of avoiding me? Knowing that I'd try to stop you if you entered?"

Her eyebrows pulled together and she let out the cutest angry huff.

"My hairstyle choices have nothing to do with *you*. Fucking self-centered-ass-fuckboy Wolff, Christ!"

Memories of stolen moments through my mind. Even though the circumstances were different, she was still the same Victoria that that enraptured me, mind, body and soul.

My goddess.

I couldn't stop myself. Blame it on the adrenaline. Maybe the anger at seeing her. The anger from her so obviously trying to hide from me. The person who had been willing to not only put their life on the line but *kill* for her as well.

Maybe it was her closeness, the smell of the sweat on her skin mixed with the bitter peachy perfume she always wore.

Or maybe it was the memory of her writhing against me— begging me not to stop—even if *both* of us knew we shouldn't have been doing what we were.

Or maybe it was just her.

The same Victoria that'd been living in my dreams and haunting my nightmares. The one I yearned for even when she wasn't supposed to be mine.

Ultimately it didn't matter why I did it. Only that in one moment we were staring at each other and the next I'd crashed my lips to hers.

It was like years of pent-up *want* exploded at the contact. The little *treat* she'd given me at the graduation party barely scratching the surface of this bone deep, unquenchable *need* for her.

I gripped her messy hair, tangling my hands in it and using it to keep her under my control as I ravaged her mouth.

I expected her to fight me after what I did. To kick and scream and force me off.

But instead, her hands wrapped around my shoulders and pulled me closer. I was on my knees in front of her and used my free arm to wrap around her waist, forcing her to straddle me. Glass embedded into my skin through the fabric of my pants, but I welcomed the bite.

A bit of suffering would go a long way in my road to repentance for putting my hands on her.

I let out a low groan when her teeth bit my lip hard enough to draw blood, shuddering against her.

"Fuck you," she growled. But before I could pull away, her hands were trailing my arms and chest. She paused in her exploration to run her fingers across the mastectomy scars hidden under my shirt.

I shivered at her touch and pulled her hair harder, forcing her head back to meet my eye.

My mouth found her neck with the same vigor as I had her lips, licking and sucking until my kisses and bites blossomed into bruises against her fair skin.

She squirmed against me, her pants filling the room.

I let go of her to run my hands up her sides, slipping my fingers into her sports bra before running them over her nipples.

"God, do you know how long I've wanted to touch these?" I groaned against her neck, biting down hard, letting her feel all the frustration that I'd be suppressing since I'd last seen her.

I had lost count of how many times she changed in front of me. I had an inkling she did it on purpose, but I never said anything for fear I would lose my chance to watch her ever again.

"Taste them," she commanded, fingers threading into my hair.

I hiked up her hoodie and bra in one go, disconnecting myself from her throat to take a look.

Victoria's perky breasts stared back at me, moving with each rise of her chest. She arched up for me, my signal to stop ogling like a teenage boy who'd never seen tits before and get on with it.

I leaned forward, but instead of taking her nipple fully into my mouth, I looked up at her as I circled it with my tongue. She gasped when I did so, telling me my little act had the desired effect on her.

I couldn't stop the smirk from spreading across my lips.

"Delicious," I said with a laugh.

Her face twisted as if she was ready to launch into an argument, but I shut her up by pulling the tightening bud firmly into my mouth and nibbling on it.

"Ah, *fuck*, like that," she moaned.

I moved to the other, doing the same and earning myself a few weakly gasped praises.

She ground against me, searching for friction I hadn't been kind enough to give her.

Without another word, I slipped my hand past the waistband of her pants, hunting for her clit.

She's wet. So wet, my fingers slipped through her folds with ease.

And all because of me. My goddess was wet because of me. The knowledge alone made my head spin.

A strangled moan came out of her mouth, drawing my eyes to hers, only to see she wasn't looking at me at all. I followed her gaze to the ceiling, heat bursting through me when I saw what she was seeing.

The two of us were reflected in the mirrors all around us, covered in blood and looking worse for wear. We were panting, our skin flushed and lips swollen from the intensity of our hurried kisses.

From this angle, I could make out her nipples shining with my spit, and my hand shoved between her legs. Even as I met her eye in the mirror, her hips kept bucking against my hand.

It was a fantasy I'd fucked myself to too many times to count. The image making my stomach clench and wet heat pooling between my legs.

"Tell me to stop," I begged, my voice thick with need. "Please Vic, tell me to stop."

VIC

BEFORE THE GAMES

If I was hoping Dylan's lackluster conversation skills would be made up for in the bedroom, I was sorely disappointed.

Like everything else in his life, my boyfriend was just fucking bumbling through it, pulling his pleasure out of my body with little regard for my own.

Sometimes, in search of his own release, he did something right. Something that was *just enough* to send a bolt of pleasure through me.

But it was never intentional and only lasted a few seconds at most.

It was pitiful, really. A big bad Legacy like him, known for his looks and sexual prowess, was actually shit in bed.

These spontaneous quickies were the worst—how the fuck did this idiot come from a *Killer* family and not even know to pull a girl's hair a little while bending her over his father's stupidly expensive pool chairs?

"Fuck, Vic, you're so tight—" he hissed as he thrust into me over and over again.

I'd laid my head on my arms, moaning like there were cameras on.

Really, I should've won an Oscar for the depth of the performances I'd given over the last couple weeks.

I'd been degraded, put into positions I'd never willingly allow.

All of *this* just for the opportunity to try and meet *him*.

Dylan's hands on my hips were perfunctory at best, missing the bite that I needed from a partner. His hips kicked a few more times, a stucco of unsatisfying thrusts that brought him over the edge with a groan in my ear.

He pulled out of me, leaning forward for a kiss at my back. "C'mere, babe."

"One sec," I said quickly, pulling my swim cover over my bare ass. Dylan threw my bottoms somewhere, and I wasn't keen to go digging before I cleaned myself up.

I planted a kiss on Dylan's stubbly cheek, darting inside for the main floor bathroom.

I'd long since gotten used to the extravagance of the house, but that didn't make it any less breathtaking. It was just another reminder of the status difference between my family and the Wolffs.

We were both the children of winners. People who'd risked their lives in the arena for the off chance that they'd get ahead.

But the Wolffs excelled where my parents failed.

The most important rule after you left the fucking games was to *live*, after all.

The thing is, the Wolffs never let go of their fascination with Devil's Playground. While my parents tried their best to live normal lives after the games, Hiram did the opposite, all but kissing the ass of The Company until he could sink his claws into them to try and crawl up the ranks.

At least it seemed to be working for them.

Couldn't say much about what that meant for Dylan, but at least he had the money to show for his triumph the year before.

If you could call third-place *winning*.

The bathroom door opened as my hand touched the handle, revealing a handsome figure in a cloud of sandalwood-scented steam.

The thrum of arousal that was left unanswered by Dylan roared back to life as I took in Kohl's sculpted chest, the reddened slashes of their mastectomy scars framing their pecs.

Kohl. Dylan's brother and my dirty little secret.

Kohl was never a part of the plan. If anything, their presence only complicated things. Turning what was once a straightforward black-and-white goal into something splattered with a million shades of gray.

Surprise crossed their features, their eyes trailing from my wet hair to the way that my bikini top pushed my tits halfway to my chin, barely concealed by a thin cover-up. Their breathing hitched as they hit my waist and hips, and I looked down, my face heating.

My cover-up was entirely see-through, giving Kohl a perfect view of my abused cunt and the slickness on my thighs.

A devilish part of me wanted to tell them about the unanswered arousal that was vibrating beneath my skin, just to see what they'd say. *To see what they'd do.*

In another life, I'd push Kohl back into that bathroom, force them to their knees, and ride that beautiful fucking face until I was shaking.

But in this reality, getting caught fucking my *darling boyfriend's* brother would seriously fuck up my plans.

They leaned forward, their hands finding the top of the door frame as the corner of their mouth hooked into a grin. "Hi, Vic."

God. All sorts of inappropriate things ran through my head at the tilt of their lips.

I swallowed hard, stumbling back a step. "Hi," I returned, my voice quieter than I would've liked.

Kohl's towel was low on their hips, hugging their flesh. The planes of their stomach were defined with the whisper of their abs, and when a stray drop of water fell down one, my mouth watered. In my mind, I was already in front of them, my tongue trailing—

"I don't know why you waste your time with that loser," they murmured, using their free hand to peel a piece of wet hair away from the side of my face. "You're worth fifty of Dylan."

Their words should've shocked me. Should've snapped me out of this spiraling need for them. But when they touched me, it was like every fiber of my being was singing. My body—*and mind*—were begging me to lean forward and taste those fucking scars of theirs.

Kohl had this sort of heavy, intoxicating air about them that Dylan didn't.

For one, I actually *liked* Kohl. Seeing them in the halls at school or even around the house was the highlight of my day—well, other than their ritual good morning and good night texts. I clung to those like a lifeline while I choked on the bitterness of having to pretend to be into Dylan.

I wanted them. Wanted them more than I'd ever wanted anything.

But every moment I fantasized about Kohl was another wasted second where I could be enacting my plan.

And as much as I wanted Kohl, revenge was my top priority.

At least for now.

It was my burden to carry, and I wouldn't let Kohl be another person on my long list of casualties. I'd make sure of it.

Kohl's thumb scored a line across my jaw as they leaned into my space, their breath ghosting over my lips. "Vic?"

I fought the urge to rub my thighs together.

"I know," I whispered, looking into their deep brown eyes.

"Then why—?"

"This is sure cozy," Dylan said from behind us.

Reluctantly, I stepped away from the warmth of Kohl's body, turning to Dylan and throwing on my kilowatt smile. "Baby! I told you I'd be right back!"

"Got thirsty," my boyfriend grunted, holding up a pair of beers. "Am I interrupting something?"

"No!" Kohl and I said at the same time.

I bounced over to Dylan, wrapping my arms around his thick middle. "Did you find my bottoms?"

"Didn't even look," he said with a smirk, reaching down to fist my left butt cheek, spreading my ass to give Kohl a look through my cover. "Thought we could skinnydip for a bit anyway."

I bit back my nasty remark, trying to ignore Kohl's eyes on me like a brand.

"Sounds like fun!"

It did not, in fact, sound like fun. It sounded like another opportunity for Dylan to get his dick wet and for me to spend another two and a half minutes pretending that submitting to an overgrown Mr. Potato Head was remotely stimulating.

Dylan led me back through the house, and I followed, my head turning as we rounded the corner to catch a final glimpse of Kohl, their jaw tight and irritated, before they headed for their room.

Now that was a Wolff sibling I wanted to be under.

I bet they liked breath play.

Kohl

I circled her clit with two fingers.

I was *so* close to pinning her to the ground, pulling her hair, and forcing her to watch in the mirrors as I fucked her.

I wouldn't be gentle. I didn't know if I knew how to be after everything.

The adrenaline that had been pumping through my veins, pushing me to destroy my victims, was begging me to destroy her in an entirely different way.

Her gaze snapped back to mine.

"*Please.* If you don't tell me to stop..." *I'll fuck you until we both can't take it anymore.* The words were on the tip of my tongue, but I couldn't speak them. Not when her hooded gaze told me she wanted me to continue.

I slipped my hand from between her legs and wrapped both arms around her, giving her time to decide.

She took my breath away. With anyone else, I would have complete control of the situation, but with her, I always found myself floundering to keep some type of hold on the situation.

Even now, she could tell me to do *anything*, and I'd gladly comply without a moment's hesitation.

"I'm pissed at you," she admitted after a moment.

"I didn't know it was you," I said, holding her. "Believe me when I say I would give my life for you, Vic."

It was more than that, but my devotion to her couldn't be said in words. I wouldn't just give my life for her. I would throw it away. Mold it into something—*anything*—she needed it to be.

She didn't even have to ask. I'd done the hardest part already, and no matter what, I planned to see it through.

Everything, *every single fucking thing*, was for her. My thoughts, my actions, every breath I took all belonged to her.

That was my gift to my goddess after everything. A way to show just how much she meant to me, the depths of my devotion.

"Your life, huh?" she said, a smile twisting her face. "And if I ask for you to prove it? What then?"

Quicker than she could stop me—I let go of her, collected a discarded fragment of the broken mirrored glass, and brought it to my heart. Her fingers dug into me. One hand on my shoulder, the other on my wrist, stopping me from pushing the glass through my heart.

"No hesitation," I said, holding her gaze as I pushed the point into my skin, forcing a drip of crimson blood to well at the surface.

If my life had to end here to extend hers, I'd do it. No problem.

Vic stared at the point of contact, but it wasn't with concern. There something in her eyes that caused my heart to skip a beat, something that looked a lot like excitement.

"Does it hurt?" she asked, her breathing shallow.

"It will," I grunted, attempting to fight her grip and push the jagged edge deeper into my skin, welcoming the pain.

Her mouth covered mine again, this time kissing me back just as fervently as I did to her. I moaned into her mouth, ready to drop the broken piece of mirror, but her wrist kept it over my heart instead of stopping its descent.

She could, at any moment, force it through chest and stop my heart. I wouldn't fight her on it. But just the little show of how much control she had, paired with the way our teeth and tongues clashed together, was enough to make my mind whirl.

"I need you to win the game," she whispered against my lips. "So don't kill yourself... but I will need some serious vows from you to be sure you won't kill me as soon as my back is turned."

"Take my top off," I ordered. She pulled back, giving me a look before doing exactly as I said. I dropped my weapon until it was off and placed it over my heart, but this time I didn't let her stop me as I dragged it against my skin.

"Kohl," she breathed when she realized the letter I was carving right over my heart.

Satisfaction burst in my chest when I saw the way her gaze darkened. The carving hurt like a bitch. But seeing how she looked at me as I branded myself as hers made it so *worth it* that I barely noticed the lingering ache.

"Have this be your proof, Victoria," I said with a wicked grin. "Proof that my body—*my life*—is yours. It always has been and forever will be. Use me how you see fit. Whether that's to win the game or throw to me away. Just say the words."

Blood leaked down my hands, spilling over my fingers and onto the floor. Pain licked at the wound. I held out the mirror piece to her, but instead of grabbing it, she leaned forward, smirking up at me before extending her tongue to lap at the bloody initial. *Her* initial.

My loud groan echoed in the room. I tangled my hand in her hair, pulling her back to look at her smoldering face.

The image of my blood staining her lips made my arousal *unbearable*.

"I can think of many uses for you at the moment," she said, her eyes locked on my lips. I leaned up to kiss her, but her head jerked just out of the way, hands running down my torso and slipping into my pants making my throat constrict.

When her hand hit my wet underwear, she let out a breathy chuckle.

"Seems like you *really* want to be *used* by me. Isn't that right, *Killer Kohl?*"

Vic

Kohl's eyes were wide with shock as I rubbed their clit through their underwear.

"Yes," they breathed, their jaw tight against a moan I knew they wouldn't release.

"You think you were the only one with a legacy they needed to answer to?" I asked, the corner of my mouth twitching as Kohl ground against my fingers.

"I know you aren't," they hissed through their teeth. "Vic, I'm so—"

"It's white rabbit," I corrected, my eyes narrowing.

Anger was making it hard to concentrate. Kohl had lied to me, nearly fucking killed me, killed Jenna.

But they were still Kohl.

My Kohl.

The watch on my wrist buzzed, a notification popping up to celebrate my increased viewership, and I grinned, an idea forming in my mind.

I needed Kohl to win this, but even more than that, I needed Kohl when this shit was over.

"Open your mouth," I ordered from where I straddled them,

trailing the piece of glass down their bare chest and leaving a shallow scratch as I went.

Surprise colored their expression. "Vic—"

"The way I see it, Kohl," I snapped, holding the jagged piece of mirror over their gut. "I could just fucking kill you right here right now, that's what you would've done to me."

"If I'd known—"

"I don't care about your excuses. Now listen to me like a good boy." I locked eyes with them, raising an eyebrow before flicking my eyes at their watch.

Kohl seemed to finally understand what I was playing at.

Sure, I was *pissed*, but more than that, we had a game to win. A grin spread over their face, and they gripped my hips, opening their mouth obediently.

I licked up the blood flowing from the V cut into their chest and spat it into their open mouth, licking the remnants from my teeth. "Swallow."

Kohl's throat flexed obediently and he let out a ragged breath. "Please, rabbit, let me make it up to you."

I should've felt relieved, happy that it was Kohl and not Dylan who was behind that mask. But as the wave of delirious gratitude dissipated, something inside me began to fester.

They'd lied to me. *They'd fucking lied to me.*

And they'd nearly *killed* me because of it.

My throat felt bruised, but I was still able to suck down gasps of air through my sore windpipe as I looked at them, their eyes wide and full of awe as they landed on my body.

"Vic, baby, please—let me make it up to you."

Under the tension that'd coiled in my psyche, fueled by losing both my parents in a single year, having to drop out of the college I'd worked my entire life to get into, and the injustice of *this*, being here, having to play this stupid fucking game...

I snapped.

"Shut your worthless fucking mouth, Kohl, before I shut it for you."

Something so delicious flashed across their eyes that, for a moment, their anger hazed. But just for a single moment. Long enough for me to form a plan.

My hand trailed their bloodied wound. My entire body lighting up when a small gasp forced itself from Kohl's lips.

"I can—"

My bloodied hand shot forward to grab their chin. There was something so fucking erotic about dirtying Kohl's beautiful face.

"You can't take directions well, can you?" I asked, pulling them forward with my bruising grip on their face. "Then you face the consequences. I'll shut it for you."

I shoved Kohl's chest, sending them flailing to the ground. I got to my feet, looking down at them where they panted on the glass strewn floor.

They were breathtaking, better than a fucking painting.

I made a show of kicking off my shoes, slowly stripping down to nothing.

They cursed under their breath, eyes wide and their breaths coming in needy little gasps.

"Do you want me to shut you up, Kohl?" I asked, dropping my tone to a low purr.

They nodded, careful not to say anything. Their thick swallow pulling a laugh from my lips.

I turned to face the mirror, bracketing their head with my knees. Their hands moved to grip my hips, but I slapped them away.

"Fucking greedy little *whore*," I snarled. "You think you have the right to touch me?"

There was a pause before they answered, their voice quivering with need. "No."

"No what?"

"No, *my goddess.*"

Their words shouldn't have turned me on as much as they did. But something about the near reverent tone Kohl used set my skin on fire. I rewarded them by lowering myself just enough that if they stretched, Kohl would just barely be able to taste my slick cunt.

"Make your mouth useful," I ordered, leaning forward to run the sharp edge of the glass down their chest until it hit the waist of their pants, leaving behind a shallow scratch. "You should thank me for giving you a chance to taste me."

They stretched, tongue darting out to run the length of my folds.

I clenched my teeth against the breathy moan threatening my throat. They didn't deserve it, not yet.

"Thank you," Kohl mumbled against my cunt. I could feel the slight tilt of their lips as they smiled.

Cocky bastard.

"That's all you can do?" I goaded, digging the sharp glass into their skin, hard enough to spill blood.

They shifted, craning upward so they could apply more pressure to my clit. I let myself push against their mouth, dragging my sensitive cunt against their lips and tongue. It was all I let myself enjoy before I teased the waist of their pants with the glass.

"Show me how wet I make you," I ordered. "Show me how twisted and fucked up that head of yours really is... How bad you want me even as I tell you how worthless you are." I shifted so Kohl could hurriedly take off their pants before settling myself right back on their face.

This time they didn't wait to attack my pussy.

Fuck, they were good at that. Not that I'd ever let them know. Not when they were so affected by it.

A tingling heat traveled through me when I caught sight of their swollen, sensitive clit. Their pussy was positively dripping, and I hadn't even come yet.

"Disgusting," I hissed, collecting the saliva that was building in my mouth and spit directly onto their cunt, using the additional lubrication to tease their folds.

They bucked their hips, searching for a harder friction that I wouldn't give to them.

When their lips wrapped around my clit, I couldn't help the whine that forced itself from my throat.

Damn it.

"Taste how much this turns you on," I ordered, and I shifted away from their mouth so I could shove my fingers passed their lips.

They sucked my fingers greedily, cleaning up their own mess. Each strong pull against my finger and every swipe of their tongue was causing more and more heat to build in me.

I jerked away from them before settling down once more on their face. I would get back at them for the way they were making me feel, but first I was going to make sure I got an orgasm out of it.

A girl had to have priorities after all.

"God, you're so useless," I panted as I dragged my pussy against their tongue. I looked up to the mirrored ceiling, watching myself as I fucked their face.

My face was flushed, the makeup the artists had done slightly smudged. I could *just* make out Kohl's mouth as they tried their best to prove their pussy-eating skill to me.

They'd completely forgotten their own predicament in search of my pleasure. Their legs wide open, wetness gathering on the floor in a puddle underneath them.

I fucking loved the way I looked riding them.

Breathtaking. All-powerful. Confident.

Like a queen sitting on her throne. No, like a goddess on her altar.

"Can't even make a girl come, huh?" I jeered, steadying myself on their bloodied chest. I couldn't help but smear the blood further into their skin and into a trail that led straight to their pussy. "So, what, last time was just a fluke?"

I groaned when they attacked my clit, not holding back. They sucked, nipped, and licked it until I was positively *shaking.*

"That's right," I praised. "Don't stop sucking. Not 'til I say so."

Fuck, they were good at taking orders.

I rewarded them by playing with their clit. They were so slippery, so *sensitive,* that even after just a few thrums of my fingers against the sensitive bundle of nerves, their body tensed like they were about to come.

"You going to come for me, Kohl?" I purred and they groaned, their pleasure making them even more eager to serve.

"No, I don't think you will…" I said slowly, still stroking their clit. "Stop yourself. You don't fucking deserve to come," I hissed. "You're gonna watch as I take the one thing you can't have. Make me feel good from your worthless lying mouth."

Kohl's returning whine made my brain go hazy.

I couldn't hold it back anymore, my orgasm ripping through me like a tidal wave. I leaned forward and sank my teeth into the soft part of Kohl's thigh in an attempt to conceal my moan.

They let out a groan of their own.

Fuck. Fuck. Fuck.

Even after my orgasm, my anger hit me. It was relentless, and all I wanted to do was take it out on them.

"Good boy," I praised, moving off of Kohl until I was sitting, with the mirror against the back. "Though I'm not satisfied just yet."

They twisted around, lifting themselves up by their forearms. The lower half of their face was a mess of cum and blood. Their eyes wide and pupils blown.

"What else can I do?" they asked, eyes trailing my body before stopping at my pussy. They licked their lips, collecting the remnants of my release.

"Beg," I demanded. "Beg for me, and maybe I'll *consider* forgiving you for the time being."

They shifted on all fours, their eyes trailing back up to mine as the shards of broken glass crunched under their knees.

Fuck, were they gonna—

They placed one hand in front of the others, their knees following behind them as they crawled on the dirty, bloody floor. Their movements slow and languid as they let me take in exactly what they were doing—like they didn't notice the mirror cutting into their knees and palms.

My core clenched like a vise at the sight.

"Please forgive me, goddess," they begged, their voice husky.

"Please. I'll do anything. Make me your fuck toy. Destroy me in front of the entire world. I don't care who sees, as long as you forgive me."

"Yeah?" I asked breathlessly as they reached my feet. When their hand came to grab a foot, kissing it before throwing it over their shoulder, I couldn't help my gasp. They left burning kisses up my calf, taking their time as they mouthed at the side of my knee.

Realization crackled through me.

"Oh, I see." I murmured. "You *like* the fact that thousands of people are watching you degrade yourself in such a *disgusting* way."

Their flush was all the confirmation I needed.

"Come on then," I said, shifting my legs open for them. "Put on a good show, Kohl. Show everyone that you're my *toy*."

They continued to kiss up my legs until they reached the junction where my thigh met my cunt, their tongue dragging across the sensitive flesh before their lips found my clit once more.

I couldn't stop my loud moan as they pushed two fingers into me, scissoring them.

"Arch your back," I said, my eyes shifting toward the mirror behind them where I could *just* make out their ass in the glow of their discarded mask and the low lights of the maze.

They did as I told them, giving me a perfect view of their wet cunt.

"See? You're nothing but a dog with no bite," I purred. "Fuck yourself while you feast, but don't come."

Their hand darted in between their legs. They were just able to rub their clit and tease their entrance from this position. It couldn't have been comfortable, but they didn't complain. Not once.

"Nothing but a useless house cat," I murmured, threading my hand into their hair. "Do you bend for all your victims like this?"

"Just you," they gasped against me. "*Fuck*. Please forgive me, goddess. Please. Please—"

"You're not saying that so I'd let you come, are you?"

"No!" they all but yelled. "Always and only you. Ever since I met you for the first time, I couldn't stop thinking of you."

I let out a hum and pushed their face further into my pussy.

With the flick of my wrist, the screen of my tracker lit, a filter of comments flying by so quickly it was hard to catch them.

"They *really* like you, kitten," I teased. "Who could've known such a ruthless Killer like *you* would embarrass themselves like this? Begging a pathetic *Ghost* to let you come."

Pings came from their tracker. It was coming every few moments now as the audience went crazy for our performance.

"Come on, Kohl," I cooed. "Make me come one more time, and I'll let you come, but just this once, okay?"

That was all the incentive they needed. I threw my head back against the glass as wave after wave of pleasure started to build up under their renewed efforts.

I wasn't sure if it was the way they begged for me or if it was their show in the mirror, but I came faster than I ever had in my life with Kohl's name leaving my lips like a fucking *prayer*.

"Show me," I demanded the second I regain control of my blissed out mind. "Up. Let me watch you come."

They were on their knees in seconds, their hands thrumming their clit. I leaned forward, taking it all in. Before I knew it, I was giving in to the impulse to let my fingers scoop up the wetness dripping from them, coating my fingers.

"Fuck, *please*, goddess."

"Oh, you want this?" I asked, sliding two fingers inside of them. Their pussy walls were already fluttering around me, but I made sure to pump my fingers in and out slowly, twisting and curling them. Anything to make my little Killer fall apart.

It didn't take long. Kohl came with a cry that bounced back at us from the glass, wetness bursting out of them and falling to the floor.

I gripped their golden blond hair, forcing their face to the floor.

"Lick it up," I ordered, a sinister smile splitting my face. "Lick it up and we're done here."

Their tongue darted out to lick up their own cum and blood off the floor. The lack hesitancy in their actions enough for me to consider going *again*.

Kohl just looked so fucking good when they were following my orders.

But we didn't have the time.

When I was satisfied with how much they cleaned up, I stood and redressed myself quickly. Kohl made a move to find their own clothes but I stopped them as they moved to put on their underwear, snapping my fingers. They handed them over immediately. I had to actively fight the self-satisfied smile threatening my mouth.

"I'm keeping these," I said, putting them into my pocket. "Get dressed."

Again, they were quick to obey.

Once they were dressed I grabbed them by the shirt and placed a burning kiss on their lips.

"You were such a *good boy* for me, Kohl," I cooed. "I can't forgive everything, but this is a good start."

The excitement in their eyes caused my chest to twist.

"Now we need a *plan*."

They nodded. "I already thought of it," they said. "I have to gather supplies and deal with the others, but we should meet back at the tunnel of love when I can ditch them."

I raised an eyebrow at them. "Seriously? The tunnel of love?"

They gave me a wolfish grin, collecting their mask and pulling it over their face. The purple of the x'ed out eyes and smiling mouth glowing throughout the dark room and reflecting in the mirrors surrounding us.

"I'm a romantic, Vic. What can I say?"

Kohl
Before the Games

There weren't many places in an Architect's house you could keep secret, but after a lifetime living under my father's reign, I'd found a way around his surveillance.

God, if he knew about the fucked-up shit I did in here, he'd fucking kill me.

I let out a ragged breath, my sweaty fist making contact with the photos pinned to the wall. Most were a little blurry—grainy images I'd stolen from the security cameras around the property. My hand closed around a handful of teal fabric. It still smelled like her.

Fuck, how I longed to force my face between her legs. For her to wrap her thighs around my head. To feel how she shook under me as I fucked her with my tongue.

Nah, I didn't want to just *fuck* Vic. I wanted to *worship* her. To bring her all the pleasure she could imagine and then some.

My fingers were working on my clit in rapid, unrelenting circles. Pleasure shot through me, licking at my spine and causing my toes to curl. I was close, even with just a few strokes against my clit, I was going to come fast.

It was always like this. As soon as I so much as *thought* of the way Vic looked under her clothes or the things I wanted to do to her, I had this uncontrollable urge to touch myself.

But no matter how many times I made myself come, none of it did anything to dampen the *need* I had for her.

It'd been only a few days since I saw Vic, but the more I stayed around her, the more I had to watch that fuckface take what was supposed to be mine. The more I found myself unable to hold back.

I needed more. I needed *her. I don't know how much longer I can hold on like this.* I was going insane. Each and every time I had to see her flirt with someone else, or have her hand brush across my brother's back, or—*fuck*—it was just all too much and slowly chipping away at my psyche.

I was turning into something I didn't like. I wanted to protect her. To serve her. But goddamn, did I want more than anything to feel her against me.

I leaned against the wall, my breathing labored. The small closet was just enough space to allow me to kneel down while still looking at my—*collection.*

I couldn't call it a shrine. It made it too real.

My eyes narrowed on the most recent leak of Vic's nudes. Not the stupid censored version that was released in the gossip mags, but the original I managed to grab before Dylan got rid of the evidence from his phone.

That fucker. I wanted to be angry—*fuck*—and I'd been furious when I realized what he was about to do. But how could I think of anything else when I saw the perfectly posed Vic sitting on her bed, spreading her legs wide, and giving me a perfect view of her swollen cunt?

I hadn't even bothered to fully undress, just shimmied my pants down my hips to allow enough room for my fingers to slip between my legs.

Images of Vic in that goddamn see-through swim cover of hers flashed through my mind. Her pussy had been so visible through the fabric, so *ready* and waiting for *someone* to give it the attention it deserved.

It should've been me.

I screwed my eyes shut, trying to bring myself back to the moment. Back to the feel of her warm skin at my fingertips.

I wanted nothing more than to lift the thin fabric and take care of her myself. I knew for a fact Dylan hadn't done shit to make her feel good. I'd listened to them multiple times. Heard the way her fake moans cut through the air.

I remembered the first time I heard him do something right. The hitch of her breath followed by a low groan I'd never heard before.

I committed it to memory. Along with the "Do that again," she'd gasped. There was such a strong command in her tone. One Dylan ignored, but not *me*. I'd never ignore a command that fell from the perfect lips of my goddess.

I'd make it my duty to see it through. My sole purpose was to make sure she came as often and as hard as she desired. Bringing her to the edge with my tongue and fingers until she begged me to stop.

It's what she deserved.

Complete and total submission.

I brought the swim bottoms to my mouth, inhaling her scent. My mind swam, yearning for the day that I would finally be able to touch her how she so desperately needed.

She could command me all she wanted, and I'd gladly comply. Truthfully, I'd let her do just about anything she wanted to me.

The obsession I had for her just continued to grow and grow, until there was no one in my mind but *her*, and I couldn't bring myself to care.

I forced my eyes open to look directly at the photo she took. The one with her legs spread and her chest popped out.

She sat on that bed like it was her fucking throne. Her skin was glowing, shining in the dim light. The fucking smile that was on her lips just made me all the more ravenous for her. She had the looks and confidence to make any man fall to his knees for just the chance to get near her.

I was no different.

There I was, foaming at the mouth, fucking myself to her nudes and discarded swim bottoms. If I'd had even so much as a *chance* to be in her presence when she was there, spreading her legs for me, I'd be on my knees in an instant.

Fuck, I'd even crawl to her.

I was salivating at the thought of the prize that awaited me. I'd kiss up her legs, trailing my tongue on the soft flesh of her thigh, until she allowed me just the *taste*.

I let out a whine as that particular fantasy made my cunt clench, warning that I was close.

I pushed myself forward, using my forearm to keep me up while I slipped my finger inside my wet, aching pussy. I couldn't tear my eyes away from the image as I fucked myself.

I was too enraptured by the fantasy playing out in my mind.

"You think you can do better than him?" Vic asked, widening her legs even further, her fingers coming to tease her folds. Her wetness was glimmering in the dim light, teasing me. I was so close that if I just reached out my tongue, I could taste her.

"Fuck," I groaned, my pussy fluttering. Even just the fantasy of her was enough to send me spiraling.

The fantasy was so vivid I could almost *hear* the words coming from her lips.

"Come on, Kohl," she'd whisper with that breathy laugh of hers. "Have a taste. Just a small one. No one has to know."

No one could know. Not with our current situation... yet some part of me wanted them all to hear. Wanted her to fuck my face while her moans filled the room. I wanted them to know how much better suited I was for her than anyone else.

I didn't care how unrealistic it was. Or how for the first time in my life I wanted someone to look down on me, to command my body to give them pleasure instead of me taking it.

I just wanted it. Wanted her. Wanted to taste her. Wanted to fuck her.

Her. Her. Her. That was all my mind was. A series of chants and images of Vic. Some that I may never see in real life, but that didn't stop me.

The sound of my fingers fucking my wet cunt filled the small closet. The air had turned warm, my groans unmistakable.

"Good boy," she crooned as my tongue reached out to run the length of her slit. When my mouth fastened over her clit, she threw her head back, a groan spilling from her lips—

My own groan forced itself out as the first wave of my orgasm hit me. I cried out, the feeling of my pussy convulsing too much while paired with the fantasy of Vic looking down at me with a smirk so sinister it caused my hair to raise on the back of my neck.

In my pleasure-clouded mind, I accidentally tore off some of the images I'd carefully taped to the wall. My eyes fell on them as they floated to the ground.

These were ones I had taken myself when she was here. But unlike Dylan, these were of her fully clothed, laughing, and smiling.

A normal person would have felt guilt for what they'd done, but all I felt was the all-consuming need for *more*.

To take what Dylan so clearly didn't deserve.

If it was the last thing I did, Vic would be *mine*.

Vic

I tried not to look at myself in the mirror as I slipped out of the house, already trying to forget the way that Kohl's fingers felt on my skin. The way they looked dirty and blood-covered on the floor—begging for more.

Classic Kohl and Vic, of course. We couldn't tear down the walls between us until it was life or death.

God, we were so *fucked up*.

Even then, there was *something* between us. The knowledge of what awaited us out there. The fear that as hard as we may try, we might not survive tonight.

It was different when I was here without them. All I thought about was what *I* needed to do to survive, but as soon as Kohl left to go find their brother, all my worries shifted to them.

Dylan was a nasty piece of work and I didn't trust him not to turn on Kohl if he had the chance.

The tracker on my wrist felt heavy as I slipped through the park, a jagged piece of mirrored glass stashed in one of my pant pockets. The gun I'd managed to grab from the games was tucked into the waistband of my pants, not that it'd do me any fucking good until I found some more bullets.

But none of that mattered. Not if Kohl kept their word.

Not if we were a *team*.

The smell of blood and the sour taste of ash filled my mouth and nose unpleasantly. When I'd agreed to this fucking circus, I hadn't considered what it would cost me if I won this thing—definitely not that it could've been the only other person in this world that I actually cared about other than my dad.

Kohl was more than just my best friend—even if they'd been a bit of a fuck-up this year. It was always going to be like this. They were always my everything.

My knight in shining armor.

The tunnel of love wasn't far from the mirror maze, but this late in the game, with the moon high in the sky and the carnival lights sparkling in puddles left from the Vultures' power washers, it made me nervous to be out in the open.

Especially *alone*.

At least when I had Jenna, she was a bit of a shield. I always knew that I was faster than her.

It hurt to leave Kohl with the wolves. Partially because I was worried that I'd never see them again. And partially because, even though they'd branded themselves for me, I couldn't quite trust that they wouldn't flip.

They were a Wolff after all. And I was nothing more than a rabbit.

Nah, fuck that. I was the white rabbit. Following in my mother's footsteps. Fast on my feet and even quicker when it came to strategy.

If anyone could win this—it was the two of us.

I just had to trust them.

Easier said than done.

I moved to follow the path toward our rendezvous, finding myself frozen as I heard Kohl and Dylan's voices.

Fuck, they found them already?

"Don't you want to show off what you did?" Dylan asked, a note of excitement in his voice that made me feel sick to my stomach.

He was different after the games.

Before, he was just a dumbass twenty-year-old with rocks for brains. Not a care in the world but spending his daddy's money and having fun.

I'd watched his games. Watched what he looked like splattered in the blood of his victims. How he laughed as he racked in point after point by torturing them.

It was disgusting.

"I left quite the mess." Kohl laughed. "Trust me—it'll be better in the replay."

Dylan made a disappointed noise, the sound of their booted feet on the concrete drawing closer.

I ducked down low, running half-hunched as quietly as I could until I turned a couple corners away, kneeling behind a garbage can.

There were so few players around, it had to be getting late.

I twisted my wrist, the holographic screen of my tracker lighting up, paired with the soft teal of my friendship bracelet. It was no surprise that after the X-rated fuck show Kohl and I provided, I'd climbed to being one of the most watched players on the field right now—but that also meant that I was worth twenty times the points. Everyone and anyone would be looking for me. And when they caught me... I shuddered at the thought.

OPALESCENT

don't trust him!!

TRIGGERH4PPY69

you guys are such a cute couple :-(too bad i'm forever alone...

B1GGYB0Y

show tits!

The tracker buzzed, an alert cropping up over the screen.

I shot my eyes skyward, finding a small, parachuted package falling toward me, a drone zipping away as I reached up to grab it out of the air. The package was a sort of mix between a popcorn box and something you'd get Chinese takeout in. Waxy to the touch and heavier than I expected, I popped the top, my mouth stretching into a grin.

Inside, was a fist full of the most exciting gift I'd ever seen. *Bullets*.

My luck was finally turning around.

I loaded my gun quickly, dumping the rest of the bullets into the side pocket of my cargo pants. At the bottom of the container was a small piece of folded paper, about the size of a fortune cookie slip. I pulled it out, flipping it around so I could read it.

Hope you don't have to put one of these in them. Cheers, wh1t3_r4bb1t!

I crumpled the piece of paper in my fist, turning to look at the closest camera and blowing an exaggerated kiss before throwing myself into a run toward the tunnel of love.

Kohl wasn't stupid enough to betray me.

I hoped.

Kohl

+1 POINT FOR CREATIVITY

With a heavy heart, I left the sanctuary of the house of mirrors.

Luckily, there was no one around as I exited. I cast my gaze over to the lights of the park. Their soft glow lighting the night sky and hiding the stars from view.

Vic being here changed *everything*.

Before the house of mirrors, I wanted to win for her. Now, I would fight to make sure she was the last one standing. It was the least she deserved after everything.

I set off back toward the games, looking to find more weapons. I wanted to gather what I could before meeting her again. Now that I had someone to protect, I couldn't rely on the brute force that I had been using for the first few hours. I could be reckless when it came to myself, only trying to see it through for the payoff at the end, but I vowed to Vic that we would get out of here.

Together.

I had a taste of her once, but this... this was something different entirely.

It was a bittersweet feeling that it had to happen *now* after all this time. Especially since we were supposed to be out for each other's throats.

But I never took myself as a rule follower.

The sound of booming laughter cutting through the night air made my head snap toward the sound.

Dylan and his friends were making their way down the walkway, totally oblivious to me.

Already? I thought I have more time before they found me.

Panic seized my throat. I hadn't prepared my spiel and I only had one chance to sell this.

If Dylan found out that Vic was here... what would he do? It was no secret that Vic practically broke his heart.

He'd been blindsided after the crash, not a cell in his arrogant being could even *fathom* why Vic had been the one to break up with *him*. It wasn't a surprise to me, or I bet anyone else around him. Vic and Dylan had been so mismatched that it'd been a common gossip topic around school. Why would *Vic* date *him* instead of any of the football players that flocked to her side.

He would hurt her.

That much I was sure of. Especially in that white rabbit mask of hers. He wouldn't be able to hold himself back.

Meaning I needed to get them away from here.

I brought two fingers to my mouth and blew. The sharp sound of my whistle making them pause, weapons readied as they looked around.

Dylan's pose relaxed immediately after spotting me.

"You should've given us a heads-up that you were off for another point." he called, laughing. "I was almost worried."

His words caused me to look down at my outfit. It was all black, but the blood had seeped into the fabric and was still wet—hard to miss. My exposed midriff was a mess, with bloodied handprints dragging down, disappearing into my pants.

Fuck. Could they tell what happened?

"I couldn't miss my chance," I said, sending him a strained smile, though I knew he couldn't see it under the mask. It was more of a reminder to myself to keep a friendly attitude with him or else suffer the consequences. "There's more though. Two at least. I think

I saw them take off that way." I jerked my thumb backward, motioning in the opposite direction of the house of mirrors.

I had three objectives.

1. *Get them the fuck away from here.*
2. *Lose them on the way.*
3. *Get to the tunnel of love.*

Easy, right? They would run at the chance to get a victim under their belt.

Pink and Yellow were already foaming at the mouth for a chance to get another point, ready to race off in the direction I pointed. Yellow even took a few steps forward.

It was Dylan who stood back, his eyes taking in my form.

Face stone-cold. Like your father's. You have seen it done over and over again. Don't let them see through you.

It was Dylan who was more likely to lose his cool. If I could just distract him for a bit, I would be in the clear.

The issue was convincing him. I cursed myself for being so unco-operative until now.

He moved his mask to the side, giving me a look at his face.

There was a chilling smirk slowly spreading across it.

"Don't want to show off what you did?" he asked, closing the distance between us.

Pink and Yellow looked over to each other, suddenly unsure of what he was doing. The tension rose, causing the hair to stand on the back of my neck.

"I left quite the mess." I said, hating the nervous laughter that spilled from my lips. "Trust me—it'll be better in the replay."

I slipped up. Already. It'd only taken a second for him to realize that I was hiding something. Just like he *always* did. He caught something he shouldn't have and latched onto it like a fucking parasite.

He came to a stop in front of me, and I had to tilt my head down to look at him. I gritted my teeth, the need to slam my fist into that face of his taking over every other rational thought in my mind.

"Seems like you had a bit of fun, hm?" he asked, turning his knife to the side and letting the dull flat of the blade brush across Vic's handprint.

I clamped down on the shiver of disgust, determined to not let him show how much his touch messed with me.

"Too much," I said, turning my voice cold. "I wouldn't go in there if I were you. I... lost myself. Opened the chest cavity and disemboweled her. We'd be better off moving on to catch up with the next one."

"Oh, sick, bro," Yellow said with a gag.

Dylan's eyes were watching mine. There was a warning in them. He was warning me that if I didn't tell him what was going on, he sure as hell was going to find it out on his own.

He could try, but I'd protect Vic with everything I had.

The sound of our trackers went off, filling the air and interrupting our stare down.

He looked at his first, but not before stepping away and turning his back on me. I used that chance to peek at mine.

+1 point for creativity

"Let's get on with it then," Dylan said, his voice stiff.

Just like that? He was going to give up? That was very much unlike him, but I wasn't going to sit there and doubt the luck I'd been granted in this game.

Looking up, I realized all three of them had their eyes locked on me. It was different than before.

Before, they treated me like Dylan's little brother. Joking and prancing around with no care in the world.

But now they were looking at me like I didn't belong there.

No. They were looking at me like I was their next victim.

The air shifted. Tension crackled between us. I was almost afraid to move. As if the next step I took would cause them to pounce.

What had they seen on their trackers?

"Then I'll just take you there?" I said, still unsure of the next steps.

Dylan had already fitted his mask back to his face, so there was no telling what he was thinking.

"Well, we have to get our points in one way or another, don't we?" he said and motioned for me to lead the way.

I nodded and turned my back to them, taking cautious steps toward the imaginary Ghosts. But even as I successfully led them away from the house of mirrors, the sinking in my gut hadn't disappeared.

"We gotta find a way to spice up the livestream," Yellow said from behind. "I'm in the hundreds now."

"Ha! I'm still over a thousand," Pink said. "Maybe they just find *you* boring."

I relaxed a little at the casualness of their conversation, though I didn't want to check how many views I had. *Especially* after what I had just done with Vic in the hall of mirrors.

It was a short walk until the tunnel of love could be seen off in the distance.

Alright, time to lose them.

"Hey, isn't that the gardens?" I asked, pointing out the dome-like building that seemed to have a permanent lean to it. Vines and dead flowers were growing up the sides, while overgrown trees sprouted from the opened roof. There was a light glow coming from within. "There's not much over here. I'm guessing they went in there."

"Nah, that's boring," Dylan said. "You know what would be an even better place?"

He came up to me, throwing his arm around my shoulders and forcing me to bend down. He pointed his blood-stained finger in the opposite direction and right to... the tunnel of love.

I had the strongest urge to grab him by his neck, throw him to the ground, and pound into that stupid fucking face until he was unrecognizable.

"Romantic." Pink laughed behind me. "Maybe the Ghosts think so as well."

Dread curled in my stomach, and bile exploding across my tongue.

I couldn't help but picture them coming across Vic and what they would try to do to her once they found her.

"That's far," I said and cleared my throat. "You forget these Ghosts aren't built like us. They can't run that far and are probably hiding in a place like there." I jerked my head toward the garden as I took a step forward. "What's the harm in checking both places?"

Both men looked to Dylan to make the decision.

"There's no fun in a midnight stroll around the gardens," he said. "If I didn't know any better, I'd say you're trying to keep us from the tunnel."

I swallowed thickly, unable to help the fear and panic that were running through my veins. If I didn't have anyone to protect, I wouldn't feel this way. I would still be able to let myself fall into the darkness of my mind. Give into the instinct to hunt.

But I have Vic now.

No matter how suspicious it looked, I needed to occupy them until I could slip away.

"You can say that when everyone in the group has killed their victim," I said, my eyes roaming Yellow. If I wasn't mistaken, the last victim was Pink's. "You said you wanted to make our family look good, how could you if you haven't killed anyone yet?"

An uneasiness passed through the other two, but Dylan seemed unconvinced.

I may not have been able to convince Dylan, but they knew for sure that the man wouldn't give two shits if they didn't do what they came here to do.

"Quickly," Pink said to him. "It will take five minutes, tops. If we don't find anyone, we move on. You know my mother will disown me if I don't have at least two kills under my belt."

Something that should have sounded so horrific coming from his mouth was so normalized that it was almost laughable.

That's right. Why was I trying so hard to convince them when their parenting and this world had already done it for me?

"There are only a few hours left," I said with a shrug. "Look, there's only a third of them left."

I pressed a few buttons on my tracker, letting the holographic screen pull up the amount of time we still had as well as the percentage of Killers versus victims.

More than a third had gotten their victims, meaning the rest of the Killers were also the ones cleaning up the rest of them and leaving none for those like Pink.

Dylan was my main concern right now, but with the way the numbers were looking, he wouldn't be the only Killer I had to look out for.

"Who knows," I said and shook my tracker so the screen disappeared. "Maybe yours is already dead."

He paused for a moment before letting out a sigh.

"Fine, but we get in and out in ten minutes, tops," he said, giving a meaningful look to the other two, who gave him sharp nods.

"Great," I said through clenched teeth and pushed past them.

The garden itself was well... a garden. The entire roof was open, letting the moonlight stream in from above. Without the moonlight, it would have been pitch black. There was the sound of running water off in the distance and trees with hanging leaves all over. Everything was so overgrown that I had to push past many of the plants to continue down the path. Though just like the outside, many of the plants had been dead or in various stages of dying.

It caused the whole place to reek.

They followed behind me as I pushed through the overgrown bushes. There was no one. Not a soul except the four of us. All of our glowing masks shone in the darkness, giving away our exact location. And yet no one was running.

I almost started to panic when there was no sign of any living creature. But then there was a sharp squeak and the sound of footsteps running.

I turned to look at the group behind me.

"There's one!" I whispered. "Go now—"

My voice was cut off by Dylan stepping forward and gripping my shirt.

The act caused my heart to stop in my chest.

"What are you—"

"You are an embarrassment," he spat at me. "I've already earned the title. I was here to keep *your* reputation, but it seems you've mistaken me for a fool."

"I don't know what—"

I tried to push him away, but Pink and Yellow were by my sides in an instant.

"We are all Seekers, you can't—"

Pain flashed through me as Dylan hit me square in the jaw.

Vic

Before the Games

I kicked off my heels, groaning as the cool air met my abused feet.

Stilettos, while gorgeous, always pinched my toes. My feet were just a little too wide for the standard of women's footwear. At least the sort of woman who could afford to spend twenty-five hundred dollars on a single pair of shoes.

Inside, the party was in full swing. I'd been thrilled when Dylan finally invited me over to his place—less so when I realized that his father was out of town, throwing my plan to meet him right into the pits of hell.

Hiram Wolff.

The name had been haunting me for years.

I just never thought I'd get the opportunity to—

"Are you thirsty?" a low, quiet voice asked.

I turned my head to find Dylan's younger sibling, Kohl, offering me a bottle of water, their dark eyes purposefully on my face. We hadn't officially met before—at least not in a one-on-one setting.

From the moment I laid eyes on them, all I could see were the differences between them and their brother. Their slimmer shoulders and handsome face. Blond hair and a distinctly South Asian nose.

Maybe they had different moms?

"Yeah, thanks," I murmured, taking the water bottle and cracking the top before taking a long drink. "Come sit."

Kohl looked between me and the stone steps uncertainly. "I really was just—"

"What, too good to sit with me? I'm a Legacy too, you know."

Not that that fucking mattered.

None of this shit mattered.

Kohl snorted, sitting beside me smoothly. "Like I give a fuck about that. The Legacy system is just another way that the Architects give us the illusion that we have any control. Really, we're players like the rest of them."

I grinned. "Careful, your daddy would beat your ass to hear you talk like that."

They shrugged. "Wouldn't be the first time."

"You are... not like your brother."

It was the understatement of the century. Dylan lives and breathes the games, practically only got hard if he thought about killing somebody. But Kohl?

I glanced over at them, my face heating at their dyed blonde hair, pushed away from their face.

Kohl was something else.

"Thanks," they said, stretching their long legs in front of them. "What the hell are you doing dating someone like—"

"Vic!" Dylan called loudly, staggering toward the pair of us. "What are you doing out here?"

He'd been drunk since I'd arrived. Normally, it wouldn't bother me—what people did with their own bodies was none of my business—but Dylan was *mean.*

And even meaner when he drank.

"Just taking a breather," I hedged, my eyes flicking to Kohl.

"You're going to miss the best part—the game is about to start—"

The Rat Race was the event du jour, meaning that the night was sure to be filled with a lot of screaming and blood.

It was my least favorite event in the Devil's Playground—I'd always thought that if I was going to enter, I'd probably play Hide and Seek. Though given my mom and dad were winners of the event the year they'd played, I had to guess at least a *little* of that was family expectation.

I didn't like to have an audience when Dylan was like this, even if it was his sibling.

Kohl tipped their head back. "What, Dyl, scared I'm going to steal your woman?"

Dylan laughed, rolling his eyes as he offered his hand to me.

But I saw it, the uncertainty. He knew as well as I did that I was too fucking good for him. But that didn't stop the hard blow that landed against Kohl's shoulder.

"Fat chance, loser."

I popped my shoes back on and took Dylan's hand, letting him haul me to my feet.

"See you around," I called to Kohl.

They waved, smiling blandly. "Play hard."

"Die famous," I hissed under my breath as Dylan led me into the house.

God, I couldn't wait until this was over

Kohl

Was killing her really necessary?

"What the fuck are you doing?" I yelled, jerking in the grip of the two men holding me back.

I managed to shake Yellow off, but Pink held strong. *Why was it always fucking like this?*

One-on-one fights I could manage, I'd trained for them while preparing for the games... but multiple people at once?

I just knew the universe was laughing at me.

I used the arm I'd pulled from Yellow to slam my fist into Pink's face, making his grip loosen. In a flash, I brought my booted foot up to his stomach and delivered a kick that sent him back a few feet.

Without hesitation, I turned on Dylan and rammed myself into him, sending both of us tumbling to the ground.

I should've taken my chance to run. I should've gotten up and ran past them to meet up with Vic.

But I never claimed to be smart. And my temper had been festering since the moment I'd seen Dylan with my fucking haircut.

I let the rage heating my veins boil over and slammed my fists into his face, one after the other. His mask fell off as I struck him, freeing me up to do some real damage.

Dylan raised his hands, trying to stop the assault, not that it did him any good.

I was too *angry.*

"Every fucking time," I growled, sending a punch with each word. "What's your issue with me? Can't you just be a fucking human? You're supposed to be my goddamn big brother, you worthless sack of shit."

I was jerked off him by arms circling my chest, heaving me backward.

I failed, grabbing the shirt of whoever pulled me away and attempting to flip us over. I wasn't sturdy enough for it to work, the pair of us falling to the side. But it was enough for me to clamber back to my feet.

Pink lay on the ground in front of me, struggling to lift himself up. I raised my foot to stomp on his back, but weight slammed into me, making me lose my balance and fall onto my brother's lackey with an "oof" of air.

"You are such a fucking dumbass, Kohl," Yellow said from overhead as I struggled to get back to my feet.

Pink shifted under me, his arms wrapping around my torso. Who I assumed was Yellow locked his arm around me in a choke-hold, completely stopping my movements and constricting my airflow.

I used my arms to try and push Pink off, but it was no use. With Yellow's grip on me, they forced me to my feet, facing Dylan again.

This time his mask was off, showing me the bloodied mess I'd made of his face.

He wiped the crimson trickling from his nose with the back of his hand, sneering like the liquid itself offended him.

I bared my teeth at him.

"What *gives*?" I choked out. "We're supposed to be a fucking team—"

"We were," Dylan said, his voice thick with irritation as he shook his head. He pressed a few buttons on his tracker, turning the lit screen toward me.

It was a single message.

They're lying. Find the white masked rabbit, and I'll give you 10K each.

The message alone was enough to make panic rise, my heart beating faster. But what made my blood run cold was the name attached to it.

Architect Wolff.

Father?

Why would he be interfering? He shouldn't be. The Architects are supposed to be neutral third parties. It was a major infraction for him to try and push the game in one direction or another. Much less his for his son. He should've *never*—

Images flooded my memory. The wrecked car. Vic sobbing hysterically as she tried to push through the police to get to the man being loaded into the ambulance. The matching marks on my father's car, parked in the garage like it'd always had a crushed-in front bumper and a massive scrape down the side.

Dylan wasn't here to save our family legacy.

He was here to cut the loose end.

Fuck.

Why? Hadn't he taken enough? Was killing her really necessary?

Hadn't taking everything from her satisfied whatever sick vendetta he had against an eighteen-year-old girl?

I'd been painfully mulling over options to get her money because of what he did. Pushed my body to the brink and back just to make some measly pocket change for her.

What else was there left to do?

But I knew it. I knew that the last thing for him to do was send someone after her in an attempt to finally cover his tracks.

If I tell Dylan who he's really going after, will he pause or...

No, I couldn't.

He'd go after her even harder. They hadn't exactly left each other on good terms.

"Father saw you," he sang, a wicked smile spreading across his face. "I wonder what you did that would make him react like this?"

I jerked against their hold again.

"Father shouldn't interfere," I spat. "Just like you should go about and find your own Ghost before the game ends. Talk about embarrassment? You've been standing back the entire time *watching* as everyone else gets their kills except you. It's pathetic, almost as pathetic as coming in worse than third on your second go."

He twisted his wrist, causing the screen to disappear. His eyes narrowed as he reached out to yank the mask off my face.

"Have you ever thought I was *looking* for someone?" he asked, fitting the glowing purple plastic over his busted nose.

Dread hit me like a truck, his plan coming together with stunning clarity.

He looked like me. In the darkness with the blonde hair and mask... *Dylan looked just fucking like me.*

I jerked against their hold again, letting out a growl.

"Dylan, don't you dare! If you do this, I'll never—"

"Forgive me?" he asked with a scoff. "I think we're past that. I don't need your *forgiveness,* Kohl. I never wanted it. Just like I never wanted to be related to you in the first place. You've been and always will be an embarrassment. A stain on my family. The product of an affair, not even with someone worthwhile. You're just like your mother—weak and *worthless.* I won't let you destroy this family's reputation with your subpar blood anymore."

"Shut the fuck up," I growled.

He let out a laugh and motioned for his lackeys to stay put.

"I'll be back," he said. "Don't let them go."

The two made noises of agreement as I struggled, my heart beating so hard in my chest I worried it would explode.

Dylan tilted his head to the side. I couldn't see his smile behind the mask, but I felt it. "Don't worry, little brother. I'll bring you a memento. How do you feel about a finger?"

"Don't—" I shouted, but he just laughed, disappearing into the greenery.

All the hope I had burst into flames and caused my entire body to deflate.

What the fuck was I going to do?

"Not so hot now, huh?" Yellow muttered in my ear.

I jerked against him.

"I'll kill you," I threatened.

"No you won't," Pink said from my other side. "You *can't*."

I needed to get to Vic. I needed to save her before—

A loud beeping came from the sky, making us all look up as a drone sped away, leaving a package floating toward us. My tracker sang out, the animatronic voice cutting through the fog of my despair.

Slowly, the popcorn-like container descended from the open ceiling to my feet, opening before I even had the chance to touch it.

My eyes widened at the present that lay snug in the box.

"Thank you," I said aloud, a grin spreading across my face. I slammed my forehead into Yellow's face, making him loosen his grip and dove for the object, the electric buzz clicking to life at the touch of a button.

"What the hell is—"

"No, don't! Please!"

Vic

He's going to fucking kill me.

When I finally came up to the building the housed the tunnel of love, the area around it was blissfully deserted. Most of the players—at least what was left of the Ghosts so far would all be in hiding now that the Killers had formed packs, hunting like lynxes to flush out their prey. But I wasn't going to stay still. That wasn't the move anymore.

Not with Kohl on my side.

We just needed some time to plan.

I climbed over the low fence and jumped into the thigh-deep water, wading until I found the low platform of the ride. The cold water was as good as nine cups of coffee, staving off the exhaustion that'd started to take root in my bones.

Inside, the tunnel was lit with warm sconces attached to the walls—*romantic*—I supposed, if the circumstances were different. I imagined coming to some place like this with Kohl, cuddling in a swan shaped boat as we sailed down the tunnel. It was utterly embarrassing and majorly cringe worthy, but in another life, I would've loved it. Because in this one, I couldn't enjoy this. Not while I was running for my life and using Kohl like a tool to get what I needed. This wasn't some cozy little make-out spot for Kohl and me. This was a hope that no one was in here looking for quick little rabbits.

I pulled myself up onto the ledge, wedging myself between the wall and the booth that held the mechanical control panel to wait. Taking the gun from my waistband, I clicked off the safety and counted the rest of my bullets. Not as many as I would've liked, I'd have to be careful.

Too bad I was a fucking lousy shot.

I shivered a little as the cool evening air seeped through my wet clothes, making me regret my snap decision to climb over the fence instead of going around. I'd just been thinking about getting up to move around to try and tease some warmth into my fingers when the faint, romantic music that'd been playing cut at the same time as the lights, plunging me into darkness.

I swallowed hard, peeking around the box I'd hidden behind, but aside from a faint whisper of moonlight from the open tunnel ahead and a fair bit of fog ambient fog from the machine tucked between the painted landscapes, there was nothing to see.

Don't panic, Vic. I chided myself, taking a deep breath.

Maybe they cut the power to up the ante or something?

I checked my watch. There were still too many hours until sunrise for the Architects to do something so drastic.

Mechanical failure, then?

A noise from the far end of the tunnel, like a slosh of water, alerted me that I wasn't alone. I gripped the gun tighter, fear making my hands shake.

When I was with Kohl, I felt like I was invincible. Like I could do anything.

But here? Alone in this creepy as fuck ride with murderers lurking around every corner? Yeah, I was scared shitless.

Footsteps warned me that my unwelcome companion was drawing closer, so in my hiding space, I raised my weapon, ready to fire the second that they turned the corner—until Kohl's purple mask loomed out of the darkness, making me sigh in relief.

"Fuck, Kohl," I said, standing from my hiding spot and holding the weapon aloft. "You scared the shit out of me."

"That so, rabbit?" A harsh growl of a voice came from behind Kohl's mask before they leaped at me, capturing my throat and using it to pin me against the wall. "I fucking knew that dumbass was hiding something in here—just didn't expect a little *reunion* to happen so soon."

I swung the gun down against my attacker's temple, trying to ignore the way that the blood was rushing in my ears.

Dylan. I knew that voice anywhere.

How did he find me? The only person who knew I was here was Kohl—

"Where's Kohl?" I rasped, fighting to speak under the flex of his fingers. He let out a chuckle that made the hair rise on the back of my neck.

"It doesn't matter," he said. "Not now that I'm here. You wanna know a secret, little rabbit?"

"No," I spat at him, attempting to bring my knee in between his legs, but he was quick, his hand coming down to catch my leg before it made contact.

"I had a feeling you'd be here," he whispered. "You see, I've been keeping tabs on you. How's that father of yours? Still eating up all your savin—"

I rammed my forehead into his. Pain shot through me, but it had the desired effect. His head shot backward, a curse ringing out through the tunnel.

All I needed was for his hands to loosen just the tiniest bit—and I saw my chance. The second his grasp loosened, I shoved him away.

He flailed wildly, knocking my hand and sending the gun flying.

The platform on either side of the thin stream that ran through the ride had to only be five feet wide, a fact I'd ignored until I watched the weapon bounce into a floating, swan-shaped boat.

He laughed, ripping off Kohl's mask as I dove for the boat, catching my ankle as my fingers brushed the butt of the gun, and pulling me back so that my face smashed into the side of the boat, my forehead opening and blinding me with a sickening wave of warm blood. I thrashed as he grabbed onto me, jumping into the water and hauling me back as I tried again for the weapon.

"See, I know all about how you're *struggling*," he said with a bitter laugh. "And what better way to make money than to play, huh? What's the point of being a legacy without the game after all?"

His arms wrapped around my neck, putting me in a headlock.

I used my feet to push against the boat, forcing us back onto the platform.

He let out a grunt and I clawed at him hard enough to draw blood. Luckily, the water had made me slippery enough to shimmy out of his grip.

But not for long.

He grabbed onto my sweater as I was diving back for the boat, forcing me on my back.

"Ain't nobody gonna come help you now. Wonder what they'll do when they find out I've killed you? Do you think they'll cry? Scream? Get *angry*?"

"Fuck you," I spat, jerking against his hold. His hand wrapped around my neck, putting enough pressure on the sides of my neck to startle me, but not enough to choke me just yet. "You look like an off-brand Kohl. Five bucks that your hair will fall out if I do this—"

I reached forward just enough to thread my hands in Dylan's hair and yank *hard*.

The feeling of his hand slamming against my cheek was enough to stun me, pain ricocheting throughout my skull.

"I should've known you were just like your fucking *mother*," he spat.

The words turned my blood to ice in my veins, panic clawing at my throat.

"The fuck did you say about my mo—"

Dylan's hand squeezing my throat caused me to choke on my words.

"I said, you're just like your *whore* of a mother," he spat. "Fucking whoever you think will get you to the top in the games.

Imagine what Kohl will think when they figure out you're just using them to get ahead? Maybe you won't even let them realize. I should tell them after this. About your plan to murder them when they least expect it."

"What are you fucking talking—"

It was getting harder to speak. Harder to breathe.

He's going to fucking kill me.

"You know? Your plan? To stab them in the back? I'll deliver the news for you, don't worry. I'll also be the shoulder they need to cry on—*god*, imagine how many points that would get me."

I tried to buck against him, but with a single hand, he dragged me across the platform until my head and upper body were over the water.

"Dylan, wait—" I begged, only to be cut off as his strong hands forced me under.

My nose and mouth filled with water as I fought against him. But he was bigger than me by about a hundred pounds, not wiry like Kohl—*fuck*, how could I have been so stupid to mistake them?

Kohl, *my* Kohl, was a lanky asshole with the walk of someone whose parents made too much money.

This guy was nothing but a cheap imitation.

I looked up at him, the water blurring his face. He was nothing like the Dylan I knew. The Dylan I knew was a stupid, self-centered bastard... but this was too cruel.

He pulled me up, letting me take a breath. As much as I didn't want to, I clung to him.

He seemed surprised by my actions and let out a huff.

"You're right," I whispered. "I will attach myself to whoever can help me win. Right now, that's you."

He carefully peeled me back from him, his eyes trailing over my face. I had to fight the sudden urge to cry, to beg for my life.

"Aw," he said, his voice turning gentle. "You're such a fucking liar."

Faster than he could keep up, I twisted beneath him, lunging forward to grab the boat in an attempt to get myself as far away from him as possible.

The gun. I need the gun.

A hand tangled through my hair, and before I knew it, I was pushed up again, my watch buzzing non-stop. Not that any of the viewers' comments or hints would fucking help me while I was being drowned in three feet of over-chlorinated water. All while staring at Dylan's sickening grin spreading further across his face as he watched me die in front of him.

This time, Dylan wasn't fucking kidding. I was a goner.

Kohl

Before the Games

I always knew my brother was capable of something horrible. He was just too much like our father.

But I never thought he would do something like this.

My hands balled into fists at my side, anger causing the blood in my veins to boil.

I hadn't meant to run into Dylan and his friends. In fact, I'd been actively avoiding them. All I'd wanted to do was go downstairs, grab a glass of water, and disappear back into my room. I hadn't expected them to be down there—drunk off their asses—and passing around Dylan's phone like it was the Hide and Seek cup.

"How the hell did you manage to get her to send you these?" one of his friends, Laramy, said, his voice practically vibrating with excitement.

I peeked around the corner, finding their backs to me. Dylan stood to the side, watching the scene unfold like a king on his throne. Another of the boys, Shaw, reached over and grabbed the phone from Laramy.

"She's spreading her legs for you and *everything*!" he exclaimed with an awestruck sort of laugh.

Dylan took a sip of his drink, sending his friends a smug smile.

"She's not like those other cunts," he said, waving his drink at them dismissively. "When I told her to send me a picture of her pussy, she listened. None of that faux-shy hiding behind a towel or sheet bullshit."

Shaw held the phone up just high enough for me to see them scrolling through Dylan's camera roll.

"Oh, *fuck*," Laramy groaned, zooming into one of the photos. "This one's going on my wall."

My entire heart dropped into my stomach when I saw the next picture.

Vic spread out on her bed, pleasuring herself. It got even worse when he swiped.

The next file wasn't a photo at all, it was a *video*.

"Fuck, you're so tight." Dylan's voice came from the phone.

His friends exploded with laughter and catcalls as they watched. Vic's obviously fake moans filtered through the speakers.

"Oh my god, Dylan. *Harder*!"

The disgusting sound of their skin slapping together made bile rise in the back of my throat.

"Damn, you should upload this somewhere," Shaw muttered. "I'd pay good money to see an ass like this."

I hated how long they watched the video.

How long they commented on Vic's body.

I couldn't take it anymore. I stormed back upstairs, closing my door with a slam.

I didn't even get my glass of water.

I regretted that I didn't confront him.

I regretted not storming into the kitchen and throwing his phone onto the tile, rendering his beloved files useless.

Not that it would've helped, everything was cloud-saved nowadays anyway.

I'd wondered why Vic didn't show up at school that day.

It'd become a habit of mine to wait in the quad until she showed up, just so I could get a glimpse of her.

Sometimes, if I was lucky, she'd even notice me and wave.

And, even less frequently, by the grace of the goddess herself, we'd walk to class together.

That little miracle happened the day before, so I got my hopes up that today would be the same.

But she didn't show.

I didn't realize why until I got home, finding Dylan in the living room on his laptop. I paused when I saw him. It wasn't like I often saw Dylan working on schoolwork, the guy barely even hung around the house during the day. Too busy with his shithead friends.

Then I saw his computer.

Legacy Victoria Miller's Nudes Leaked.

He scrolled down, and right there were two slightly blurred pictures of Vic. Even with the filter, what was happening was obvious.

I did what I should've done that night.

I stormed over, grabbed his computer, and chucked it across the room, the device hitting the hardwood with a clatter.

Dylan shot up. "What the fuck, Kohl—"

I pushed him back down on the couch, towering over him.

"Is this what you did with them?" I hissed and motioned to the computer a room away. "God, do you have any fucking decency? You piece of fucking shit—"

"What the fuck are you talking about?" Dylan seethed, throwing his hands up. "You just come in here spouting nonsense—"

"She didn't come to school today because *you* leaked her fucking nudes," I growled.

He closed his mouth and opened it again, a slow, vicious smile spreading across his lips.

"So, you've been keeping tabs on my girlfriend now?" he asked.

"Don't try and change the subject," I huffed. "You leaked the nudes of a high schooler."

"She's eighteen," he shot back. "And why are *you* accusing me? I've seen how you watch her, maybe it was *you*. *Wanted a bit of* revenge for her getting with me and not a *freak* like you, huh, Kohl?"

I snapped.

One moment I was standing over him, white-hot rage licking up my spine, and the next I was on my back with Dylan straddling me, his ham-like fists raised.

His face was bloody, the liquid running from his nose to splatter onto me. Dylan's eyes were purple and starting to swell as he breathed heavily.

My fists and arms ached.

I'd never been much of a fighter. My slight build and natural inclination toward being quiet generally kept me out of trouble. But in that moment, I fit the puzzle pieces together about what happened.

He'd gone too fucking far.

His fist slammed into my face, once, twice, a third time before he was yanked off of me. Through the ringing in my ears, I could just make out Dylan and Father screaming at each other.

I glared at him through my blurred vision.

Father forced him out of the room, barking a command I didn't hear.

As I forced myself up, my hand came into contact with something cold and metal.

I strained my eyes to make out Dylan's phone.

Don't do it, my inner voice told me. *Don't fucking unlock it.*

But I did. I knew his passcode since we first got phones. He never changed it.

Standing, I went straight to the photo album to see if the photos were still there.

They were.

My thumb hovered over the delete button. *Just do it.*

But even as my mind was chanting at me to do the right thing, instead I hit the share button and dug into my pants for my own phone.

I'm so sorry, Vic.

VIC

My lungs and eyes burned as I kicked and thrashed, finally catching Dylan's face and causing him to loosen his grip.

If I didn't get the gun, he was going to fucking kill me.

I took it for the lifeline it was, taking the opportunity to throw myself into the boat, panting for air.

The gun. Kohl. *No, fuck Kohl. The gun. The gun.*

He was on me in an instant, his fingers closing around my throat. In a flash of oxygen-deprived insanity, it was like I was with Kohl in the house of mirrors again, their breathing ragged as they prepared to take my life.

My fingers brushed the gun where it had fallen onto the floor of the boat, and I stretched to the point of breaking, black clouding my vision and the world starting to slip.

Finally, I was able to get the weapon close enough for me to grab it, turning the gun on Dylan and pulling the trigger. The loud, sharp sound of the bullet firing reverberated throughout the tunnel. There was a pause, like both us were waiting for something, *anything*, to happen. But his grip never faltered.

"HA! You fucking lousy shot! I'm close enough to *touch* and you still missed?"

I cursed under my breath, fumbling to touch the gun to him.

Fuck, how hard was it to shoot this goddamn asshole?!

Another. Just one more time, Vic.

This time I jammed the gun against his shoulder, my weakening finger trembling as I fought for the strength to pull the trigger.

This time, the bullet embedded itself right into his shoulder. He howled and fell back backward, the sweet relief of oxygen filling my lungs.

I coughed and spluttered, forcing myself onto all fours. "Kohl chokes me harder than that when we fuck," I taunted, my voice hoarse. "You're losing your touch, Wolff."

Dylan snarled, his hand shooting out to grab my ankle to yank me backwards.

If I'd thought Dylan was strong before, if was nothing to now. He grabbed me, forcing me underneath him and my head over the edge of the boat to hover above the waters slowly moving surface.

"You hear that?" Dylan asked, referring to the pings coming from his tracker. "They *love* watching me kill you. Do you know how many are begging me to go even *slower*? I've bagged ten extra points just by playing with you, Vic."

"You're fucked in the head," I hissed, struggling.

"Maybe," he hummed. "But does it really matter when the games will make me rich? I don't think so."

I thrashed against him again, my fight slowly leaving me he was just too goddamn heavy.

Fuck... was this it?

I couldn't help but let my mind wander to Kohl. Where was he while Dylan was here?

I hoped they'd make it out alive. At least one of us *had to*. I hated how I wouldn't be able to experience what our lives would be when we were free of the arena—that I wouldn't be able to tell them that I had already forgiven them for something they weren't even truly a part of.

"Dunk her again," he read aloud from his tracker. "Ooh, this one's fun. Dunk her until she passes out, then give us a little show.

What do you say, Victoria? Want one last time together before I send you to hell?"

"No one wants your puny shrimp dick," I hissed.

"Aw," he said in mock disappointment, a feral grin overtaking his features. "Well, I can't say I didn't try."

He pushed my head forward, the water brushing my nose.

"Wait! Dylan, stop this now—"

"No, I don't think I will," he said with a laugh, the sound dampening as the water filled my ears.

Kohl

I left the garden, breathing heavy and clutching the taser in my hand and Dylan's blue mask on my face.

Thank fucking God for my viewers.

It had been awful trying to fight against both Pink and Yellow. They were nothing if not my brother's lackeys, and they tried their damn hardest to make sure that I wasn't going after him.

But they underestimated just how much I was willing to do for Vic. Just how much of a monster I was willing to become for her.

It was *they* who should have been thanking the viewers for sending me a taser and not a rifle. I wouldn't have hesitated to litter their bodies with bullets as I let out my anger on them.

It was the same anger that pushed my aching body toward the tunnel of love.

I wasn't going to say sorry to Vic again. I couldn't. After everything she'd been through, *we'd* been through, I wasn't going to let another person stand in my way... even if they were family.

I ran to the tunnel of love, ignoring how my body screamed at me to stop. The only thing on my mind were images of Vic and my brother. I knew he had a temper, one that he would be all too willing to take out on her.

When I pushed through the tunnel of love's entrance, the first thing I noticed was the music. The melody was familiar, almost comical. Something that was played in old TV shows and movies whenever there was a romantic moment between the characters. But the warpedness of it coming from the crackled speakers made the tunnel all that more sinister.

Next, I noticed the sounds of rushing water. The sounds of the boat hitting the sides of the tracks.

And then the splashing.

I walked the short entryway, and there was only a small turn before I came face-to-face with the loading dock. As I got closer I could make out grunts of effort that pushed me faster, until I was rounding the corner with dread sitting heavy in my stomach.

That's when I saw *them*.

It was far too quiet for what he was doing.

He was bent over her, forcing her face into the water. Vic's hands flailed as she tried to grasp on to something, but he had her gripped so tight that she had no way of getting away from him.

He turned to me, a crazed smile spreading across his face.

"Just in time!" He called, yanking Vic out of the water. Her pained gasps and coughs cut through the space. "Look, your dog has come to save you."

Vic tried to tilt her head to look at me, but Dylan was faster. He pushed her head back underwater, keeping his eyes locked on mine as he hurt her.

"But you won't be doing any saving, will you?" he asked smugly.

"Let her go!" I growled and took a step forward.

"Oh? Don't tell me you're really going to try this? For a Ghost? Do you know how embarrassing it is to see you drooling all over this bitch? I guess some people find sloppy seconds hot, but *damn*, the things my comments said about you two—"

"Dylan, let her up!" The terror in my voice surprised even myself.

"Why do you care so much?" he asked, his eyes narrowing as he lifted her again to let her breathe.

"Don't let Dad continue to run your life like this." I begged.

There was a point growing up where I looked up to Dylan. When the blind confidence he had was something more innocent. When the power he had to make every single thing go his way was so *magical.*

Sometimes, if I squinted hard, I could still believe that little boy who used to push me on swings was still in there somewhere.

But that time had long since passed.

The look on his face as he held Vic, gasping and whimpering just over the surface of the water, solidified once and for all that the brother I knew was dead. Whoever—whatever the fuck had come back out of the arena wasn't Dylan.

It was a replica of our father in his place.

But unlike Father, Dylan had no ambition of his own. He continued to take orders from our worthless dad, even going so far as to kill someone he *must've* had feelings for at some point.

And for what?

Was Father's approval really worth selling his soul over? Or was it the people watching? The fame that awaited us outside the metal walls of the arena that called to him like a whisper in the night?

"Oh, don't do that," Dylan said with a groan. "I was having so much *fun,* and now you're ruining it. I hate when you get all up on your high horse."

"Just let her go," I said, taking another step forward. His answer was to pull Vic closer to him and force her to look at me.

"What d'you think?" he whispered to her. "I don't think we've had our fun yet, do you?"

"Fuck off," she growled, baring her teeth.

Dylan laughed.

"Still have that useless fight in you, huh?" he asked. "Maybe if you beg for Kohl to come save you, I'll consider letting you go. At least then you would've learned your fucking place."

The silence was pressing as Vic slammed her mouth shut. Broken only by her terrified breathing.

Just do it. My eyes pleaded to her silently. I gripped the taser in my hand, suddenly fearful that if I tased him while he was drowning her, that I may hurt her as well.

Just say it.

But the fire in her eyes told me she wouldn't.

"See, this is why you shouldn't have thrown your family away for a *Ghost*," Dylan said with a huff. "I'll rectify that. She'll be my first kill tonight."

Then, with more force than before, he forced her head back in. Her scream, even muted by the water could be heard throughout the tunnel.

It was the thing that spurred me into action. I crossed the space between us, intent on tackling him to the ground, but a smile spread across his face. One so bone-chilling that it caused my blood to freeze in my veins.

"I knew you couldn't leave it alone—"

I cut him off by slamming my body into his.

It was too late to turn back.

Whatever he was planning, I would just have to take it. I tried to keep a grip on my taser, but as soon as Dylan twisted to fight me, it was knocked from my hands.

I gripped at his hair, forcing his head back and delivering a punch. Instead of trying to protect his face, he let me hit him while wrapping his arm around my waist and slamming me to the ground.

The air was knocked from my lungs.

Damn, that fucking wrestling club. I had always thought he looked so stupid flipping people over on the mat, but now that I was in the same position, I started to regret not watching him closer.

But I had prepared for this too.

When I couldn't push him off, I dug my teeth into his shoulder. It was enough to make him rear back, but what I didn't expect was the cold barrel of a gun to be pushed against my forehead.

"See, you always get this fucking *look* in your eyes whenever you think I'm doing something wrong, and it *pisses me off*," he growled. "You think I don't know how you looked down on me since high school? Or how much worse it got after I was in the games?"

"Dylan, we're family, don't—" I tried to reason, but he wasn't listening.

"I know you don't believe that bullshit. Not like I do, and not like Dad. *No.* You throw away family for a fucking Ghost whore that won't even look at you. It's *pitiful.*"

I tried to push up, but he forced the gun harder against my forehead, his finger brushing against the trigger.

"You let that bitch in your head. You think Father and I are in the wrong because we enjoy what we do," he said. "And you think you're *so* much better because... what? Because you don't want to be here killing these *poor innocent victims?*"

The way he said "poor innocent victims" in a baby voice made my blood boil.

"Newsflash," he seethed. "You aren't better than me because you don't enjoy this. If anything, I think that you're just lying to yourself. This is the world we live in, Kohl, and because I can recognize an opportunity when I have it, I will finally bring some respect back to the Wolff name."

"No Dylan, don—"

A shot rang out. Blood splattered across my face.

I hadn't realized I had shut my eyes in preparation for my murder until Dylan's body fell on me with a hard thud.

"God, he was fucking annoying."

VIC

BEFORE THE GAMES

The heaters in Kohl's car were barely keeping up against the frigid February air. I huddled in their passenger seat, waiting for them to return with our drinks.

Today was *not* my favorite day.

Arabella Williams had stomped on my fingers so hard in cheer practice that they were purple and ached every time I moved them. I'd gotten a D on my history final. And my nudes had been leaked to the press a couple days before, meaning that everywhere I looked, I saw *and heard* myself in a compromising position.

Honestly, I couldn't think of how it could get any worse.

Kohl opened their door with a gust of icy air behind them, jumping into their seat and slamming it shut behind them. "Jesus Christ, I hate winter."

In the last few months, we'd gotten pretty close. Helped along by the odd biology project or late practice—Kohl always seemed to be hanging around the school studying late, so they were perfectly primed to bring me home, or, y'know, to see my boyfriend, after cheer practice.

If only I was going home to someone else.

I was sick of the person I had to be for Dylan, bending and breaking to his whims just to keep the fucking peace. And the closer the games got, the more it was all he talked about. How he couldn't wait to enter.

It made me sick.

It made me want to punish him. Especially knowing that he'd leaked my fucking photos to the press.

Did he really think I was stupid enough to send something like that without a watermark?

I was going to fucking kill him. But before I could make my move on Dylan, I needed to get to Hiram first.

Priorities, Vic.

I took the hot chocolate from Kohl's outstretched hand. "Thanks."

At least they weren't a total shitbag.

Kohl leaned back in his seat, taking a deep drink from his own cup. "I'm so—"

"Please don't tell me you're sorry," I whispered, staring a hole into the side of their head.

"I wasn't," Kohl said, the side of their mouth hooking into a grin that I had the sudden urge to kiss. "I was *going* to say I'm so glad you didn't have practice tonight so I could see you. I want to talk about something."

Panic shot through my veins as Kohl shifted forward, my eyes dipping to their lips.

Sure, I'd known that Kohl had a bit of a crush on me. But I'd never dreamed—never expected they'd be so bold to—I jerked back in my seat.

"Kohl, I— It's not a big deal, but I can't do this. I don't want to come between you and Dylan—and—he's my boyfriend, and —" The excuses I was making sounded weak even to my own ears.

We both knew I didn't care about Dylan, at least not enough to deny myself the person that I really wanted.

"I don't understand why the hell you're willing to let him walk all over you."

"You don't have to understand, Kohl. I like him."

How I managed to keep a straight face through the lie was beyond me.

I didn't give a *fuck* about Dylan. But I did give a fuck about Kohl, and I didn't want them to become collateral damage when I finally got what I wanted out of their family.

If I let Kohl do this, if I allowed myself to fall in love with them —or even into bed—I was running the risk that my entire plan would be smashed to pieces.

"Vic, please, I—"

"No," I said. "For Christ's sake, Kohl, he's your brother. Isn't it enough for you to just be in my life?"

No. Not when I want to touch you like this. Not when I can see the way you are looking at me, and I know that it would feel ten times better to touch you than it does him. Not when I can see my future staring at me behind your eyes.

Kohl blew out a breath, setting their drink in the cupholder with a thunk as they put their hands back on the steering wheel. "Okay."

"Okay," I whispered back, my stomach tightening into a knot.

Why did doing the right thing have to suck so bad?

Kohl

I don't know why I cradled Dylan in my arms. In the moment, it felt like the right thing to do, but as I looked over his blank expression and the gaping wound in his head, I couldn't help but regret my actions.

All it did was make me feel something for him.

It was a small ghost of a feeling, It started in my chest and moved down to my gut. It was hot and heavy and felt a lot like guilt.

But what did I have to be guilty for?

His words rang in my head.

You have this thing in your head. You think Father and I are in the wrong because we enjoy what we do. You're lying to yourself.

Was I? Was I lying about what I was doing here?

I came here for Vic, no one else. For Vic, I changed into something. For Vic, I murdered.

I hated the games and what they stood for, but we *both* came in. Maybe for different reasons, but I was just as guilty as he was. My murders, no matter what they were for, were just as real as his were.

And the feeling of adrenaline and excitement I got from them was too hard to ignore.

My eyes shifted to Vic. She sat on the ground, her hand coming to rub her neck. She still held the gun in her shaking hand.

"Are you okay?" I ask.

Her gaze lingers on me for a second before nodding. She has this look in her eyes. One that I have never seen before. Her eyes are darting back and forth, her breathing heavy but not from the near drowning.

She was searching for something.

The same adrenaline I had felt with my kills was now pumping through her veins.

I looked back down at Dylan.

It was nasty. His face was almost unrecognizable on the right side with the back of his head open. It reminded me of the first time I ever saw someone get killed in such a manner.

"Do you hate me for it?" she asked.

It was the replay of my father's game. The one he made me watch every single fucking year so that when I was ready, I could follow in his footsteps. He thought showing me how he smashed a guy's head in with nothing but a spare brick, causing blood and brain matter to splatter everywhere, would give me some ideas on how to handle my own games.

I hate that he was right.

"Never," I said, making quick work of dragging my brother's dead body to the water.

I could never hate her. I could hate myself, but never her.

Dylan's actions were caused by *my* oversight. His rage and carelessness were all his own, but if I had been more careful, maybe we wouldn't have been in this position.

The water bubbled as he sank to the bottom, the corpse letting out the last of the air in it. Hands grabbed my face, forcing me to look back at Victoria.

Slowly, I took off my mask and laid it on the ground, and as soon as I did, Victoria's eyes searched my face. A shuddered breath left her. I took a deep breath of my own, nodding when she copied my movements.

"This isn't your fault," I said, noticing her still rapid breathing.

There was worry in her eyes, and I feared that if I didn't calm her down soon, she may just go crazy.

I ran my hand down her face, cleaning up the blood splatter. I tried not to cringe as the sticky substance coated my skin.

I exhaled my breath as I wrung out the bloodied water from her hair.

She did the same.

I almost lost her. I *almost lost* her. Because I was late. Because I had been too fucking stupid to realize that I was being played.

The moment Dylan received the notification from Father ran through my mind. I still couldn't understand what possessed him to do that.

Goddammit. I thought I was better than this. I thought I could save her. *Why was I so fucking useless?*

We took one more breath together.

"That's right," I praised. I let my fingers linger too long on the side of her face. Victoria noticed too and moved to sit up. "We are okay. You are okay. I'm not mad."

The movement caused a sourness to fill me, and I leaned back, letting her sit up on her own. Water seeped into my clothes, chilling my skin, but I didn't show any of the discomfort on my face.

This isn't about me right now. She's spiraling.

"I killed your brother Kohl, *family*," she said, her voice giving me a glimpse at just how worried she was.

"I know," I said, keeping my voice low and soft. "He was going to kill us. There was no other way."

"But—"

"Vic," I breathed, and I took her hands in mine. "Trust me, okay?"

"They won't like this," Victoria warned, and as if she spoke it into existence, pings echoed through the hallway.

Comments from my viewers ranged from anger, to excitement, to swoon-worthy.

G4AMEME1STER69

You should kill that bitch. How dare she go after
a Killer?

ELLEMAEBOOKS

OMG!!! Are we going to fuck again?

AUTHORBEXDEVEAU

Oooh shit, was this planned? Did y'all want to
fuck with the gamemakers? Damn, I can't wait
to see what happens.

"Kohl..." Victoria breathed. I looked up at her, and my entire heart
felt like it fell into the water below us, floating away with the dead.
She hesitated and moved to the side, like she wanted to hide it
from me.

"Show me," I growled and grabbed her wrist to take a closer
look.

GAMEMASTER

wh1t3_r4bb1t wants to be a Killer now,
does she?

My blood ran cold, and all the air left my lungs. I don't know
how long I stayed staring at the tracker, but no matter how many
times I read over the message, I couldn't wrap my head around
them.

Why? Why, after everything?

She had such a hard, sad life because of everything, and now?

We both knew she wasn't meant to be a Killer.

Anger rushed through me. Almost too fast for me to contain.

It was unrealistic for me to jump to conclusions, but I couldn't stop the image of my dad's face flashing in my mind as I pleaded with him to help.

Was he watching now? Was he wishing something like this would happen?

Or maybe...

I didn't let my mind spiral any further. Instead, I brought her hand to my lips, giving it a kiss. I didn't stay around to watch how she reacted. I turned back to the ledge, noting the still-lit-up purple and blue masks.

I reached for them, wiping off the blood on the blue one before turning back to Victoria.

"I'll help you," I promised.

She shook her head, eyes widening. "You and I both know that's just asking for them to fuck with us even more."

I gave her a smile before fastening the mask on her face.

"You got this," I vowed, tucking her hair behind her ear. "Remember? I'll give my life for yours? And that includes making it out of here with more money than you've ever *dreamed* of. It's me and you, forget about everyone else."

Her eyes searched my face as if trying to find the lie, but she wouldn't find one. I didn't care how fucked up it was that I was willing to slaughter innocent people just so the woman in front of me could get out of here, and not just that.

Get out of here and live the life she could have had if her family had never been intertwined with mine.

It had been years since I'd seen a genuine smile from her, but I swore to myself that I would do *anything* I had to see it again.

Vic

Looks like you can be trained after all, kitten

The sound of my own breathing was howling in my ears as I looked at Kohl.

I'd come so close to never seeing them again.

I'd come so close to never seeing *anything* again.

"Vic, are you okay?" they asked, cutting me a sidelong look as we headed for the opening to the tunnel.

"Okay?" I asked, my voice sounding tinny, hollow.

I'd killed somebody. That's who I was now, a murderer.

And it'd been so *easy*.

Kohl stopped us just outside of the moonlight's glow, gently taking my hand and pulling me to their chest. "You did what you had to, Vic. That doesn't make you a bad person."

I looked up into Kohl's face, their dark eyes swallowing the little light in the tunnel, my tongue snaking out to wet my dry lips.

When I reached to touch their face, reminding myself that they were here, that they were *whole*, my hands were shaking so violently I couldn't stop them.

Sure, killing somebody didn't inherently make me a bad person. I knew that.

Enjoying it, though, that was a whole other problem. My soul was already tainted, swathes of black growing like moldy spores I wouldn't be able to scrub off no matter how hard I tried.

Kohl put their hand over mine, and I sucked in a breath.

Every fiber of my being wanted to rip myself to shreds. To tear and destroy until there was nothing left.

"I-I-I feel so out of control," I admitted in a harsh whisper.

For a moment, I'd thought they'd killed them. That Kohl was somewhere out there, broken and bleeding and dead by that worthless scumbag's hand.

I wouldn't have even gotten to say goodbye. They wouldn't even know how I—

"Hurt me," Kohl murmured, gripping my fingers and pulling them from their face to lie against the initial over their heart, hidden by the heavy fabric of their cropped hoodie.

"What?" I asked, aghast, even as my blood started to pump harder. My heart picking up at the thought of listening to Kohl beg for me again.

I shouldn't want that. I should want to kiss away their hurt. To build them up into something magical. Not to reduce them into a snotty, sniveling mess as they wailed for me.

But I couldn't deny the way that my body reacted to the idea.

There was something twisted in me that needed to use them.

"Hurt me, Vic. I can see you're spinning out." They cupped their hands around the back of my neck, pulling me in for a kiss. "Let me give you an outlet. Hurt me like he hurt you."

Kohl tasted like blood, sweat, and ash. Like sin incarnate. My own personal slice of hell brought to life.

"Purpose," I whispered, giving them another sweet kiss.

The darkness was threatening to swallow me up, dragging on my limbs and making my mind race. But the moment I circled my hand around their throat and saw the way that their breathing took a sharp uptick before I closed off their air, it started to quiet.

Kohl's hands snaked around my waist, their fingers firm against my bare skin as I tightened my grip.

"Get on your knees."

There was a flicker, hardly more than a second where I thought that Kohl would disobey me. The dark, pulsing mass in my mind swelled with anger, and I dug my nails into their flesh, making them yelp.

"I gave you an order."

They dropped to their knees on the hard concrete, their eyes on the floor.

I gripped Kohl's shaggy blond hair roughly, jerking their head back. "Look at me when I'm fucking talking to you."

Kohl's dark eyes met mine, the irises lost to their blown pupils. As much as I needed this game, as much as I loved using and abusing them, they craved my wrath just as much. "Yes, my goddess."

We really were a fucked-up pair.

I tucked a finger under their chin, my thumb brushing against their lower lip. "Looks like you can be trained after all, kitten. *Good boy.*"

Kohl shivered, turning their head to kiss my palm. "Thank you, my goddess."

I stepped away, moving toward one of the unmoving swan boats. I climbed inside, settling on the wooden bench. There was hardly enough room to stand, much less kneel in the cramped space, but Kohl was just going to have to make do.

"Crawl to me," I ordered, patting my thigh in a clear order.

Kohl jerked into motion, hand over knee, as they made their way to where I sat.

"Look at you," I crooned softly, the tightness in my chest starting to ease as my hand rested on the butt of the gun sticking out of my waistband. "Big bad *Killer Kohl*, reduced to a Ghost's plaything."

"I'm not—" they started to argue, their jaw flexing, and I stood, my boot slamming down on their fingers as they got to the lip separating us. Kohl yelped, and I leaned into their face, my breath fanning across their cheek.

"What was that, kitten?"

Kohl gasped as I ground my foot down on their hand, hard enough to hurt, but not to break any bones. This was a game. A tug-of-war between us—just like when we were in school. The picture-perfect cheerleader and the fucking quarterback.

I didn't want to hurt them, at least not more than what would allow us to get the fuck out of here in one piece.

No, I wanted to *destroy* them.

I wanted to own them, mind, body, and whatever damaged, broken part of a soul they had left.

They were mine. And no one, not even the gamemakers, could change that.

Kohl pressed their lips together, their eyes dropping to the ground.

"I want to hear you say it." I rasped, my breathing coming in eager pants. "Tell me that you're my plaything. That I *own* you."

"You—" Kohl wheezed as I applied more pressure onto their hand. "You own me. I am yours. Your plaything. Your worthless—"

"Kiss my boots." I hissed, barely audible. "Prostrate yourself for your mistress, Kohl."

Their eyes lifted to mine—that's when I saw it. Kohl wasn't just enjoying this. No, Kohl was having the time of their fucking life. Our games played into the same dark, twisted parts of them that they did with me.

The masochistic little *freak*.

Kohl kissed my boot where it rested on their fingers, whispering their praises to me as they cleaned the blood crusting on the toe away with their tongue. I watched, enraptured as this gorgeous, unattainable creature lowered themselves to this. Praising me and cursing me in the same breath.

Begging for the release that only I could offer. For the control that I could exert over them.

I wouldn't just destroy Kohl. No, I would make them anew. Mold them like clay into something else entirely.

When I pulled my boot away, Kohl made a noise that could only be described as disappointment. But I was sick of watching and waiting. I needed to touch them.

I stepped back into the boat. "Strip and hand me your clothes."

Kohl swallowed hard. "The whole way?"

I raised an eyebrow. "What? Are you shy, kitten?"

"Vic, there are cameras fucking everywhere—"

"And you already put on a show in 4-fucking-K, so take your goddamn clothes off before I cut them off you myself," I snarled.

Kohl's eyes lit in their hesitation, the moment gone so quickly I could've imagined it before they started to undress.

"You'd like that, wouldn't you?" I whispered, resisting the urge to press my thighs together as they shed their cropped hoodie, baring their bitten, bruised skin to me. The letter V proudly carved over their left pec was crusted with dried blood now, angry and red.

Kohl nodded slowly, like they knew what it would cost them to admit it.

The watch on my wrist was going haywire with notifications, viewers barking suggestions for what I could do next. But I didn't need their help to ruin Kohl.

I knew exactly how I wanted them to fall apart for me.

Kohl undid their belt, the metal clinking as they moved to take off their pants. They met my eyes as they did so, and I smirked as I watched them bare their cunt to me.

Cutting off their underwear in the house of mirrors was a great idea. If only because they were no longer a factor.

They handed me their clothes, moving to lower themselves back to their knees, but I grabbed their shoulder to stop them.

"No, sit there." I pointed to the bench, and Kohl's eyes widened. "And spread your legs."

"Vic—"

"Do as you're told," I snapped. "Or face the consequences."

Kohl climbed into the boat, settling onto the bench and spreading their legs obediently, baring their glistening pussy to me.

"You dirty little fucking *freak*," I hissed, swiping my fingers through their arousal as I settled onto my knees between their legs.

"Are you dripping for me because I *hurt* you?" I twisted their nipple with my free hand hard enough to make them cry out. "Or because there's five million people watching and there isn't a single thing you can do to stop me?"

Kohl hissed through their teeth, their breath coming in desperate pants and gasps that shook their whole body. "Vic—please—"

It was like a fucking symphony to hear them beg for me.

I breathed deeply, feeling the tension in my shoulders leave as I pulled out the gun, trailing the muzzle along Kohl's side.

They hissed at the kiss of the metal against their skin, their eyes wild and jaw slack in anticipation.

But I wasn't in a rush.

"Please what, kitten?"

"I need you," Kohl whispered. "Please, Vic—"

My mouth tipped into an unkind smirk as I nudged Kohl's clit with my fingers. "Do you want me to fuck you, Kohl? Does my little *killer* want me to dominate them?"

"Vic—fuck—" Kohl shook with restraint, their knuckles white where they'd wrapped around the bench.

"Or do you want me to hurt you, baby?" I whispered, kissing their knee before dragging my teeth along the sensitive skin of their inner thigh.

Kohl's hips bucked toward my face. "Touch me—please—I can't take it—"

I laughed, relishing in the silence that Kohl's voice brought me. The darkness purring like the engine of a European sports car.

"Hurt you, it is."

I couldn't deny how it made me feel inflict pain on Kohl. I loved seeing them squirm in pain as much as I loved seeing them squirm in pleasure. *But only* if it was my doing.

I could hear the pings of messages echoing through the tunnel. All of them no doubt egging me on. Or maybe they too were degrading Kohl in the comments. I wanted to read them to him. To make them come to the degrading messages from the fans.

Kohl's eyes fogged over. No doubt they were imaginig something similar. Their breathing was heavy and their eyes hooded.

Such a pretty picture.

I dug my teeth dug the sensitive skin of their inner thigh. They bit their lip, trying and failing to stifle their groan.

My fingers picked up pace on my clit, causing their groan to turn into a moan. They tried to cover their mouth with their hand. I sent a sharp smack to their clit.

That wouldn't do.

"The freak still has enough shame to try and muffle themselves?" I asked with a cruel laugh. "You're here, *sopping wet.*" I shoved two fingers inside of her, hooking them. Showing them just how easily their body reacted to me. "Spreading your legs for the cameras and begging to be fucked, yet you still have the gall to try and hide?"

"I w-won't," they said breathlessly. My chest was heaving, my heart racing at a thousand miles per second. "Please, *please,* Vic–"

Their cries cut out when I trailed the gun between my legs. I loved they way they shivered. It igniting something dark in me.

They froze. From fear or from arousal I did not know, but their way their cunt gushed around my fingers gave me a good idea. I dragged the still-warm barrel of the gun down their thigh, right where I had bitten.

Their skin looked so beautiful marked by me. First the initial and then this... *perfect* and all *mine.*

"Oh, come on now, we have an audience. Let them know just how much you want this," I purred. I removed my fingers to trail the gun down their pussy, gathering their wetness onto the barrel before nudging it against their clit.

They shuddered against the feeling. I dug my nails into their thighs, trying to pull them back to the present. They couldn't get too lost in their pleasure just yet.

"Tell them, Kohl."

"I want this," they said through moans. I moved the gun against their clit in hard, horizontal strokes. "I'm your worthless, pathetic plaything, and I want you to fuck me already."

I let out a mock, scandalized gasp before dragging the gun down their fold to push against their entrance. Their cunt started to suck the gun in greedily.

They threw their head back. Obviously enjoying my ministrations but being a good boy and not begging too much. I ran the gun up and down their folds until they were bucking against my movements.

Greedy. Greedy boy. Power thrummed through me, igniting something inside of me. It was easy to get addicted to the way Kohl submitted to me. To the way they begged me for more.

"Oh no, that won't do," I teased. "Getting an attitude?"

They opened their mouth to speak, but I brought my hand back to their clit again, cutting them off. I pushed the gun into them. Just a taste, before pulling back.

They were so *so* wet. I hoped the audience could see just how turned on they were by this.

"Look into your mistress's eyes while she fucks you, Kohl."

Kohl forced their eyes back down to me and took in as I pushed the gun further inside them. I couldn't help the wicked smile that spread across my face.

Their mouth fell open, curses and moans following out with ease. Their body started to tremble. They were close. Too close.

"Only good boys get orgasms," I said and stopped my assault on their clit, pulling the gun out entirely.

"Vic no, *please*—"

I pushed the gun against their lips, giving them a sharp look. Without my prompting, they opened their mouth and licked the length of the gun.

Fuck. It was so hot to see them lick their own come from the gun. A gun that I could fire any second.

But they didn't care. They would do just about anything I asked of them.

"That's right, kitten," I cooed. "Show us that you deserve the orgasm."

Their hand came to grip my own, directing it to the side so I could get a better look at the way their tongue ran the length of it.

The pings were getting louder now, more jumbled as people tuned in. I jerked the gun back with a harsh sigh.

"I'm turning this fucking thing—*oh*." I curt off when I saw the first few comments. All of them degrading Kohl. *Perfect.* "That's right, slut, clean your own mess up. God, they're so fucking disgusting, look how turned on they are. Keep begging, you freak."

I let out a laugh. They loved it. I could see it in the way Kohl's eyes widened. In the way their body began trembling without me even touching them.

The sound of a splash caught both of our attention. I leaned to the side, ready to jump right out of the boat, but instead of an intruder, there was a box floating down the river.

Kohl reached over and grabbed it right as it was about to float on by. When I caught sight of what they sent, heat spread through my body.

"Naughty, naughty viewers," I breathed and tore it out of Kohl's hands. I tore open the box and pulled out a brand-new, all-white vibrator. I tested out the buttons on it until the bulbous head started to vibrate. The harsh sound of it breaking through the music and pings. "*Make them cry.* How sweet."

I looked up at them with that a smile. *Now how good of a boy will you be for me Kohl?*

"You heard them, my goddess."

Perfect. Kohl was so fucking perfect I couldn't get over it.

I placed myself back between their legs, wasting no time with foreplay, and placed the vibrator right onto their clit.

"Which setting, hmm?" I asked and turned it to the lowest.

"Highest," they gritted out.

I let out a laugh and turned it up. *Whatever the good boy asks.* Their entire body seized and almost immediately an orgasm shook their frame. Their mouth was wide open, pained moans coming out as their pussy clenched around nothing. Their wetness leaked down onto the boat, soon it would create a puddle.

"Let's see how long it lasts," I murmured, using my free hand to start pumping two fingers into them at a furious pace.

"No," They whined. Each slam of my hand hit the vibrator, pushing it harder into their clit. I wanted to see them lose it.

"*Yes.*"

I stopped my movement to push my palm against the vibrator and hooked two fingers inside of them, massaging their G-spot at the same time.

Wetness exploded all over my hand.

"So fucking filthy," I cooed. "You're a deranged little slut, you know that? Getting off like this while all these people watch? I bet you've been waiting for a moment like this your entire life."

"Yes, yes," they let out a groan as their pussy clenched around my fingers. They were going to come again with little rest between.

I pushed the vibrator harder into them, pulling a harsh cry from their lips.

As soon as the waves subsided from their orgasm, they tried to jerk away from me, but I didn't let them. I kept my pace, feeling as their pussy squeezed tighter and tighter around me until–

"Again?" I asked. "My god, how long has it been since someone fucked this pussy correctly?"

I leaned forward in an attempt to pull their nipple into my mouth, but they jerked back. I merely smiled at me and leaned down, and down, and down, my teeth digging into their upper tight so hard their hands shot out to grip the seat.

"Too much," they breathed. "Fuck. Vic, please. No more."

"But you're not crying yet," I said in a sickly sweet tone. "We told them I'd make you cry."

I began pumping my fingers in and out of them again, fitting a third in before fucking them again. I removed the vibrator and leaned down to lick at the swollen nub.

They were so delicious.

My teeth raked against the bundle of nerves, forcing a guttural cry from their mouth. I then sucked it into my mouth—*hard*—before I continued fucking me.

They kneeled over me, their hands flying to my hair. *It wasn't enough. I needed to see that beautiful crying face of theirs.*

I picked up the vibrator again, placing it on their clit. That was the last straw for them. They thrashed around. Bucked their hips. Cries fell from their lips louder and more frequently than before.

As soon as my hand pushed against the bulbous head, their orgasm finally overcame them.

Tears fell then, finally.

Started at the corner of their eyes. Their face a mix of pain and pleasure as they cried out for me. They came easily. One after another running down their face as they attempted to gasp for air.

"God, you look so good with tears running down your face," I said, my still wet hand coming up to wipe them.

"Enough, Vic, please."

"Enough? I don't think this is nearly en—"

The boat jerked and made both of us fall. Kohl caught themselves just before they crushed me, both of us looking back at the tunnel.

"Someone must have turned it on," I whispered. "Get dressed!"

Kohl jerkily put their clothes back on, body still not fully recovered from the show we just gave. The boat was slow enough that we were able to jump off before entering the tunnel.

As soon as we were off, Kohl took the time to check their comments.

I hadn't liked how it ended so soon, but Kohl was right. This had been a perfect way to get my head back in the game.

I just hoped I'd have more time to play with my toy before the games ended.

"Later," I said, pushing them back toward the entrance. "We have a Hider to kill."

Kohl
Before the Games

A *fucking dinner?*

Was Dylan planning to make it *official* or something?

I shifted in my seat, trying not to look Father in the eyes as he sat down, taking his place at the head of the table. We'd been going through one of those multi-week fights again. The ones where he forgot just how angry he was until he looked me in the eyes.

This time it'd started over me making a snide comment when we had company over. Charlene—the Inner Circle member du jour that my father was ass-kissing—laughed it off, but Father saw through it.

What the woman brushed off as a joke, he saw the malice underneath. Something that someone in his *position*, a man vying for the top, wouldn't stand for.

Luckily, he was still on a phone call, his voice echoing throughout the dining room.

I cast a glance at the empty seats in front of me, trying not to let my temper bubble. Instead of the normal single plate placed carefully for Dylan, there was an extra.

It didn't take a fucking rocket scientist to figure out who it was for.

The only thing making this evening even worse than it was, was that he decided to bring her to *this* dinner. The one where Father would get to stand up, making his stupid fucking speech about how hard he had worked to provide us a life, and then let us know that he *finally* got the title of Architect.

It wasn't a surprise, though. He had been vying for this position for a long time and made the whole goddamn house aware whenever he *wasn't* chosen. Sometimes it took the cleaning crew weeks to clean up the mess from the fallout. Last time they had to replace multiple spots of drywall.

I had marked this day on my calendar for years as a reminder to prepare myself for the inevitable. But this time around, when promotions were handed out, the house had been oddly quiet. There was no shouting. No punching holes in walls. No need to hide as Father searched for something to take his anger out on.

Just... *silence.*

And then a few hours later, he came to us, letting us know that our presence would be expected at dinner.

I hadn't expected Dylan to bring Vic here though.

Father knew about her, of course, he knew about almost everything that went on inside this house. But this was still the first time she had met him.

Other times, Dylan had made sure to bring Vic around when Father wouldn't be in the house. Or at least that's what I thought he was doing. After all, Father had never been interesting in our personal lives besides what we were doing to upkeep his oh-so-impressive legacy. Inviting people over while he was here would just annoy him.

When the sound of the door slamming open and shoes squeaking across the floor hit my ears, I straightened. My eyes immediately went to Father.

"Right," he said, his eyes shifting to the open door that gave him a perfect view into the hallway connecting the living room and entrance. "Let's talk about it on Monday. I have some guests."

Without waiting for the person on the other line to respond, Father hung up and placed his phone on the dining table.

I saw the moment when he laid eyes on her. Saw how the skin around his mouth grew taut. How his gaze narrowed. I couldn't tell if it was disappointment or something more dangerous. For a moment, I thought he stopped breathing, but it was gone as soon as it came on.

"Welcome," Father said, a smile spreading across his face. His mask was firmly in place, and if I wasn't so worried for Vic, I may even appreciate the change of pace her being here had brought.

"Dad, Victoria, Victoria, Dad. You can call him Hiram," Dylan said and made a show of walking her to the table and holding out her chair for her.

Vic gave my father a tense smile, her gaze locking on to his. The intensity of it gave me pause.

Normal people in her position would pause, especially when faced with an alumni like my father. He was well-known, and given the history of her family, it was unlikely that she didn't know who the fuck she was staring down.

Fear shot through me.

I was normally at the end of my father's wrath, but I sure as hell didn't want Vic to be his target.

But the news earlier that day seemed to loosen him up, and all he did was return her smile and sit down.

"Nice to meet you, sir," she said, her voice sickly sweet.

"Hiram," he said. "There are no such formalities between families like ourselves. Did your parents tell you we knew each other?"

We were interrupted by our personal chef bringing out our meals. Vic sent the girl a smile as she placed a plate down in front of her before turning to my dad.

"I know a little," Vic admitted. "Though my parents don't talk about the games much anymore."

Father nodded, "Last I heard, they had chosen jobs outside of the games, is that true?"

When Vic hesitated, I shifted. Dylan didn't so much as look at her, too focused on devouring the food in front of him.

"Seems more like a reunion than meeting the girlfriend," I commented.

Father's eyes shifted to mine, the command there was obvious. *Don't you talk back to me.*

"It's fine," Vic said, her foot coming to brush across mine. But instead of it being like a kick, her movement was soothing, as if she could tell I was defensive on her behalf.

"My parents left the games behind for good," she said, taking a bite of her own food. "Though am I to understand there is something exciting happening about your role in them?"

Father positively puffed at this. His eyes glimmered in the light, and his hand swept out to grab the cup of wine at his side.

"I got promoted to Architect," he said, sending her a mock cheer even though none of us had anything but water in our glasses.

"Congratulations," she said and leaned forward. "Anything juicy you can tell us? Maybe help prepare us for the next games?"

He waved her off.

"It's so uncanny how much like your mother you are," he said with a wistful sigh. "She once told me that when I was an Architect one day, that I would be able to help our kids through the games. She always seemed to believe in me."

His words caused my heart to stop in my chest. *Our* kids? Surely he meant something else? Maybe as friends?

His lips pursed, and he paused for a second, then took a swig of his wine.

"Yes, well," Vic said with a sigh. "She always was the type of person who believed in those she knew would do well. It was like a sixth sense. Pity, she never really thought I would do much with the games."

Vic's face was pained when the words left her. She never talked about her mother much. Maybe that was why.

"It's not for everyone," Father said and cleared his throat. "How is she? It's been... well, years since I heard anything about her."

Vic's eyes widened before falling to her lap. I leaned forward, trying to get a look at her, but her hair had fallen over and covered her face. Only then had I noticed how tightly her hands grasped her shirt.

"You don't know," she murmured.

"What was that?" Father asked.

Vic lifted her head, giving him a sad look.

"I thought most winners and the Inner Circle would have heard the news..." her voice trailed. "Truly, you heard nothing?"

My gaze shot to Father, and I was taken aback by how abruptly his entire mood had changed. He had been somewhat happy about his accomplishment and the ability to brag, but now his face was tight and reddening slowly. His jaw was set, the sound of his teeth grinding could be heard even across the table.

Even Dylan had paused his eating to take a look.

"What happened to her?" Father all but spat out.

Vic opened her mouth and shut it.

"Father, maybe this isn't dinner conversat—"

Father didn't hide his glare at my interruption.

"She's dead. Cancer, we didn't catch it in time."

There was something in the way Father's face slackened. The way his eyes shot toward her. The way his hand clenched into fists before releasing.

Whatever news this was, it was enough to catch Father off guard. He was a pro at concealing his emotions, had to for his job... but his mask had slipped just enough to give me a glimpse into what he was really feeling.

Anger?

"How?" he asked.

Vic shrugged.

"I guess no one really noticed anything off, and one day my father came home and found Mom passed out, and—it just progressed really fast. That's all there is to say, sir. They were never really close. Since I was born, there had been this wedge in between them, one my mother put in between the both of us, so it was easy for us to miss the signs."

What was even more jarring was the way Vic stared at my father. Just like when she sat down. Her gaze was almost daring him to say something.

He stood, the sound of the chair screeching against the floor causing me to wince.

"Sorry," he said, though his expression told me he didn't mean it. "I forgot that I have a call. It was nice meeting you, Vic."

We all sat there in shocked silence as Father stormed out of the room.

"Well," Dylan said, leaning across the table to grab Father's cup of wine. "More for me."

"Vic," I whispered, leaning my head against her bare legs.

It had been a few hours since Father stormed off. Dylan was to the side of us, passed out after raiding Father's alcohol cabinet. His snore barely audible over the sound of the action movie he had forced us to watch.

I turned to look up at her when she didn't answer.

She swallowed thickly and clutched at her shorts.

"Kohl," she said back, though her voice held more of a warning to it.

"You know I'll support you with anything, right?" I asked.

She gave me a stiff nod.

"And I you," she whispered.

I leaned forward, brushing the barest hint of a kiss against her knee.

"Then I think it's time you be honest with me," I said.

I couldn't get the image of Father reacting to her news about her mother out of my mind, nor could I get the way she stared him down out either.

This time, instead of fighting me, she brought her lower lip between her teeth.

"We're friends," I said, trying not to wince at how bitter the word tasted in my mouth. I trailed my hand up her leg in a soothing motion. "You can tell me, whatever it is. Hell, I'll even help you if you want."

Her eyes widened at my admission.

"You don't know what you're getting into," she muttered, shaking her head. I turned, shifting to sit on my knees and face her fully.

"I don't *care*," I said, trying to fuse as much power into my words as I could. "Anything. I would do anything for you. Don't you know that?"

"Kohl—"

"No," I said quickly. "Let me finish. I would stand by your side even if the goal was to watch the world burn. Fuck, I'd hold the kerosene. *Please*, just let me in. Whatever, *whatever* it is, I promise to be the one to help you with it."

Her eyes searched my face, no doubt looking for any hint that I was lying to her.

Just as she opened her mouth, the harsh sound of her vibrating phone cut through the air. I tried not to groan aloud when she picked it up.

"Dad, I thought you were—"

Her eyes widened, and her mouth dropped open. Her shaky hand came to try and cover the slow crumbling of her expression.

My heart dropped into my stomach.

"Vic—"

"My dad—he got into—oh my god."

She dropped the phone into her lap, her other hand coming up to cup her mouth.

"Vic, what's wrong with your dad?" I asked, my hands coming to her caress hers, but as soon as she flinched away, I paused.

"I need you to drive me somewhere," she said, her voice muffled.

"Yes, anywhere," I said, this time not hesitating to pull her into a standing position. She leaned into me, taking deep breaths as she tried to calm herself.

For the first time, I didn't feel the rush of warmth when her skin touched mine.

"Vic, wait–"

But it was already too late. She was rushing out of the car and into the rain before I could stop her.

The rain was pouring down, obstructing my view, but even so, bright red and blue lights flashed back at us.

I threw the car into park and darted out into the rain after her.

There was an abundance of uniforms scattered throughout, directing traffic and keeping the scene clear. Bright yellow caution tape was blocking off the side of the highway where it dipped into a small wooded area. One that was too dense for anything big and metal to make it through.

People honked at Vic as she sprinted past. Uniformed men raised their hands to stop her from approaching.

"Stop, miss, you can't be here!"

"That's my dad!" she screamed, her voice already hoarse as she tried to yell over the barrage of noise that hit us. "Please, I need to see if he's okay. Let me through!"

I ran up behind Vic, grabbing her arm and forcing her to me.

"Don't!" she yelled and shoved me back, then turned to the man. "Where is he?!"

The man's lips pushed together in a thin line.

"Let me direct you over to my partners, they will be able to—wait!"

Vic pushed past the guy, running straight toward the drop-off of the highway. I darted after her, not wanting to know what they would do to her if she pushed them hard enough.

Legacy or not, there was only so much protection we had in the outside world.

I grabbed at her, curling my arms around her waist just as she reached the edge. I had gathered a sense of how bad it was on the car ride, but nothing had prepared me for how catastrophic the crash was.

The slope into the wooded area was steep, with little space between the highway and trees. The car had not just veered off the road, but it looked like it was going at a high speed because the way the front had crashed into the trees caused the entire front to become smashed metal.

The windshield was completely shattered, giving us a look at the blood-splattered interior.

Vic let out the most heart wrenching sound.

"Please, Vic," I begged, pain filling my voice. "Please, don't look."

I attempted to cover her eyes, but her hands were there, clawing them away.

"I must," she gasped. "Don't you fucking interfere."

Her words made me jerk back.

Men in uniforms flocked up, none of them looking like they were willing to play nice.

I reached out one again to try and bring her close to me, try to stop the pain that was surly tearing through her entire being, but stopped short when she sent me a glare so filled with hate I started to wonder if the Vic I had known all along was the real one, or was it the rage-filled, vengeance-driven person I was seeing then?

It would be another four hours before I trekked back into my house, clothes sticking to me because of the rain. A chill had settled over me long ago, causing my fingers and toes to become numb, but I pushed off all of it.

The image of Vic's tear-stricken face flashing through my mind. The sounds of her hoarse yells echoing through my mind.

Why her? First her mom, and now her dad?

Out of all people, why did it have to be her? They had said he was barely alive when they pulled him from the crash.

It was too unfair, too cruel. The games had been part of my reality for as long as I could remember, but somehow normal, everyday life had seemed much more brutal.

I walked throughout the house, noticing that Dylan was no longer passed out on the couch.

I was glad. I didn't know if he would be pissed that we had left him, but in all honesty, I didn't have the energy to talk to him. All I wanted to do was yell. To scream at the world and demand answers.

There would be no coming back from this. I just knew it. Something in my gut told me that it would be almost impossible to get close to Vic again after this.

I walked around the house aimlessly, not too sure where I was going, just that I couldn't stop moving. Because the second I did, all the painful memories of Vic's face would slam right back into me.

Rolling my shoulders, I made my way to the garage, knowing there was at least one cold beer there waiting for me. I didn't normally condone drinking to drown your feelings, but I didn't know what else to do in that moment.

I opened the creaky door to the garage, flipping on the light, though as soon as I did, I regretted my actions.

I stood there, shocked as I took in my father's car. It wasn't strange for it to be parked in the garage. What was strange was the state it was in. The bumper was askew, more on the right than left. I walked to the side, my blood curdling as I saw the dents and scratches that made up almost the entirety of the right side.

No. It was too much for it to be a coincidence.

But then why did Father leave like that? Why had he looked like his entire soul was crushed when she said those things about her mother?

And why was the car still dripping with rainwater?

I never thought I could hate my father more than I did, but that night solidified that some people, once they entered the games, left a part of themselves there.

Vic

The thought of killing someone should have made me feel nervous, maybe even a little sick. I certainly shouldn't have felt like it was exciting, if not a little irritating.

I was a legacy, sure. But my parents were Ghosts. Killing wasn't in my nature. All my life, my dad had been vocal about his distaste of the games. He hadn't wanted this life for me.

But yet there I was, and Killer no less.

I shouldn't have liked the way the adrenaline rushed through my veins. Shouldn't have enjoyed the flush of power it brought me.

I *should* have been disgusted... but I was far from it.

Would my dad be ashamed of what I was becoming? Would he be angry that I'd become a Killer?

What about my mom?

It didn't matter. I had no choice, once the Architects decided you were going to do something, you did it. Or the punishment would make you wish you had.

Kohl's warm hand in mine was grounding as we made our way through the park.

It was kind of nice not to be afraid. To walk with them like equals instead of having them chase me like I was prey. I cut a look at them sidelong in their mask, the purple neon glowing ominously at me and obscuring their features.

"Hey, Vic...?" they asked, voice weaker than I would've liked.

I squeezed their hand. "If you have something to say, Kohl, just say it."

"I'm—I'm sorry. About lying to you."

I bit the inside of my cheek, stopping us just outside of the area with the games where I'd first gotten a good look at them in their mask.

"I so want to be mad at you," I admitted. "For everything. But *I can't*. It would be unfair for me to hold this over your head."

I haven't been the most honest myself, was what I wanted to say. Their vulnerability was almost enough to make me spill everything that had been bottling up inside.

They squeezed my hand back, an action that caused my heart to set alight.

"You know..." They trailed their gaze, looking out at the arena. "If our lives weren't on the line, this may have been a bit romantic."

I couldn't help the laugh that fell from my lips. *Of course, Kohl would try to make me feel better about the shitty situation.* It only made me fall harder for them than I already had.

I hadn't known it was possible to need them any more than I had for the last few years, but ever since the house of mirrors, I felt closer to them than I ever had.

I also worried for them more than I ever intended.

I wanted to be selfish. Wanted to be able to be cold and shrug them off when needed to get ahead.

But all I could think about was my initial carved into their chest. Their face as they looked up at me through their lashes. Their flushed face as they begged me for mercy.

Seeing them like that was everything I thought I could never have. They were a selfish delusion I only allowed myself when the lights were off, and I was snuggled deep in my soft duvet.

"If I had a choice on our first date, I'd go for something a bit more simple than fucking being covered in blood and on the dirty floor," I said with a laugh.

"Oh ya? What would that be? Brunch? A coffee shop? Library date?" they teased, pushing their side against me. The small, teasing gesture lifted the weight on my shoulders, even if it was just a bit.

"No, something *better*," I said in a teasing tone. "I think it'd be nice to take my dog for a walk. I ever have the perfect studded collar in mind."

"A dog? What about Bingsoo? I can't imagine them agreeing to a *dog* in the house."

I gave them a long look. When it finally dawned on them, bright red traveled up their neck. I gave them a wink and let the laugh that had been bubbling in my chest out.

The pings on both our trackers told me the audience liked our playful banter as much as I did.

Just for fun, I pulled up the comments to show Kohl.

"Oh my god, look, someone even offered to send us one if we—"

"You fucker!"

We both turned at the loud voice. Kohl moved in front of me almost immediately, blocking me from view.

I leaned to the side, taking in the tall men with pink and yellow masks.

They were with Dylan.

Alarm bells rang in my head, and my legs itch to move. Did they know about Dylan? They had to have, right? Or else they wouldn't be here...

"You guys were holding me up, I had no choice," Kohl said, their voice light and not at all like they just watched their brother get shot. "Plus, the taser didn't hurt *that* much, right?"

"We were knocked out!" Pink said, throwing his hands in the air.

"Yeah, we could have died!" Yellow crossed his arms over their chest.

"But you didn't," Kohl said. "Now, if you excuse me, we have to go. Last I heard, Dylan was going to go find you two, so—"

"See, that's what I don't get," Yellow said, his head tilting to the side. "I'm pretty sure Dylan wouldn't have let you off, especially after what your father was willing to give us for offing that pretty little rabbit you were hiding. Don't think you can fool us by giving her a Killer mask. We aren't *dumb*."

Their father? Anger shot through me. I pushed forward, ready to give them a verbal beating, but Kohl held me back.

"He called Dylan off," they said. "I made a different deal. One that you're not privy to. Now run off before the architect gets mad."

They looked at each other, obviously lost at what to do without their leader.

Kohl turned slightly, gripping my shoulders and readying us to make our break. Then the pings on their trackers cut through the air.

They stood still, their chests not even moving.

"That's Dylan's mask," Pink breathed.

"No," Yellow whispered his hands coming to clutch his head. "No. No. *NO!*"

They were charging us before we had a chance to ready ourselves. With a yelp, I turned and pulled Kohl along with me.

"God, my father's such a fucking prick!"

KOHL

DOWN, BOY.

I should have killed them.

I should have fucking killed them.

It was all I could think as I ran after Vic, Dylan's lackeys chasing after us with a vengeance.

At the time, all I was thinking about was getting to Vic before my brother did, but now I wish that I had just taken the precaution to kill them.

I won't make the same mistake twice.

Vic was faster than me, faster than them, but I fell behind. So much so that it was only a few minutes until one of them tackled me from behind.

We fell to the ground in a heap, pushing the air out of my lungs, but unlike last time, I wasn't going to allow myself to be overtaken. Not when Vic's life was on the line and she had come so close to dying just moments before.

I promised her my life, and I would make damn sure that she would make it out of the games.

I locked my arms around his neck, trying to replicate a move I had seen Dylan do so many times over, and when I finally got him into a headlock. He struggled against me, his words becoming a garbled mess in his throat. I felt the presence of Vic coming up to our side.

"Beat it, or I blow his brains out," Vic warned, the sound of her cocking the gun filling the space between us.

Pink stopped thirty feet away from us, his eyes darting to me and then to Vic before settling on his friend.

What was she doing? The gun tucked in the back of my pants was accessible if I needed it. If anything, I would have preferred she ran away while I fought these two. I was confident in my ability to get at least one kill in after they lost their leader.

"I'm going to let you up," I warned. "Be smart."

He nodded, his hand coming to slap my arm three times. I let him go, watching his back as he crawled away from me.

The humiliating act caused a thrill to run through me. I stood slowly, unable to take my eyes off Pink as Yellow helped him up. I could kill them. Right then and there.

Vic had a gun, I had a gun. It's the least they deserved for trying to hurt Vic. My hand twitched, the urge to grab my gun filling me.

"He's in the tunnel of love," I said, taking a step forward. "Shall I show you where?"

It should have pained me to even think about my brother. For the images of his dead body sinking to the bottom of the canal. But instead, all I could think about was the horror that would twist their faces. Of the shocked gasps they would have to conceal. They would be overcome with rage, but the shock would render them frozen.

And then, when they were least expecting it, I would raise the gun and—

"Down, boy," Vic all but purred as she came to my side. "We don't know what other consequences the games have in store for us."

And just like that, the invisible leash she kept tied around my neck was yanked back.

Vic pointed the gun at them and raised her brows, daring them to try again. They cursed under their breath, both looking at each other before Yellow was finally the one to shake their head.

I lowered my head and waited with her as they ran away, shooting daggers at us as they escaped.

"Getting antsy?" Vic asked, my eyes darting to her. Even though the majority of her face was covered by my brother's mask, those piercing eyes showed through and making my heart stop in my chest.

Still, after everything, I couldn't believe that she was by my side. That she allowed me to touch her in a way I only dreamed of. That she trusted me as nuch as she did.

I won't let her down. She was my reason for existing, to let her down would be unthinkable.

I was scared to think of the after. Of what would happen when we left the walls of this island. Would she move on? Would she leave me, only to exist as a distant memory in her mind?

Sirens blared overhead, making us jump. That same haunting sound that made the blood rush through my veins now pushing fear to take hold of me.

"Three hours remaining. Three hours remaining. Six Hiders still alive. Six Hiders still alive."

We both shared a look. *One of those was Vic's.* And if we didn't find them soon, she would be out of luck. But that wasn't the only problem we faced in the final hours...

These last few hours would be the most dangerous. Once all the Ghosts were found, the Killers would start turning on themselves. Each of them hoping to knock others off the scoreboard. They were not supposed to, and many faced consequences, but most were willing to risk it to be number one.

"We have to get someplace safe," I said and grabbed onto Vic's wrist. "Just long enough so we can hide out and plan out our next moves."

"Just enough time to get our shit together," Vic said. "Remember your promise."

"I'd never forget," I said, forcing as much sincerity into my tone as possible.

The corner of her eyes crinkled playfully.

"Well, the Killers will be forced to comb the park searching for the last Ghosts," she said, looking around. "So that means there aren't many places we can—oh!"

Her sentence ended with a light huff of a laugh. I followed her line of sight, looking off into the distance at the Ferris wheel. Its slow-moving boxes swayed in the wind slightly, causing my stomach to twist.

But it was perfect. Not only would it take about thirty minutes to go all around, but it would also give us the perfect view of the entire island, and we could watch as the Ghosts ran to their places.

"Let's go find you a Hider," I said, wrapping my arm over her shoulders.

"I have something better planned," she said, the smile obvious in her voice.

"Fuck, do you know how long I've waited to taste your pussy?" Vic asked as she kneeled between my legs, her tongue running the length of my slit.

I just about came right then and there. Here was Vic, a girl akin to the goddess Aphrodite, kneeling at *my* feet and giving *me* pleasure.

I let out a groan, my hips bucking when she teased my clit with her tongue. "I don't deserve this," I panted. "Please, Vic, let me please you. Use me how you want, you don't have to waste time—"

A sharp slap of her palm against my clit had a sharp yelp coming from my lips and my body jerking. The box we were in tilted along with me, causing my heart to catch in my throat.

"You aren't to tell *me* how I'm wasting *my* time," she growled. "If I want to eat my pet's cunt out until they're shaking, I damn well should be able to do it."

She leaned toward the soft skin of my thigh, her hot breath brushing across it.

I don't know when I decided I was comfortable being almost completely naked in the area, with thousands if not millions of people watching me, but there was little I would go against Vic with.

If she told me to get on my knees and beg, to bark like a dog, or even spread myself while she spit on me, I would fucking do it.

"You're right," I breathed. When she sank her teeth into my thigh, I let out a pained moan. She pulled away to drag her tongue along the marks.

"Say sorry," she commanded.

"Sorry," I said quickly, spreading my legs even wider for her. "I'm *sorry*."

On the way up, it was hard to ignore our surroundings. The Ferris wheel was moving so slowly that I was afraid someone might just take the chance and jump on our box, but once we got higher and Vic distracted me with hot kisses trailing down my blood-stained skin, the world fell away.

"Do you mean it?" she teased, her tongue just brushing across my folds.

"Yes," I moaned. "I'm sorry. You tell me what you want. Whether that's fucking you or being fucked by you, I will gladly oblige."

She let out a light laugh and rewarded me with a kiss to my clit.

"How would you fuck me?" she asked. "Tell me and don't stop."

I swallowed thickly, my eyes making contact with hers as she leaned forward, ready to pick up where she left off.

"I want you against the glass," I said breathlessly. "I want your tits out and pushed against it so everyone down there could see you."

"*Naughty*." She rewarded me by latching on to my clit, her fingers drawing mind-numbing patterns in my thigh as they came closer and closer to where I wanted them.

"I want them to be jealous of what I have," I admitted. I want to show them how much you enjoy my mouth on you. I want them to watch as I make you come and as it drips down onto me—*oh fuck.*"

I opened my mouth, but no sound came out as she fit her fingers into me and curled them sharply. She wasted no time massaging a place that caused me to jerk against her.

The heart-stopping movement of the box swinging back and forth only heightened the feeling of her fucking me. She pulled her mouth from me with a loud, wet sound.

"Continue, or I'll stop," she threatened.

I let out a whine, unable to help myself. "I want you to make a mess of me. I want you to come so many times the whole area knows what it sounds like when you come."

She leaned forward, using her tongue to trace circles around my clit. She pulled her fingers out, only to slam them back into me again. The motion was so hard, so sudden that it made me jerk again.

She must have felt the way my pussy convulsed when the fear of the box rocking ran through me.

"If you want, I would use my hands," I said. "But not until you commanded me to. I'd want you in charge the whole time. Tell me what to do. Teaching me how to please you."

My words earned a long suck.

"I love how you taste," I admitted. "I fucked myself to your scent hundreds of times."

"My scent?" she asked, pulling away. Her free hand came to strum my clit as she looked up at me, a playful look crossing her features.

Heat flashed through me, but instead of answering, I spread my legs further for her. A silent command that I wasn't sure she'd obey.

A wicked smile teased at her mouth, her fingers pounding into my cunt at a mind-whirling pace.

I couldn't stop the moans escaping me, embarrassingly loud in the confined space.

"Your swim bottoms," I gasped. My pussy was gripping her fingers. Heat filling my body, licking at my spine, and threatening to explode from the inside out. "I kept them. Used them whenever I fucked myself to you."

"You dirty boy," Vic said with a gasp of mock horror. Just below the surface I could make out the absolute *delight* she was trying to smother. "How fucked up are you that you'd jerk off into my bikini? Fuck, I should have known you were the perverted little *freak* who took them."

I couldn't hold it in anymore. Her words alone were enough to throw me violently over the edge, my release coming with a wail of pleasure that made her practically vibrate with excitement.

Vic fucked me through it, her hands keeping pace until I slumped, entirely spent against the hard backing of the seat.

She stood, shimmied off her pants, and climbed into my lap. My hands found her skin like she was metal and they were made of magnets.

"Lift my shirt just like in your fantasy, *Killer Kohl*," she demanded in a soft whisper.

With shaking hands, I did just that, my mouth watering when I caught sight of her pert tits and erect nipples—just begging for a taste.

Her hands were gentle as she cupped my face, pulling me closer to her chest.

"Come on, kitten, you don't just want to look at them, do you? Make your goddess feel good."

I let my tongue trace her nipple, the pattern similar to when she'd when she teased my clit.

There was something different about the way we joined together this time, something gentler. More settled.

The craze from before had lifted. Maybe it was because we had escaped with our lives so many times that we were just tired. Maybe it was finally the fact that we had some time where we wouldn't be interrupted... or maybe it was something more powerful.

Maybe it was something that the violent feelings from before hid.

I brought her nipple into my mouth, sucking gently. She let out a breathy sigh, almost like my actions soothed her. My hand trailed between her legs, teasing her dripping folds.

The way her body reacted to me, even after so many times of being together during our games, still managed to cause pride to swell in my chest.

Slowly, I pushed two fingers into her. Gliding them in, then out lazily.

For now, there was no rush. For most of the night we'd been racing to the finish line for fear of being caught. But in here? It was just the two of us, no one to interrupt.

What a gift.

Her hips met my hand, her light moans filling the space.

"That's a good boy, Kohl," she groaned.

I took my mouth from one nipple to switch to the other but paused before I did so.

"You're so beautiful," I whispered, taking in her flushed face. She had always been beautiful to me, but even more so when she was covered with blood and panting because of the things *I* was doing to her. "I've always thought so. From the moment you first opened your mouth, I was smitten."

She whined when I nibbled on her other nipple and sucked it into my mouth.

"If you keep talking like that, you're gonna make me come too fast," she said with a light laugh.

"Do you like it?" I asked, pulling away from her so I could fully see her as she rode my hand. "When I tell you how crazy I am about you? When I tell you how fucking *obsessed* I am?"

Her cunt fluttering around my fingers was the only answer I needed. Her whimpers music to my ears.

"Yes—"

"Every night," I admitted. "Every night I fucked myself to the image of you. Those nudes—fuck, I was so pissed—but I couldn't help myself."

"You didn't," she gasped, her movements stopping. But I didn't let that stop me. I used my hand to steady her hip while I drove into her.

"I did," I breathed. "Fuck, I imagined so many times being at your feet and licking your cunt while you degraded me. I couldn't get enough of it. I was going crazy just *imagining* how you tasted."

"Stop—*fuck*—I'm gonna—"

She didn't even finish her sentence before her orgasm overtook her. Just like I imagined, her cunt was leaking all over my hand.

"But now I don't have to imagine, do I?" I asked with a wicked smile, bringing my hand up to lick all of her wetness off my fingers.

"Don't get cocky like that again," she warned before forcing my fingers from my mouth and covering my lips with hers.

I moaned into her mouth, tasting myself on her tongue.

She pulled away, spit connecting us. It was so erotic, so embarrassing knowing that this was being livestreamed, but *fuck* did it only make everything that much stronger.

She dropped down beside me and reached for her pants. I did the same, both of us dressing in silence. It wasn't an awkward silence, it was like the sex—comforting, peaceful, because for a little while... it was still just *us*.

She cleared her throat, drawing my eyes.

"Why are you okay with me using you like this?" Vic asked, her voice weary.

Using me.

Yes, it'd been obvious from the beginning. I was nothing more than her guard dog, ready to attack whenever and wherever she commanded.

"It's an honor to be used by you," I whispered. "All I want in life is to see you succeed. To see you happy. If anyone tries to take that from you, I wouldn't hesitate to slit their throat."

"Even family?" she asked, still not looking at me.

"Even *family*," I said. "Anything. You don't even have to say the words. I'll already be there, waiting for my moment to serve you."

She let the silence spread between us before nodding.

"You're the best little pet, *pretty boy*," she praised, making heat burn up the back of my neck.

"I aim to please," I murmured and scooted closer to her.

She let out a light laugh. The slight tension that had built up between us dissipated.

I meant what I said and I wouldn't stop until I proved it to her.

"You can see everything from up here," Vic said, leaning against me. "We're just at the top."

I couldn't help but pause and lean over her. I gave her shoulder a kiss as we looked out the window together.

Then my eyes caught something.

"There they are," I breathed as I looked out the window.

People dressed in yellow seemingly appeared out of nowhere, bagging bodies for clean up.

"I always wondered how they got in and out without anyone seeing," Vic said, leaning closer to me. Her hot breath against my neck made me shiver.

"There are rumors among the Architects," I said, my mind flashing back to all those parties my dad used to throw. I was never allowed near them, but oftentimes I found myself sneaking downstairs to get a sneak peek at what they were talking about. "Some say they are here the entire time, hiding until they find a dead body."

"And others?"

I couldn't stop the smile from spreading across my lips.

"*Tunnels*," I whispered just as the two Vultures I was watching looked around, as if checking if they were being watched. Then they kneeled near a trash can before shimmying it out of the way, and—

"Holy shit," Vic whispered. "They were using them the whole time?"

The two jumped down, taking the body with them.

"We'll hide there," I said. "We'll first find your Hider and then stay in there until the games are over."

"Is that even allowed?" she asked.

I opened my mouth to answer, but there was no need, because

right before our eyes, in a bird mask, ran a victim who had the same idea we did.

"I don't even remember seeing her in the crowd," I murmured.

"She's the one," she said, the conviction in her voice making a shivers run down my spine.

God, I couldn't help but love how bloodthirsty she is.

Vic

Before the Games

I was such a fucking idiot.

Did I really think I could go toe to toe with an *Architect* and nothing would go wrong?

Takeout boxes littered the kitchen as I crouched to feed Bingsoo, the fat white Persian meowing balefully for his dinner.

I knew Hiram had something to do with the accident, but I had no fucking proof. Which meant that I was fucked.

But at the very least, there was one thing I could do. Ditch his shrimp-dicked loser of a son. Because fuck *that*.

I checked the time on my phone and scratched Bingsoo behind the ears.

"Be home soon, bingy-bear," I called, grabbing my keys on my way out the door.

The drive to the bar where I was meeting up with Dylan wasn't far, but it was enough for me to calm my nerves. It's not like I could stop what I'd done at this point anyway—the emails were sent, the graphics were designed, and the final images were already sent to the printers.

God, I loved revenge. Almost more than I was going to love putting my fist right into Dylan's rat-ass face.

I pulled into a parking spot, noticing that Dylan's silver Lexus wasn't parked anywhere yet.

Fine.

At least I wasn't going to have to make a big public scene. I could just wait for him out here.

The press would do the rest for me anyway.

I grabbed a printed photo from the passenger side and crumpled it up, shoving it into my pocket as I climbed out of the car to wait for my soon-to-be ex-boyfriend.

He didn't disappoint, tires screaming into the parking lot about five minutes later. He flashed me a wink as he parked his car, a backward baseball cap perched over his long, dark hair. He'd been growing it out the last few months. In a way, it sorta made him look like Kohl.

If Kohl was a ham-fisted shithead, that is.

"Baby," Dylan said, getting out of his car and coming to meet me. "You look—"

"Let's get one thing straight, dipshit," I snapped, putting my hand into his face and shoving him away from me. "First of all, I'm not your *baby*."

"Vic, what the fuck—"

"Second," I said, my voice raising as I cut him off. "I know it was you who sent my nudes to the press, you fucking—"

"Vic, baby, who the hell put that in your pretty little head? Did that loser Kohl—"

"Third," I was shouting now. "Every hair on Kohl's goddamn cunt is twice the man you'll ever fucking be, so keep their name out of your fucking mouth."

Dylan's face went from pleading to angry in a second, his hand reaching to grab me, but I moved out of the way. "Listen, you little bitch. You were a fun piece of ass for a minute, but I'm not going to let you—"

"Let me?" I laughed, a manic note entering my voice. "Dylan, you haven't been in control of this situation since we started. And you sure as fuck aren't now." I pulled the paper from my pocket and threw it at him, getting into the car and rolling down my window as I turned over the engine.

Dylan caught it, opening it up. His jaw dropped, voice taking on a deathly serious note I'd never heard before. "What the fuck is this, Vic?"

I grinned at him. "A goodbye present. I thought fair was fair, since you sold my nudes to the press, I used yours to make a little *advertisement.*"

"I don't have—you fucking *cunt*—"

"Might not, *baby*," I said, reaching into the passenger's side and throwing a fist full of printed flyers out the window. "But nobody reads the fine print anyway."

The advertisement was simple but extremely effective. Dylan was undoubtedly busting his load after a pathetic two minutes of unskilled thrusting with a splash of text decrying the rise in syphilis and begging the public to use a rubber. As promised, the fine print did state that the image was just a model, but really... no one was going to read that.

What they were going to read was that Dylan Wolff had an STI, which probably meant he had cauliflower cock.

Fuck. You. Bitch.

Dylan jerked forward as if to grab my door, but I threw the car into reverse. "I'll kill you!"

"You can try," I said snidely. "But if memory serves, your family isn't very good at finishing the job, douche weasel. Say hi to your daddy for me, Dylan."

And with that, I was speeding away.

Point Victoria, now I just need to send in my documents, and I'm off to the games.

It'd be pretty fucking hard for Dylan to kill me if I was already dead.

Kohl

I'M SORRY, KOHL. A POINT IS A POINT.

"That's it," I whispered. "I got you, just let go."

My hands gripped onto her hips as she lowered herself, and then with little hesitation, she dropped straight into my arms.

It would be a lie if I said I put her down right away instead of pulling her to me and reveling in the way her body fit perfectly with mine.

I left a kiss on her neck before placing her gently on the ground.

Darkness enveloped us, there were few lights throughout but many were off and the ones that weren't dimly flickered. There was no evidence that anyone had been here before us, even though we had just seen people enter. And eerier silence spread throughout the tunnel the only thing breaking it was our breathing.

The tunnels themselves were cleaner than above ground and wide enough for multiple people to carry bodies through them. The clanging of metal and the sound of rushing steam echoed through-out, giving me the impression that there may also be some access to the underside of rides.

Water dripped from above, but there was nobody above us, so I wasn't quite sure where it came from.

We looked around, trying to figure out if we should follow the tunnel that expanded to the right or to the left of us. On the wall there were painted signs, things like "Ferris Wheel," "House of Mirrors," and "Merry-go-round," in legible white letters and arrows pointing in the corresponding directions.

"Rock-paper-scissors?" Vic asked, a playfulness in her tone.

I shook my head and let out a huff of a laugh.

"One time. I win, we go left," I said.

"Right for me then," she said and lifted a closed fist. "Ready?" I nodded. "Rock...paper...scisso—"

"Fuck, why are you always so good at that," I grumbled as Vic knocked her two fingers against my spread-out hand.

"You're predictable," she said with a laugh and turned down the hallway leading right. "Come on, pup. No time to waste, we got a game to win."

We walked the hallways with silent footsteps, pausing every time we heard so much as a rustle.

We passed the underside of the House of Mirrors and Merry-go-round, each having a ladder up to the surface.

It made it startling clear how insane the level of detail the Architects needed to have in order to not only build these, but have them be used over and over again, no matter how the surface changes.

"I've never seen these on the streams before," Vic whispered as we peeked into what I assumed was the underside of a small lake. There were puddles on the floor, the water sparkling in the darkness, and while most of the carve-out was empty, there were some large boxes on pallets that littered the space.

I checked my tracker quickly. I still had a large number of viewers, three hundred thousand, to be exact. Comments were coming in steadily, all of them talking about the tunnels.

"They haven't shut off our streams yet," I noted, showing her what I was seeing on my tracker.

"Because we bring in too much money," she said with a huff. "Do you know how many ads they could fit on yours alone? For three hundred *thousand* people?"

She had a point. A good one.

We came here for one reason and one reason only, to win. But that didn't mean that the elites who ran the game wouldn't try to milk us for everything we had.

There was a flash in the room. Like someone running. It took me a moment to get my head back in the game, but Vic had already raised her gun and started firing.

The person cursed, and I blinked a few times to try and make them out in the darkness of the room.

They didn't have a mask, but their all-black uniform and tracker told me they were a part of the game. A different person than the victim we saw earlier, but they would do.

I promised I would help Vic with this, and I would damn sure keep it.

"Let me," I said, darting toward the person. They were smaller than me and already panting, with blood splattered all over their faces.

We aren't the first to find you, but we will be the last.

It was almost too easy to tackle them to the ground. They fought like hell, kicking, punching, and swinging their fists at my face, but they were too weak.

For the first time since the games started, I felt like I was in control. I felt like I was in charge of what would happen in this room. And that single-handedly I could win the game for us.

It was an intoxicating, powerful feeling that made a burst of excitement run through me.

This must have been what Dylan felt. I had gotten a glimpse of it when I killed Vic's friend, but it was never like this. Because this time, I was doing it for *her*.

I dragged the young man by his hair to Vic, kicking the back of his knees so he was forced to kneel in front of her. The way her chest puffed as she looked down at him sent heat rushing through my veins straight to my core.

Finally, people would see Victoria the way I did.

Could see the way she was meant to tower over those weaker

than her. To see how good she looked when she was looking down at a squirming, crying coward.

A goddess looking down upon her kingdom, ready to enact her righteous justice

Jealousy flared as Vic placed the gun under his chin, but it was quickly extinguished when her eyes lifted to me with a teasing wink.

Fuck. Even such a simple move threatened to make me a puddle at her feet.

We were in this together. Deity and beloved servant.

"Please," he begged. "We still have time. You don't have to—"

She pushed the gun to his forehead.

"A point is a point, right? Don't take it personally," she said.

I had thought I'd fallen in love with Vic long ago. It was slow at first, when I watched her with her friends or snuck out to see her whenever she had a spare moment from my brother. Then one day it fell all together, and I couldn't *stop* the feelings of warmth in my chest when I looked at her.

I thought *that* had been love.

Laughable.

It was clear to me now that in this moment, holding her enemy still at her feet—ready for her to claim their worthless life and begin the road toward reclaiming everything my family had taken from her, I fell more deeply for her than I could've ever imagined.

All encompassing. *Eternal.*

"Surely you can't miss now," I teased, unable to help myself.

She let out an exaggerated gasp. "Oh, you'll pay for that later."

I didn't say anything, just pushed the man's head harder into her gun. I moved to the side, making sure I wasn't in the line of fire.

She tilted the gun slightly before firing. The powerful shot reverberating off the walls, silencing even my most insistent thoughts.

The feeling of the bullet forcing its way through the man as I held him was something I'd never experienced before, but the sigh she let out afterward made it all worth it.

I pushed the body to the ground and took a step closer to her.

"Congratulati—"

A shrill sound came from her tracker. We both looked down at it.

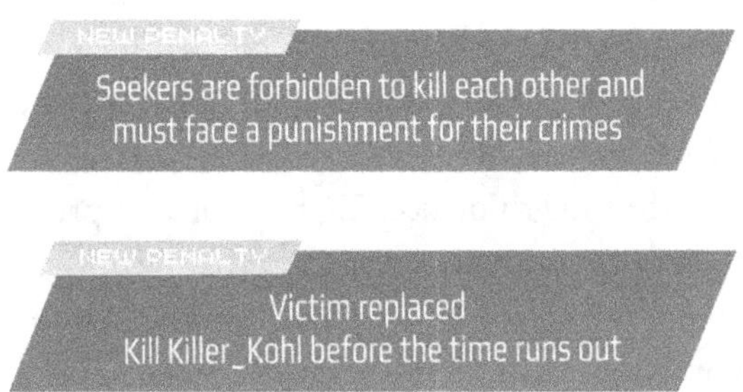

My heart stopped in my chest.

"What?" I asked. "No, that was a victim—"

I looked down to the supposed killer. They didn't have a mask. *Where the hell—?*

I stormed to the corners of the room, peeking behind the pallets of boxes. I couldn't hold in my gasp when I caught the bird mask and dead body crumpled to the ground, blood pooling underneath.

Next to the body lie a bright red, glowing Seeker mask.

"Shit, Vic, the Hider is—Vic?"

She was staring at the body on the ground, unmoving.

I took a few strides back to her but paused when her head slowly swung up to mine. Her mind was spinning. I could see it in her eyes. She was thinking of a way to get us out of this.

"Vic, it's okay, we will find a way," I promised and took a step forward.

The arm that was holding her gun swung up... pointing right at me.

No. She wouldn't. Why?

Why are you letting me use you like this? Her words rang through my mind.

I stuck by what I said... but I'd always envisioned myself by her side. There to help her. Serve her.

But I never thought–

"Vic?" I asked. "What—" I swallowed the knot in my throat. "What are you doing?"

I held my hands up and slowly fell to my knees.

I wasn't going to run. Not from her, I *couldn't.*

A pain so powerful ripped through me that it caused my breath to catch and my eyes to tear. I wanted more time with her. But there was no way I would stop her.

Not when the only thing keeping her from her prize was *me.*

"Vic—please listen to me. I promised that I wou—"

She took a few steps forward, the hurt and pain clouding my mind made way for fear. I didn't tell my body to move, but before I knew it my hands were on the floor, dragging myself away from her.

Tratourius body. My mind wanted to sit still. Wanted to wait patiently for her to shoot me and get it over with.

But my heart hurt. Hurt so bad that my body acted on it's own.

"Please," I begged. "Don't do this. We mean something to each other, right? You can trust me to—"

"I have to win this, Kohl," she said, her voice sounding colder than I'd ever heard. "This is what they do. They put us against each other. You know that all too well."

I know! I wanted to scream. But the words died on my tongue. Instead, panic filled me.

"But we are in this together!" I cried, my throat aching at the desperation in my voice. It was no use. I couldn't hold back my fear or the pain her actions caused.

"No," she said. "It's never been *us* together. Ever since the crash, it's been me and me alone, and I won't let my dreams fall aside because my heart is weak."

I didn't know what to say. All I could do was beg that the love of my life wouldn't put a bullet in my brain.

I can't do it. I can't be her savior. I thought I would do anything for her, but this—

"Victoria," I said. "Please. I know it seems like you don't have any options, but you do. I can hel—"

"I'm sorry, Kohl," she said. "A point is a point."

Vic

The light flickered overhead, the soft buzzing that followed the fluorescents setting my teeth on edge.

Kohl's eyes were wide with betrayal, which made my heart beat as quick as a rabbit in my chest, my breath coming in quick pants.

The instructions were clear. Kill them or lose. The sun would be up soon, I was running out of time.

"Please, Vic—"

I took a deep breath, trying to still my shaking hands as I pressed the gun to Kohl's forehead. Slowly, deliberately, as I held their terrified eyes, I adjusted the stained bracelet on my wrist.

We both knew someone was pulling the strings of this game. Someone who wasn't going to let their Legacy die with my finger on the trigger.

Kohl's eyes followed the motion, catching on the sun-shaped charm as the lights went off.

It was as good as I could do without totally fucking over my last-ditch plan.

If anyone realized that I wasn't willing to—

"Stop!" Hiram's voice boomed, followed by a slam and the sound of feet shuffling over the concrete.

I squinted in the dim light provided from our masks.

When the lights came back on, blinding me momentarily, I had to blink to make sense of what I was seeing.

Hiram Wolff, his hair askew and suit rumpled like he'd had to fight his way in here, stood panting in our tight corridor. What'd looked to be a solid wall before had slid open to reveal separate tunnels.

No wonder they hadn't turned off our cameras.

The tunnels we *thought* we'd infiltrated must've been just another setup they'd put here to see who was daring enough to go for an adventure. The *real* tunnels hidden within plain sight, just beyond the walls.

No matter, it wasn't the knowledge of the game that made a burst of euphoric satisfaction rise in my chest. It was that Hiram looked positively *desperate*.

Good.

I'd waited what felt like a lifetime for this moment. For him to finally realize that *I*, the person whose life he *destroyed*, would be the one to do the very same to him.

"You think this will change anything, little girl?" Hiram spat, taking a slow step toward me.

He was panicking, trying to stall. I could see right through him, but I *doubted* he could see anything that was going on inside my mind.

That was the thing about victors like him.

Their heads got so big after the games. Made to believe they were the chosen ones. Special. A lie reinforced by the publicity they got when they entered society as "heroes."

On the outside, it looked like they were just living their lives. But it was a lie, they were in this fucking arena as much as I was. They never fucking left. Never stopped playing.

Unlike my father. He'd tried his hardest to forget about what he had to do to survive. Not that it'd done him any good. Here we were, still playing.

No, that wasn't his fault. It was Hiram's. He'd dragged us all back in.

And now he was paying the price.

"Oh, I think it'll change a lot," I said breezily, nudging Kohl's head with the muzzle of the gun. "But somehow I have the feeling you don't *really* think that I'll end your Legacy here and now." I clicked my tongue and trailed the gun down Kohl's face, hovering it just over their lips.

God, they'd been so beautiful when I defiled them with a gun.

Kohl's eyes widened, and their eyebrows pushed together. There was something beautiful going on in their head as they slowly put the pieces together.

I raised an eyebrow and opened my mouth, miming for them to do the same.

They did, allowing me to tease the gun at their lips and tongue before placing it back on their forehead.

It was the twinge of their lips and the relaxation of their body that told me my little pet had finally caught up.

That's right, Kohl. Play with me, baby.

"You've already taken my son—isn't that enough?" Hiram asked. "You know the pain of losing family, don't make a mistake you will regret."

A feral smile split my features. "What's there to regret? You've taken *everything* from me. Why the fuck should I give up the opportunity to do the same to you?"

"Vic, please—" Kohl begged, the fear in their eyes had turned to something lighter. An excited flash in their eyes made heat flush up the back of my neck.

Filthy little freak.

Truthfully, if I'd truly wanted to kill Kohl, I'd had more than enough opportunity.

I knocked off the safety, putting my finger over the trigger.

"Wait! Wait! Okay, let's *talk*!" Hiram shouted. "Money! It's the money you want, right?"

"How about two parents and a life where I didn't have to

become *this*?" I said coolly. "How about a mom who wasn't so hung up on you that she left me out to dry?"

"That wasn't my fault. You think your mother was the only one who couldn't stand what their life had become after we were separated?" There was a twinge to his voice, something more vulnerable than I thought someone like him would ever be capable of.

But it was too little, too late.

Hiram, just like me, had made his bed. But unlike him, I knew what I had to do to make my dream become a reality. He acted out of fear, cowardice.

I acted out of sheer revenge.

"That seems like a you problem," I hissed, my eyes flicking down to Kohl as the lights started to flicker again. "Maybe in the next life we'll meet again, kitten."

KOHL

BEFORE THE GAMES

This moment was supposed to be every young adult's dream.

After twelve years of work, I'd walk across the stage, smile at the crowd, and go off with my diploma in hand to start my new life.

So why did it all feel so fucking *shallow*?

Why had it been so hard to walk up that stage and look at the crowd with the smile I knew would be plastered over the gossip blogs and magazines before the day was out?

I knew my role. I'd been used to the attention, despite not really enjoying it. It was tolerable.

But after the wreck? It just felt downright *disgusting*.

Father was in the crowd somewhere, though he would sneak out soon. Before, I'd written off his aversion to crowds as PTSD. But now I knew what it really was, he just didn't give a fuck.

No one who'd done what he did could have a shred of humanity left.

I walked across the stage, the cheer from the crowd making my ears ring. I forced a fake smile on my face. The consequences for fucking around would be worse now that I was an adult. No more watchful teachers to ask about bruises and wait for feeble excuses. I walked across the stage, feeling like my shoes were made of lead, and put on a good show for the cameras.

I could barely make out the principal's face, flashes of the cameras in the crowd were too bright. I fought my instincts to pull away when he grabbed my hand.

This photo op was longer than the others, no doubt trying to get a historic picture of a Legacy with an *Architect father* before their debut.

Not like my whole graduating class wasn't full of them. Over half the student body had a winner in their immediate family.

When it got too awkward to stay anymore, I nodded to him and walked off stage back to my seat.

I kept waiting for it to hit me. Kept waiting for the euphoria of *graduating* to fill me... but as I watched my classmates cheer and whisper excitedly to each other, I couldn't feel a damn thing.

That was until a prickle at the back of my neck pulled my attention from the stage and to the far right, my eyes widening as they landed on a real life ghost.

Someone I hadn't seen in *months*.

Vic.

She was hardly recognizable in a pair of baggy jeans and a loose T-shirt—long gone the short skirts of her cheer uniform or the cute little sundresses she used to wear—her hair pulled up into a messy ponytail.

She was tired, that much I could tell from my distance. Especially given she didn't have a speck of makeup on to cover her dark circles. But none of that mattered, not really. When she met my eyes, I couldn't stop my stomach from giving the flip it always had when Vic was around.

"Congratulations, Kohl," she mouthed.

I grinned, standing to close the distance between us, but she put her hand up to stop me.

Her lips pushed together, a hint of a smile playing at them before she turned and disappeared into the crowd.

"Graduates, you may now turn your tassel to the left, and—" the principal started.

I zoned him out, too focused on watching Vic as she left.

Cheers broke out, hurting my ears. Caps were thrown all around me. Friends bounded toward each other, jumping into each other's arms.

Everyone was celebrating... everyone but me.

I turned back to where Father had been sitting to see if he was still there, but just like I'd guessed, his seat was empty.

I don't even know why I had bothered to show up to the party.

It had been an invite from another Legacy that I had barely talked to through my entire high school career.

At least there was free booze.

I leaned back on the wall, the extravagant wallpaper feeling sticky against my exposed arms. The place was packed with new graduates, not just from our school, but it would seem any Legacy within at least ten miles was packed into the mansion.

The pathetic show of something that wasn't even theirs to begin with caused my mouth to sour. I took a swing of lukewarm beer I had been nursing for nearly an hour.

I should have left within the first twenty minutes, right after I heard the first loud declaration that a drunk teen would be joining the next Hide and Seek game.

People cheered around him, stocked him up on alcohol, and he was shuffling around, words slurring, a mere half an hour later. I was sure that by that time he'd probably be passed out in one of the rooms.

Definitely *not* someone who would make it through, even as a Seeker.

I hated watching them. Hated that they cheered as people swore their lives away for the measly chance at winning big. Most people didn't. Most people are delivered, body bags zipped up and bloodied to be dropped on their parents' porch in the wee hours of the morning.

But no matter how disgusting I found it, I stayed. I stayed because, just like them, I hoped for the slim chance that I too would win big.

My prize that night came wrapped in a loose-fitting dress. One that showed just enough of her curves to make my mouth water. Her hair had been placed up in a messy ponytail, dark makeup covering her eyes. She paired it with stockings that caused my entire body to heat.

She carried a drink with her, careful not to let it get hit by the various moving bodies, and she pushed through the crowd.

She must have felt my eyes because they darted around right before finding exactly where I was.

In that moment, pure panic filled me. I didn't want to scare her off. All I wanted was to go up to her and pull her into my arms.

She had broken up with Dylan after the crash. Something he complained to me relentlessly about. Something that made the shimmering prize at the end of the tunnel seem that much more attainable.

To my surprise, she headed straight toward me. I stood up, clearing my throat and smoothing down my wrinkled T-shirt.

"Congrats," she said, her voice just barely audible over the pumping bass that filled the house.

"What?" I asked slightly louder, not at all missing what she was saying but trying to do anything to get her closer to me.

A smile tugged at the corner of her lips, causing the tension in my shoulders to subside, only to make my body freeze when she took a step closer, invading my space and leaning up to whisper in my ear.

I leaned down slightly to make it easier for her.

"*Congratulations,* Kohl," she said, then pulled away to give me a smile that didn't quite match her eyes.

"Congrats to you as well," I said, hitting her plastic cup with my glass bottle. "I know we're both ready to get out of there and move on to the next biggest thing. Have you finalized your schedule yet?"

Her smile dropped.

"I still have time," she said, her eyes falling to my chest. "After my dad's crash, I've had some time to think about what I want in life."

"Like breaking up with Dylan?" I asked, raising my brow at her. It was an attempt to lighten the mood, but it didn't stop the feeling of dread that had accumulated in my stomach.

I didn't like how her face had hardened when she uttered those words.

Her eyes searched mine. "Yes," she said pointedly. "Actually, that's a big part of the reason I came here."

I cocked my head to the side. "Because of Dylan?" I asked.

She rolled her eyes.

"To say goodbye," she said. Before I could register her words, she stood on her tiptoes and brushed her lips across mine. I was almost too shocked to move, but boy did I scream at my limbs to fucking do *something*.

I wrapped my arms around her, careful not to spill anything on her, and deepened the kiss.

My mind told me to stop. Told me that I should give her space. That I should let her grieve. That the person who was here kissing me was not doing this because she wanted *me* but because she needed a release.

But *fuck* did I want to be her release.

She clings to me, and our tongues slid across each other. Her hand tangled in my hair and pulled me close so she could pull my bottom lip into her mouth and sucked—

I gasped as liquid splashed all over my right shoulder. Vic and I pulled away, her cup not empty and the contents all over my shirt.

It caused the fabric to stick to my skin in the most uncomfortable ways.

"Oh shit, Kohl. I'm *so* sorry—"

"It's okay," I said quickly, not wanting to ruin the moment. "You stay here, I'll go clean up in the bathroom."

Before waiting for her confirmation, I high-tailed it toward the guest bathroom. By some miracle, it was empty.

Goddamn it, why does the world just have it out for me and Vic?

I cursed under my breath as I tore the shirt off, threw it in the sink, and doused it with water. My skin had a sticky film over it that caused me to shudder.

Then, as if things couldn't get worse, there was a knock at the door.

"Just a minute!" I yelled, not even bothering to conceal my frustration.

"It's me," Vic said from the other door. "I snagged a shirt from one of the bedrooms, let me in."

I stilled, my eyes coming to look at myself in the mirror.

My hair was disheveled from her hands running through it. My lips were puffy from the kiss. My gaze traveled down to my bare chest, the two almost identical scars feeling far too dark in the bathroom light.

Alone. In a bathroom.

I didn't let the panic consume me. Instead, I turned right to the door, yanked it open, and pulled Vic in.

"Thanks," I said, giving her a smile. "Sorry, I thought you were someone trying to steal the bathroom from me."

She gave me a smile that caused my chest to warm and handed me a dark gray shirt. "I think it's her dad's."

I shrugged and placed it on the counter so I could continue to clean myself up.

"It'll do," I said and turned back to the sink. I grabbed one of the hand towels, wet it, and wiped it across the skin of my chest.

The weight of her gaze on me was hard to ignore. So was her reflection as she stared at me through the bathroom mirror.

There was one time when I caught her looking at me like that. I had been coming out of the shower only to run into her without any bottoms on.

The memory caused my entire body to heat.

"If I didn't know any better..." I trailed, reaching across my side to get my back. "That look tells me you did this on purpose to get me alone."

The smile that spread across her face caused my heart to skip a beat.

"And if I did?" she asked, taking a step forward.

I turned back toward her, looking down at her as she closed the space between us.

"I would ask why," I murmured. "I would ask why here and why now."

"Because it's a goodbye," she said. "And I have been holding both of us back for far too long. Let me indulge a little, won't you?"

She leaned forward, her mouth level with my nipple. Her pink tongue darted out to swipe against it.

I couldn't conceal my whine. Her eyes lit up at the noise.

"Do you want that, Kohl?" she asked, her lips tilting. "To indulge a little with me?"

She stood on her tiptoes once again, but this time I was faster. I pulled her to me and forced her lips to mine.

Her gasp allowed me to deepen the kiss. To force my tongue in and explore her mouth like I had always dreamed to.

Back in the crowded party, I had only gotten just a taste. But this time, I let myself take advantage of what she had been offering.

How long has it been since the first time I had fantasized about squeezing her hips and forcing them to mine? How long had it been since I fantasized about the taste of her?

Her body fit perfectly against mine. Just like I knew it would.

Our movements are in sync. Hungry with the need to devour each other. Making me come to the shocking realization that Vic wanted me as much as I wanted her.

Her arms wrapped around my shoulders, only to tangle her hands in my hair and force it back so hard I let out a whine. She broke the kiss, looking at me through hooded eyes. The intensity of her gaze caused me to shudder.

She licked her lips before her mouth, came into contact with my neck, and then she sucked hard on the sensitive skin. Hard enough to cause heat to flow through me.

I dug my fingers into her soft skin, trying to keep myself contained.

"Fuck," I moaned. "I've wanted you for so long."

"What are you going to do with me now that you have me?" she asked, the flirtation obvious in her tone.

Her words caused my stomach to flip. "Worship you."

The seductive tilt of her lips caused my pussy to clench. I was scared of the fantasies I could see playing behind her eyes, but *fuck* would I drop to my knees right in that moment to prove just how much I was willing to bend to her will.

"Lift me up on the counter," she ordered.

I didn't think twice before I reached down, grabbed her thighs, and forced them around my waist. I turned us around so I could plop her on the counter.

My hands pushed up her dress over her ass. My eyes traveled down to her stocking-covered thighs.

She trailed her hand down my arm until she grabbed my wrist and brought it in between her legs.

"You feel that?" she asked. She used my hand to trail her core through the fabric of the stockings, making it crystal clear that she had not been wearing any underwear underneath.

The only thing separating us was a thin layer of stockings.

I let her guide my hand just the way she wanted. Let her run my fingers through her folds. Teasing her entrance before moving to her clit.

"I wonder what else you have planned in that wicked little head of yours," I murmured, putting more pressure on her clit. She let out a breathy sigh.

"I'm afraid I may scare you off if I'm too loose with my words," she said, then spread her legs for me. "Do you want to taste?"

My mouth watered at the thought.

How had I gotten so lucky that Vic was here offering herself to me like this?

It caused my mind to whirl, but I didn't hesitate. It had been my dream for so long to be between her legs like this. To bring her pleasure. To watch as she fell apart in front of me.

I clumsily pulled her legs and ass to the edge of the counter so that I could lean down right where she wanted me.

Her wet pussy was so clear through the stockings, the thin fabric all but mocking me, showing me that I had gotten so close yet not close enough to actually touch.

I kept my gaze locked on her as I hooked my arms under her legs, keeping her in place so that I could lean forward and trail my tongue from entrance to clit, moaning at her taste.

My back was going to start aching by the time I was going to bring her to an orgasm, but I didn't care. Not when one of her hands came to push my head closer, the other pushed against the mirror behind her so she could grind down on my tongue harder.

She gave me the illusion of control. She let me make a mess of her as I lavished her clit with attention. As I circled her folds with my tongue. As I tried to push through the thin fabric into her entrance. But the entire time, she had my head locked right where she needed it. If I had gone too slow, she would buck against me.

I listened to her moans, pinpointing the little things that would make her shudder with pleasure.

I was consumed with the way she writhed against me. Obsessed with how her moans filled the small bathroom.

Unable to take it any longer, I shifted her legs over my shoulders so I could use my free hand to rip the stockings right over her cunt.

A loud tearing sound cut through her moans.

When I looked up at her, her gaze was still hooded, but she was watching me with an almost curiosity to see what I was going to do next.

I licked her pussy again. *Once. Twice,* before I fastened my lips to her clit. Now that it was unobstructed, it was easier for me to grab a hold of. I forced two fingers inside of her, pumping them slowly.

The little jerks of her hips caused satisfaction to run through me. She was chasing the pleasure *I was* bringing her.

"Harder, Kohl," she moaned. "Be a good boy and make me come."

Heat licked my spine.

I wanted nothing more than for her to say that again.

I sucked her clit into my mouth harder, using my teeth to scrape at the sensitive bundle of nerves. I picked up my pace on my thrusts.

Her breathing was getting heavy. Her movements were uncontrolled. She pulled down the neck of her dress, baring her breasts, and removed her hand from my hair so she could pinch her erect nipples.

She was going to come. *I* was going to make her come.

I could see it in her eyes. The way her breathing stopped. The way she tilted her head back and screwed her eyes shut as the first waves of her orgasm ran through her.

Her mouth opened with no sounds coming out as her pussy convulsed on my fingers. I sucked harder, fucked her without restraint.

I wanted her orgasm to last as long as possible. I wanted to hear those moans come from her mouth. I wanted to hear her—

"Oh god, Kohl, *please* keep going."

Who was I to say no to a goddess like her?

I couldn't stop, even if I wanted to.

Her command had done something to me that I never felt before in my life.

She wanted more, so I would give it to her.

I forced another finger into her and curled them. I removed my mouth from her clit and used my other hand to rub hard circles in it.

I was fixated on the way her pussy convulsed around me. On the way, her cum leaked from her. On just how easily her pussy sucked me in.

She pushed her legs off my shoulders. Her slim fingers grabbing my neck and forcing me up so she could crush her mouth to mine again.

I moaned into her mouth. She kept one hand on her throat as the other slipped between us and forced itself into my pants.

"Keep going," she warned against my mouth, her teeth biting into my bottom lip.

Even against her warning, I paused when her hand came into contact with my aching cunt.

I let my forehead rest against hers, unable to keep kissing her as her fingers confidently stroked me.

"I *can't*," I forced out like a whine. I tried to keep up the pace but as her strokes grew bolder, harder, and as she used my wetness to trail up to my clit before rubbing horizontal strokes against the aching bundle of nerves... I began to lose myself.

"You can't come so easily, Kohl," she teased. "I barely even touched you."

"Your pleasure feeds mine," I gasped out as my hips jerked against her skilled fingers.

"You made me come like a good boy," she said. "So I thought you deserved a little present. Who knew you're so sensitive?"

As if to prove her point, she pinched my clit, pulling a deep moan from me.

There was a loud knocking on the door.

"Hurry up!" someone yelled from the outside.

"Yeah, *Kohl*," Vic teased. "Hurry it up."

I cursed under my breath and tried to focus on bringing her to another orgasm, but the way she was playing me was too intoxicating. I buried my head in between her shoulders, biting into her neck as a tingling heat spread through my body.

The position made it harder on her arm, but she didn't pause in her assault on my clit.

"Come for me, Kohl," she whispered into my ear.

I groaned as my orgasm shot through me faster than it ever had before. My body shook with the ferocity of it. I whined against her, attempting to push through my own pleasure to continue fucking her.

"Harder, Kohl, *faster*," she ordered. "You don't want to make the people wait any longer."

Her voice was breathy, her pussy tightening around my fingers. She was so wet it caused my fingers to slip into her easily. She may have put on the front that she wasn't affected, but I knew better.

"Tell me," I gasped and lifted my face to watch as another orgasm reared its head. "Tell me how much you've been waiting for this. Tell me how much better it feels with me."

Her eyes widened, but her face gave almost nothing away. Too bad her pussy told me how much she liked those words.

I gave her a wicked smile. Slowing my pace and using my knuckles to apply more pressure to her clit.

"People are waiting—"

"I don't give a damn," I hissed. "Tell me what I want to hear."

Her groan sent a thrill through me. She was just on the cusp of her orgasm. With just the slightest bit more pressure, it would explode inside her. Her body was already shaking with the intensity of it.

She leaned her head back onto the mirror, her lips so close to mine.

"I've always wanted you, Kohl," she whispered. "Every time I had to take care of myself, I *always* thought of you."

I lunged forward, capturing her lips with mine and pushing her into her orgasm.

I swallowed her cries, moaned against her as her cunt fluttered around me.

The knocking on the door sounded again, but this time, both of us ignored it.

"This isn't goodbye," I gasped after pulling away from her. We removed our hands from each other, but I kept close, not wanting to break the spell that had come over us. "Promise me you won't do anything reckless."

Her eyes searched mine. There was a sorrow in them that caused my heart to shatter in my chest.

"*Please*," I begged.

"I won't," she whispered, her eyes darting to the side. I cupped her cheeks, gently pulling her gaze back to mine.

"I will support you through anything, remember?" I asked. "But *please* stick with your plan, okay?"

"It's gone," she whispered.

"What's gone?" I asked. Her lower lip trembled.

"My college fund," she said. "It's all gone. Used it to try and keep Dad alive. He can't even breathe on his own, Kohl."

The hurt in her voice caused my chest to clench. Images of my father's beat-up car flashed through my mind. I couldn't help the guilt that crashed over me.

If she had never gotten with Dylan, would things have turned out differently?

I should have tried harder to pull them apart instead of feeding into my own obsession with her. Tried to do anything to get her away from us.

And now, we took away everything for her. *How could I possibly ever repay her for what we have stolen?*

"I'll figure something out," I vowed. Her eyes shot toward me, hope flashing through them. "I will, just give me time. Remember our promise."

She nodded slowly.

"Here," she said, taking one of the bracelets off her wrist. I hadn't fully noticed them when she came in, but now that we were close enough, I could make out the threaded material with a small, half-heart dangling from it.

My breath caught in my throat as she put it on me.

"Is this a friendship bracelet?" I asked, my throat tightening.

"Something to remember our promises to each other," she said, showing me hers. Then she guided her charm to mine, and they snapped together, forming a heart.

"I'll never forget," I vowed. She gave me a smile that didn't quite reach her eyes, like she knew what was going on in my mind.

I owed her this much. A way for her to get her life back together... but in order to do that, I had to break a promise.

VIC

WE HAD BEEN CUT OFF.

I turned on my heels, firing a shot at Hiram. The sound ripped through the room as the bullet hit the stone behind him.

I wasn't aiming to kill, and the shot was far off, but it was enough to cause Hiram to freeze. As if on instinct, he put his hands up, showing he wasn't a threat.

Hilarious, really. After all, it was his crimes in the past that caused us to end up right where we were.

"How many points do you think killing an Architect is worth, Wolff?" I asked, taking a step closer to Hiram. Excitement flared through me. *This was it. Everything I'd ever wanted.*

Kohl let out a breathy laugh as they stood behind me. I heard the sound of them brushing the dirt off their pants. A nonchalant move that made it obvious just how much they despised his father.

There was no rush to save him. Not that they could.

"Enough to win a game for sure. Can you imagine what the views would be like for that?" Kohl said.

I didn't take my eyes off Hiram as I twisted my wrist to get a look at my tracker.

In the corner, where the number of viewers normally were, was a big, red zero. No way all viewers would have fled, *especially* when things were just getting good.

We had been cut off.

The Company would do anything to save its ass in order to continue bringing in obscene money for this country and themselves.

"It would seem like the place you've dedicated your life to is cutting ties," I mused, making a show of aiming my gun right at Hiram's chest. "How does it feel? Knowing that no one is coming for you?"

The gravity of the situation seemed to dawn on him then. His eyes widened and his face turned impossibly red. He looked like he was about to blow and I couldn't wait to get a front row seat.

"You sneaky little—"

"Uh oh, I wouldn't say something you might *regret*," I said playfully, waving my gun.

"Kohl," he growled, his eyes shifting to the figure behind me. "Please, talk some sense into her!"

"You almost killed her father," Kohl said. "I saw your car that night. You know you ruined her life?"

"All of it," I said, anger boiling under my skin. I couldn't take it any more. All of the pent up anger. The sadness. The grief. It was too much. "You took it all from me. Every penny drained from my accounts so I could keep his husk of a body still alive. And for what, jealousy? Pitiful revenge for my mother picking someone other than yo—"

"He deserved it!" Hiram's rage was palpable. His voice bounced off the walls and struck my chest. "If he really cared for her, he would have noticed the signs! If she had just kept her promise to me, I would have seen it! She would still be alive today!"

"So your answer to that was trying to *murder* him?!" My voice tore at my throat, all the pain and anger was coming out of me, bursting through the seams. My body was shaking with the force of trying to keep it contained.

"It had to be done!" he spat. "Don't you want revenge for her? Don't you want to make the man who made you lose your mother pay?"

I stepped forward, my hand shaking as I pointed the gun at his head.

"She never loved my father or me," I hissed. "She was passive. Never once caring about me *or* him. Sometimes I even doubted if she was my real mother. Her death was a fucking godsend. It reminded me that with or without her, my life was the same. At first I mourned, but you know what really made me want to kill you?"

He stayed silent, his eyes narrowing at me.

"That fact that it was *your* name she called out on her deathbed." My voice broke at the end. The memory still haunted me. It wasn't me or dad she cared about. *Just him.* "I couldn't help but replay it in my mind over and over again, and once the sting of her death wore off, you know what the first thing I did was?"

Realization dawned on him. His eyes widened, and his jaw fell slack.

"You tried to whore yourself out to my son," he breathed.

"Don't you fucking talk like that to her," Kohl barked, their hand coming to grip my shoulder. *Like a good guard dog.*

"You're right," I said with a laugh. "But somehow you were a step ahead of me."

It was Hiram's turn to let out a bitter laugh that caused my insides to twist.

How could he still be so evil, even with all the odds stacked against him?

"I enjoyed it," he said through laughs. "I replay it in my head. The moment your sorry excuse for a father realized what I was doing. Better yet, when he saw my face? Ha! I'll remember it for the rest of my life."

I fired the gun, aiming for his face, but it flew right past it.

Kohl stepped forward, their face hard.

"Don't!" Hiram growled. "I'm your father, Kohl, for fuck's sake, we share the same blood! Stop her!"

KOHL

FOREVER BROKEN.

"It doesn't matter if we share the same blood or not," I growled, closing the space between us. "You're a fucking disgrace. You hid behind your title, ruining lives for something that happened in the games. About someone who wouldn't even look twice at you. Don't you realize how fucking stupi—"

His hand shot out, squeezing my throat. His face twisted with anger. His eyes were wide, and his breathing came out in pants.

I had seen my dad angry before. Angry at me. Angry at my brother. Angry at his job.

But this was something completely different.

Father wasn't just angry, he was furious. He was hurt.

"You wouldn't understand," he spat. "You're a spoiled fucking brat that only knows how to whine and complain. You entered the games and were supposed to prove yourself to the world, but instead you went and fucked it all up."

"I fucked it up?" I choked out as I tried to push him away. His arm was shaking with the ferocity of the grip he had on me. "You were a *jealous,* weak man that murdered an innocent father and ruined Vic's life just because you couldn't get what you want—"

"You and your brother are a fucking stain on my life," he seethed. "I should have ended it as soon as I knew that whore was pregnant with you. I thought I could pretend. Thought I could create the perfect Legacy family. Raise kids that would become the perfect clones of myself. But you've only disappointed me."

It became hard to breathe. Tears filled my eyes, and the strength left my limbs.

What hurt even more was the fact that Father didn't care about us. Not me. Not Dylan. And sure as hell not Vic.

He claimed to do what he did out of love. Because in another world, my father knew how to love someone. But just like everything else in this world, after the games, that too became twisted and gnarled, turning into something horrific. And nothing could ever bring you back to the person you were once the games were done.

You were forever changed. Forever broken.

And for what?

It was a cruel realization. To look back on my life growing up. To see how hard Dylan and I had tried to make him love us when all he wished was to use us for his own gain.

How many times had he looked at us, wishing our mother was someone else? How many times had he fantasized wrapping his hands around our throats while we were sleeping, just like he was now, so he could take back the mistake he made all those years ago?

"I hate you," I forced out.

He gave me a bitter smile, a laugh falling from his snarling lips.

"Not more than I *hate* you."

Hands wrapped around my waist at the same time people dressed in bright yellow grabbed my father and pulled him away from me. He tried to fight them, yelling over his shoulder and twisting in their arms, but it just made more of them show up.

Coughs racked my body as I collapsed into Vic. My chest twisting in pain as I tried to gulp for air. She made soothing sounds as she lowered us both to the cold ground.

"What's it like, Wolff?" Vic yelled as Father struggled against the vultures as they tried to pick him apart. "To have your own, perfectly molded child turn against you? How does it feel to have everything you ever dreamed of stolen from you?"

"You little fucking—"

"Get ready for jail, Wolff. I heard they *love* Architects in there!" she goaded.

One of the men in yellow slammed his hand over Father's mouth before forcing him back into the secret door he came from.

"Let's not incriminate ourselves anymore," one of the men grunted.

The door slammed closed after them, leaving us alone in the bowels of the arena with nowhere else to go but up.

A pinging from my tracker called my attention down. My heart stopped in my chest when I saw that my viewership was in the hundreds and my rank was—

"Second to last?" Vic yelled, her voice echoing through the room.

"At least you're not last," I said, giving her a smirk and showing her mine. She let out a gasp.

"Kohl, oh no, what do we—"

"We go up," I said, stretching my hand out to her. "That's all we can do."

Vic

Before the Games

The smell of stale beer and cigarettes drifted down the hall as I made my way toward the light seeping under the door of my dad's study.

As much as I hated to admit it, since Mom died, he hadn't been the same. Spending long hours alone in his office instead of watching shitty reality TV with me or cooking dinner together in the evenings.

While Mom had been sick, and even before, Dad had been my rock. But now? He was just so... sad.

Unreachable in his grief in a way that a kid shouldn't have to feel about their parent. Especially not while enrollment was drawing nearer. Preseason interviews would start soon with the rest of the Legacies, and despite my insistence that I wasn't going to enter—I had to admit I was tempted.

There were expectations as a Legacy, and even though my mom was kind of a piece of shit now that she was *gone,* my inner child was struggling with ways to earn her approval from beyond the grave.

I pushed the door open with my free hand, a plate of dinner in the other.

My dad was sitting at his desk, a glass thing with metal legs that stood before a wall of books and achievements. Indicators of a full life rendered suddenly empty with the loss of his partner.

The bitch didn't even value him, and here he was mourning her.

He was folded over the desktop, his cheek pressed into the glass as he stared at a family photo, empties piled on the workspace beside him and littering the floor.

It hurt to see him like this. My dad was always a pretty normal, happy guy—this person who replaced him after we buried Mom was practically a stranger to me.

"You hungry?" I asked hopefully, nudging the plate until it rested against his arm. "I made your favorite, chicken carbonara."

He sighs, his eyes still on that fucking photograph.

I want to throw it across the room, to beg him to come back to me.

Losing my mom was one thing, but if I lost my dad too—I didn't know if I could take it.

"You know," he slurred, his voice raspy with disuse. "I met Lydia in the games."

I sighed. "I know."

"She was a Ghost—our event was Hide and Seek. I found her a couple times, nearly killed her."

I'd heard this story a hundred times before, but something in the way Dad's talking makes me take notice. I climb into the chair across from his desk, bringing my knees up to my chest. "Why didn't you?"

"Couldn't catch her," he admits. "Of course, now I think it's horrifying. That's the thing about the games, when you're in the arena, you lose all sense of yourself. Some people never really come back from that."

He turns the photo toward me, and my eyebrows raise. I'd been expecting the family portrait that'd sat on his desk the last couple of years, taken just before Mom got sick. But instead it's an image, pulled directly from a newspaper, of my father, mother, and a man I didn't recognize, a championship cup held high above my father's head where he stands in the middle.

"It's like they never work out how to get back to the person they were before they entered. Killing people, even when you have no choice, has a cost. It taints you, makes you *wrong*."

"Dad, you aren't—"

"*Wolff* was like that. We were best friends when we entered, laughed about how we'd spend our money when we were done. But everything changed when I won instead of him. He never expected —" He laughs, dragging himself to sit with a hiccup. "He never saw me as much of a threat, but that's what made me such a good competitor, Vic. They never saw me coming. Scrawny thing I was, Hiram didn't think I had a chance of outranking him. But then *I did*."

"Why are you telling me all this now?" I asked softly. "What difference does it make?"

"Because you don't deserve to have the only parent you have left lying to you."

I shake my head. "Dad, Mom never gave a fuck—"

"Your mother was deeply in love with someone else and was forced into a political marriage of which you are the result of, and no matter how you feel about it, you won't fucking disrespect her."

It was like being slapped across the face, the way that his words stung. No wonder she'd always been distant. I'd spent my entire life blaming myself, working ten times harder than everyone else in my life just to please her, but the cards were stacked against me from the start.

"She was having an affair," Dad said, the sadness and anger combining in his voice to shake. "I knew, I've always known, but I loved her, Victoria. I wanted her to be happy. Even if that was in secret. Even if that wasn't with *me*."

"Who?" I choke, trembling with the effort to stay in my seat. It wasn't like I could choke the life out of a ghost anyway.

Dad's eyes slipped to the photograph—it was all the response I needed.

"I'm going to eat dinner," I said, standing on wooden legs. "Come join me downstairs when you're ready."

I don't expect him to.

I expect him to stay right there, drinking himself stupid over a woman who never deserved him.

I'd watched my parents' games countless times with my mom. I thought she was trying to teach me strategy, that she wanted me to learn how to survive. But that wasn't it at all.

She was reminiscing about someone else.

All this time, I thought that there was something wrong, broken in me. But it was *her*.

And now she'd hurt him—my dad.

Enough was e-fucking-nough.

I knew Hiram. He'd come to the house a few times for barbecues with his kids when I was little—his eldest son, Dylan, was a bit of a womanizing prick, but that would only make him easy to manipulate.

Hurting me, that was one thing.

But no one made my dad feel like he wasn't good enough.

Better watch out, Hiram. I'm coming for you.

KOHL

YOU REALLY GOING TO BE SHY NOW, KITTEN?

"I'm gonna kill them," Vic hissed.

"Who?" I asked, leaning to brush our sides together. "Not like you're gonna storm into whatever stuffy boardroom they discuss this shit in and start cutting throats."

We were dirty. Blood sticking to our clothes. Exhaustion weighed me down, but still... I couldn't help but love how close we were. Just being by her side was enough.

I was pissed about what happened, angry. I wanted to get revenge for her. But most importantly, I wanted her safe. I wanted her to be happy.

And I was fucking relieved that we both made it out of the games alive.

"Watch me," she growled under her breath, her hand finding mine to twine our fingers together.

We—along with the remaining players—stood in the waiting area, our eyes trained on the large screens. Just a few hours ago, this place had been packed so close it was hard to breathe while brushing up against someone, but after the games were over, there was more than enough space for the remaining players.

I caught Yellow and Pink easily, both of them staying as far away from us as possible. They had scored pretty well on the leader-boards, but nothing to brag about.

Pink looked our way, their eyes turning into slits as they glared. Yellow nudged him causing him to look forward.

We weren't allowed to kill each pther now, but I could give them a reminder if they so much as threatened to invade Vic and I's little bubble.

It was a little disheartening that out of five hundred Ghosts, only thirty-seven made it out alive—even fewer unscathed. It wasn't always like this, with so few of the players remaining, but this year had been especially brutal.

Even the Seekers had taken a major hit. We stood tall, our colorful masks lighting the early morning. But not without serious damage.

Clothes were torn. Some were still bleeding. Others looked like they had bathed in a pool of blood.

Horrific sight.

We'd survived the night, but at what cost? All the lives we took meant nothing to The Company, but would weigh on us for *years*.

I glanced at Vic, taking in her blood-streaked face and deep scowl.

"They tanked our fucking rank, Kohl."

I glance at the big screen, slightly obscured by the orangish sky. Three pictures appeared, two Seekers and a Ghost, with their user-names in big font along with their scores. The rest of us who had survived the night had our names scrolling along the side of the screen, much smaller than the others.

Who cares that you lived if you didn't win?

"This is bullshit," Vic grumbled as the winners moved to take the podium. "We should be up there!"

She was right, of course. Viewership made up a lot of your final score, and since the mirror maze, we'd been sitting comfortably in spots one and two.

I squeezed her hand. "It's rigged, we know that."

"Fucking bullshit," she said again, her grip on my fingers crushing.

The Seekers were looking worse for wear as they climbed up onto the stage. But still, they cheered. They cheered with the blood of multiples on their hands. Smiled with the weight of the dead on their shoulders.

The Ghost looked better than the others, but hadn't escaped unscathed. She had a split lip and was holding her arm, which looked to be dislocated, but she was alive. And that was more than many of the other Ghosts could have dreamed of.

Vic practically vibrated with anger beside me.

The once-excited crowd was subdued—getting a taste of the games would do that to the players. I didn't doubt that they'd be reliving this night for years to come. And not as the dream that our parents and the media made it out to be.

As a nightmare.

Many thought this would be easy, that they would come out of the games unscathed—but the silence surrounding us told me just how wrong they'd been.

"They were going after *Seekers*," Vic said, her voice dropping low. "You see the scores? The next highest is nearly half what theirs are."

I did already notice, though I'd tried not to. Really, what I wanted was to go home and wash all the dry, sticky blood off my body.

I'd been one of the stupid fucks who was cocky enough to think that my soul would stay intact after I left the arena, and now I was paying the price. *Sort of.*

"Can I come over after this?" I asked, looking down at her. "There's the survivor's party tonight... but I'd like some time to decompress," I swallowed hard. "With you, if you're comfortable."

Vic looked up at me and turned her mask to the side so I could get a better look at the smile splitting her muddy face.

"How many times did we fuck each other in front of millions of people tonight?" she asked. "You really going to be shy now, kitten?"

My face flushed, and I had to clear my throat before continuing.

"I meant everything I said," I whispered. "You're my whole *world*, Vic. I'm just making sure I'm not stepping over any boundaries."

"Are you mad at me?" she asked. "After knowing everything I did to try and get back at your dad?"

"Never," I said, shaking my head. "He deserves everything that he's gonna get and more. My only regret is that I couldn't help sooner."

She took her mask off fully, tilting her head to the side so that her teal hair shifted behind her. "I haven't cleaned up... not that there is much to clean up," she said. "But I'd love for you to come home with me. If you don't mind a very icy shower."

My entire body seemed to relax at her words. Someday I'd have to face my empty house, my brother's body bag waiting for me on the doorstep... but that could wait for another time.

"I'm sure I can think of a way to warm us up," I hedged.

Vic laughed. "Let's get the fuck out of here, I'm sick of looking at these losers."

"Okay."

She tugged my hand, leading me toward the exit where the final stretch of our games waited.

The press line.

The *"winners"* got there first, the remaining players slowly making their way to the doors themselves.

I couldn't help but tense as we got into closer proximity with each other. It was only a couple of hours ago that they were trying to kill us.

That I was trying to kill them.

Out of all the stages of the Devil's Playground, this had to be my least favorite.

"Ready?" I asked Vic, planting my feet just out of view.

She put her nose in the air, fixing a blinding smile on her face that left me speechless for a few long moments. "Let's show them what a real pair of winners look like."

This woman might be a fucking demon, I thought, stepping onto the red carpet to a barrage of noise from the reporters. *But goddamn if I don't love it.*

"Look over here!"

"Come here, sweetheart! Tell me how it felt to push your friend in front of the Killers so you could run away!"

"Penelope! Has your sister's body been delivered to your house?"

The screams from the reporters sounded all around us. Clicks and explosions of light—camera flashes—filled the air.

At our feet, the deep red carpet looked too similar to the blood covering our bodies. We waited patiently for our turn, Vic studying the other players with an irritated twitch to her lips, invisible to everyone but me.

It was always like this. People scrambling to get pictures of those who ended up surviving the games. Many of them waited out here all night, streaming different players on multiple screens, so they knew exactly what to ask when they came out. The clips and pictures that came from this walk would be shared for the next year, even longer if a specific winner caught the eye of the public, which meant they were worth their weight in gold.

I'd been so busy trying to make sure that we survived that I hadn't even thought about how to prepare for the attention we'd get when we were done.

But Vic? She was made for this.

It was like a bomb went off.

One second, every reporter on the press line was yelling at the other players further down, taking photos, and doing interviews— and the next, we were the center of attention.

A couple reporters literally *screamed* when they caught sight of us.

"Mask off," one of the armed guards standing outside the entrance ordered me.

Biting my tongue, I did as he said, revealing my bruised, bloodied face.

Vic gave my hand a firm squeeze before pulling me along beside her. "I got you," she swore. "We just gotta get through this and we can go home."

I nodded, fixing my face into a smile.

"Victoria! One Wolff wasn't enough for you?"

"Kohl, how does it feel now that there's no competition between you and your brother?"

"Victoria, how'd you get Kohl to roll over like a dog for you? What dirt do you have on them?"

"Victoria, Kohl! Come on, give us a *show*! Make Kohl cry for us again!"

"Kohl, have you always been a pathetic little pet?"

Vic's easy, press-ready smile flipped into a snarl in an instant as she lurched forward. "Say that again, *bitch*! I dare you!"

I narrowly caught the back of her hoodie to pull her backward.

What we'd done in the arena was risky. We both knew that. Though, I'm not sure either of us fully understood what it would mean. That everyone and their dog would think they were free to degrade me like she did.

Especially not the reporters.

The reporter who'd called me pathetic nearly fell over in surprise, trying to back away from Vic. She snapped her teeth at him.

"Not so fucking brave now, are you? You forget that I don't need a fucking gun and an arena to—"

"Vic," I warned her, eyeing the other reporters. "Play hard."

"Win, win," she hissed, flipping the cameras her middle finger.

There was a chorus of disappointed sighs as hundreds of perfectly good images were ruined by the action. Sure, we were murderers and villains, but society still had some decorum.

It was a move that brought a genuine smile to my face.

Many tried to get us to stop for interviews as we passed, but Vic was on a mission now. Her mask had already slipped, and she wasn't keen to fix it back in place. The only thing that stopped us was a white van that'd pulled up right to the end of the red carpet.

Men with guns—not just guns, fucking semi-automatic assault rifles—stood aside the open doors, motioning for us to get inside.

I stepped in front of Vic protectively, not that I stood any chance against people armed like that.

"Get in," one of them ordered. "They want to talk."

"Who's *they*?" I asked, squaring my shoulders.

The taller man looked me up and down like I was some kind of joke.

"You know very well who *they* are," the other spat. "Get in."

"Fine, fine." Vic walked forward with a sigh, "I knew it was too good to be true."

"You're fucking joking, right?" I growled, slamming my hand down on the table. "Not only did you tank our ratings, but you really think *fifty-k* is gonna be what settles this for us?"

The man at the front of the long, polished table twisted in his chair with a sigh.

An hour.

It'd been a fucking hour since they dragged us to the financial district, forced us into an elevator with yet another set of armed guards, and led us to a fancy conference room with a single suited man sitting at the end of a long oval table.

He was in his mid-forties, with salt and pepper hair, someone the entire fucking world knew all too well. Tristan Wilde, CEO of The Company, and the richest person in the *world* by several hundred billion.

His picture had been splashed on every single magazine, news-paper, and social media website since he took over for his mother five years ago.

He has yet to have a single scandal and has been named the richest person in the world multiple times over.

He was practically untouchable.

"It's more than fair," he said, giving us that stare that I had a feeling got him into this room in the first place.

"It's fucking *robbery*," Vic snarled.

There was no hiding how much these games made this man. Hell, the profit it made for the entire country was such an inflated, far-out number that it was laughable.

People paid good money to see the games from their smart devices. The people were enraptured. They could act horrified in public, spew crap about how the games needed to be stopped, but in the darkness of their room where no one could see them, they were the same type of people to drop hundreds, if not thousands, of dollars on stream add-ons.

Things like channel switching, highlighted comments, *gifts*, all of it costs money, and the games took a majority of it.

But that's just viewers. The thing that was the most valuable?

Their attention. Ads were running non-stop on streams, there wasn't even a premium option to turn them off. And with the whole world watching... who wouldn't want in on it?

"Then, pray tell, what will make you satisfied?" he asked.

"Killing Hiram is non negotiable," Vic says. "On top of that, we need way more than you're offering. You think we haven't seen our viewership?"

There was silence, and then the idea hit me. *Perfect.* We had seen our viewership. We'd watched as they climbed and climbed and climbed. People couldn't look away, not with the show we were providing.

"Give us all the ad spend from our streams and half of all future spend whenever our faces are shown," I ordered.

He sucked on his teeth before sighing. I could see it in his eyes, he was doing the numbers like I had.

Smart man.

It was a hell of a lot of money, but this was easier to negotiate.

The hard part was putting a price on what *we* thought we deserved, but they did all the hard work for us.

All we had to do was cash it in.

"One stream," he said. "And you only get future ad spend if you help with the next games."

It wasn't what I wanted, but it was more than enough. Hope swirled in my chest. *This was it. With this, Vic could finally go back to school! She could get out of debt!*

I didn't care about what it meant that I had to join the games again. I would do it for her. I'd done it once already, so what was one more time if she could live the life my father had stolen from her?

I tried not to show the excitement on my face when I looked at her, but when I did, my heart dropped.

Where I'd expected to see acceptance in her eyes, I only saw outrage.

Vic

"**I**'m not entering again," I said, forcing the words out of my mouth.

What kind of fucked up deal was this?

We won our games fair and square. *They* were the ones that botched our ranks.

And for what? To save face after one of their own literally admitted to attempted murder after interfering with our match?

Which was still a crime outside the game. It was almost comical with how well my plan worked out.

But then this fucker had to come in and try to take it all from me.

Back in the games, I could taste my victory. It'd been so close.

It was a sweet, comforting feeling that I had never thought I'd be able to feel... but I *did*.

I wasn't going to give it up now.

Fuck them and fuck this.

"We *can* negotiate," he said, a feral smile spreading across his face.

In that moment, it felt like we were prey in front of an apex predator. The contrast between now and how it felt in the games was stifling.

I couldn't help but wonder if this is how all the winners before us felt. How they'd look back at their games, remembering how much *control* they had, only for the world to remind them that on the outside, they were still *painfully* ordinary. Controlled by The Company like cockroaches that could be dealt with at any moment.

"Whichever has more viewers, and our lives cannot be at risk," I added after a moment. "Don't think you can pull a fast one on us."

Wilde's sinister smile spread wider. It was chilling.

"I remember the year your mother entered," he said. "Have you watched her games?"

"This isn't the time to reminisce," Kohl spat. Their hand squeezed mine, the reassuring gesture was the only thing keeping me in my seat.

I was still so hyped up on adrenaline that it took everything I had to keep myself calm. Even the threat of armed guards staring at us through the conference room's windows wasn't enough to stop me, not really.

But I wouldn't do that to Kohl.

"You're a lot like Lydia," Tristian said, his eyes moving to the ceiling as a light fog covered them. "She made us a lot of money that year. The snide comments to the cameras were one thing, but that love triangle?" He let out a sharp whistle. "People ate that shit up."

I *had* seen it. After she died, I'd gone to look at all her footage.

Another slap to the fucking face. To watch her pine for Hiram when my dad was right fucking there.

"A lot of people compare us," I said, giving him a sickly sweet smile. "But *unlike her,* I have no problem continuing my winning streak *outside* the games."

His gaze darted to mine, holding my stare. I could see it weighing on his mind. Thinking about whether it was a better idea to get rid of me or keep me on a leash.

"Oh, the money you will make," he said with a laugh.

"Then give it to us," Kohl growled. "Stop fucking around."

"Alright! Fine, I think I have the perfect plan," he said. "One that will guarantee you money for the rest of your life and get us more viewers than we've ever had. Just say yes, and I'll get you every-thing you need."

The leash it was.

I looked at Kohl, but they were already staring at me.

"After the next event, we're gone," they said, their eyes darting from me to Tristan. "I'd like to be home *before* my brother's body starts decomposing."

He let out a laugh that made the hair stand on the back of my neck.

Disgusting.

I tried to search Kohl's face to check if there was any lingering hurt, but there was too much going on and not enough time.

"That I *can* promise you," he said, standing and buttoning his crisp suit jacket. "Sign the contract, and you have yourselves a deal."

A tablet with a digital version of the contract was forced under our noses. I looked it over, and it outlined exactly what we'd agreed on. No more, no less.

Suspiciously bare.

I looked at Kohl.

"Are you really okay with signing your life away?" I asked.

"Just one more game," they whispered. "One more game and you'll finally get the life you *deserve*."

The sincerity in their voice made my heart pound in my chest.

Looking down, I held my breath and used my index finger to sign my name. It showed up with a slight delay, shimmering on the screen.

Kohl took it right after me, not hesitating to write down their name.

The act caused something to flutter inside me. An emotion I hadn't dared name while we were in the games.

For me. They were doing this all for me.

They didn't have to go to these lengths. They could've just left me here to deal with this on my own.

I was the one threatening to pull the trigger.

If they wanted to, they could probably just say they didn't want anything to do with me—and because of Hiram's position, they might've just let them go.

But they didn't.

They signed those papers with me. *For me.*

I could do this. One more time and I was out. One more time and I would be richer than I ever dreamed possible.

One more time and Kohl and I could make a life for ourselves. One untainted by the game's ruin.

When they signed the digital line, the document disappeared. Tristan called our attention by clapping his hands together.

"Come, we don't have much time to get you cleaned and fitted before Rat Race starts," he said, walking out of the room with the clear expectation for us to follow.

It made me wonder what the fuck we'd just signed up for.

KOHL

"God, I'm fucking obsessed with you," I moaned against Vic, our wet bodies slipping against each other.

"I know," she breathed, nipping my shoulder and making me groan.

The water was starting to go cold where it beat down on us from the showerhead, warning that we were well past our allotted twenty minutes, but I didn't care, not when Vic's hands were threading through my hair and for the first time I was able to run my tongue across her skin in *private*.

"I can't believe we're here," I said through kisses as I trailed my mouth down her shoulder. "Can't believe I can finally touch you again."

"You haven't had enough?" Vic asked. The small laugh she let out was like a fucking drug. I wanted to hear more of it. Wanted her to laugh louder as she forced me between her legs and rode my face without any hesitation.

"Never," I breathed, falling to my knees in front of her. "How many times do I have to say it, Vic? I'm yours. For as long as you want to keep me, I'll be by your side, loving you, pleasing you, protecting you."

I ended my sentence with a light kiss on the tuft of blonde curls between her legs.

When I looked up at her, her eyes were hooded and her mouth was slightly agape. I held her gaze as I leaned forward and ran my tongue up the length of her folds.

The breathy moan she let out went straight to my core.

"Finger yourself," she ordered. "Ride your hand while you eat my cunt, but don't you dare come."

It was my turn to let out a laugh.

I placed her leg over my shoulder before letting the same hand fall between my legs. I let her get a good look at me rubbing my clit before I leaned forward again.

"Only if you ride my face like you mean it," I said, my voice husky from the pleasure that was coursing through me.

I wanted her to see me come undone. I wanted her to know that it was because of *her* that I would fall apart without her even touching me.

Her other hand came to tangle in my hair, and she used it as leverage to grind down on my mouth.

Her gasp rang out in the shower when my tongue darted out to lap at her clit.

"If you're a good boy and fuck yourself, I'll consider never letting you go ever again," she purred.

I did as she said, pulling my fingers away from my clit entirely so I could force them into me. I moaned into her cunt as I ground on my hand.

She was doing most of the work. I tried to keep up, sucking her clit or teasing her entrance with my tongue, but Vic had one thing on her mind: her own orgasm.

"That's right, Kohl," she moaned. "Fuck, you feel so good. Are you making yourself feel good, baby?"

Her pet name caused butterflies to unleash in my stomach, and if I wasn't careful, that single phrase could have tipped me over the edge.

Her degradation was intoxicating, something that could make

me, even in my most sane mind, crumble. But her praise? God, her praise was like getting a blessing from my very own goddess.

I moaned into her, letting her know how good she was making me feel. Her light laugh that unraveled into a moan caused my pussy to clench around my fingers.

There was a pounding on the door.

"You're on-air in less than thirty, and you haven't been fitted yet!"

"You hear that?" Vic asked, her movements getting more erratic as she fucked my mouth. "Better hurry up, baby. Be a good boy and come with me?"

I couldn't stop the whine from my mouth. There would be no problem with me coming at the same time as her. If I moved my fingers over my clit, I would explode right in front of her.

"Oh fuck," she moaned. "I'm coming, Kohl. Are you ready? Come with me, baby."

I tore my fingers from my pussy to rub them on my clit as I pulled her clit into my mouth and gave it a large, hard suck.

Her cry drowned out my moans as we came together. The pounding got louder on the door, and in return, Vic only cried louder.

"If you don't stop, imma make my fuck toy go for another round. Is that what you want?"

It was all the intruder needed to stop pounding on the door.

Vic pulled me up by my hair and forced her lips to mine. I positively melted into the kiss, pushing our wet bodies against each other.

"Tell me you love me, and I'll promise to never let you go," she ordered, pulling away and staring at me intently.

There was something that passed her eyes... something that looked too similar to fear to let slide.

I cupped her face, bumping my nose against hers.

"I have and will always love you, Victoria," I said. "I was made to belong to you, and I wouldn't want it any other way."

"Truly?" she asked. "You're not joking?"

"I've never been more serious in my life," I admitted. "I love you, Victoria Miller, and I would be honored if you kept me."

A smile split her face.

"Good," she said. "Because I seem to have fallen for my little pet. I love you too, pup."

My heart threatened to burst inside my chest. I had fantasies so much about Vic, but somehow, never once, even in my wildest dreams, ever imagined that she would *love* me.

"They can wait," I said, and I grabbed Vic's legs to place around my hips.

Her laugh echoed in the bathroom as the pounding began once more, but this time we didn't stop, not until my name fell from her lips.

"Welcome back to Devil's Playground: Paradise Pier," Vic said, her bright cherry-red lips putting on more of a grimace than a smile as she looked into the camera. "In a short few minutes, we will introduce you to some of the players in the Rat Race. But first, I think it's time for an introduction, don't you think, Kohl?"

"What else is there to say?" I said with a huff. The itchy fabric they forced me into was already getting on my nerves. "They already saw us fuck, I'm sure they know us more than they ever wanted to."

Vic let out a laugh.

"And now we're here, against our will. But hey, at least we are getting paid. The least those fuckers could do after fucking our rank like they did," she said, motioning to the area around us. "Getting paid one hundred k per fucking minute. Can you believe that?"

"Not to mention the thirteen million dollar payout we got in advertiser spending," I muttered. "But who's counting?"

The producer on the other side of the camera motioned for us to go on.

"Okay, well, let's get into the maze contestants," Vic said. "It won't be as entertaining as watching Kohl on their knees for me, but beggars can't be choosers and all that."

"Vic," I hissed under my breath.

"Oh, don't get shy now, Kohl, we all know you secretly like it," she tutted.

"Anyway," I said after clearing my throat. "We have a few contestants we have our eye on for this year. Let's bring them up."

"First is Camilia Slater, going by cam_g1rl this year—Oh wow, that's... an outfit," Vic said, hardly concealing her laughter.

An image of a muscular brunette with a cowboy hat and a tank top stretched tight around their chest showed up on the screen. They didn't look like a Killer for sure, not with the blinding smile they gave the camera.

"Coming from a private school funded by The Company, we are looking forward to what type of show they put on," Vic said, leaning her head against her palm in an almost annoyed fashion. "If The Company invests *that* much money into their education, they have to be deadly."

"Next we have Aubrey Westion, known in this game as w1ckd_w3st—"

"Someone who went to the same school as us," Vic piped in. "Watch out for this one, babes. Head cheerleaders are known for two things: their flexibility and ruthlessness."

We should have been unnerved at seeing someone close to us, but neither of us paused. Maybe it was the thousands of dollars being deposited into our bank account every few minutes that caused our apathy.

"And then last but not least, Hiram Wolff," Vic said, this time looking at the camera with a sinister smile. One I had only seen her show in the games. "We all know what he did to get in here, and I'm sure so *many* of you want to take your anger out on an Architect, but let me sweeten the deal for you."

Vic leaned forward, putting her hands on the desk in front of us and staring right into the millions of viewers watching our stream.

"Whoever kills Hiram will get paid out a million dollars, *regard-*

less of whether you win the games," she said, her lips twisted. "Hell, I'll even cut the check myself. If you can make me laugh while you're doing it, I'll double it."

She was the most twisted and evil thing I'd ever seen... and I fucking loved it.

TO BE CONTINUED IN RAT RACE

I also update my novellas on there every other week and they are the FIRST to get ARCS of all my newest releases!

Check it out here or go to https://www.patreon.com/ellemaebooks

ACKNOWLEDGMENTS

Besides our lovely readers, Bex and I also had the idea to thank each other lol.

We use these cowriting projects as treats for each other when all of the stress from writing and life get to us. I literally cannot tell you how many times we broke down in sobs because we were laughing so hard while writing this (not because it's funny but because the sheer unhinged mess this book turned out to be).

Thanks for your hard work and patience Bex, here's to the next!

About Ashley

Bex (Ashley Pines) is a cat-mom of three, wife and spicy romance enthusiast living in Edmonton, AB. You can usually find her curled up on the sofa surrounded by a hundred pillows and reading on her kindle (or, y'know, writing.) Becoming her best friend is easy! You just need an undying love of all things sweet and be cool with watching the same five movies on repeat.

About Eden

Eden Emory is a contemporary spicy pen name for Elle Mae. This pen name will mostly focus on spicy dark wlw romance that pushes the boundaries and incorporates troupes normally seen in f/m romance.

Eden Emory was born out of a want for more. More spice, more wlw, and even more smutty vibes with little to no plot.

Loved this book? Please leave a review!

For more behind the scene content, sign up for my newsletter at https://view.flodesk.com/pages/61722d0874d564fa09f4021b